The Obvious Game

Rita Arens

The Obvious Game
Copyright © 2013 Rita Arens
All rights reserved.
ISBN: 0985148373
ISBN-13 (print): 978-0-9851483-7-9
ISBN-13 (ebook): 978-0-9856562-0-1
Inkspell Publishing
5764 Woodbine Ave.
Pinckney, MI 48169

Edited By Deb Anderson.
Cover art By Najla Qamber

DEDICATION

—for my parent

Prologue

1987

When we were in seventh grade, Amanda and I snuck out of her house one foggy Saturday night to meet her boyfriend, Matt. We spent more time planning our escape than we did actually conducting it.

We'd made a list while pretending to do our homework:

Wrap flashlights with black electrical tape. (check)

Make fake bodies out of pillows to hide in our sleeping bags. (check)

Booby-trap her bedroom door with string across the threshold so we could see if her mom had tried to check on us. (check)

Assemble all-black outfits, complete with stocking caps, so we would blend in with the shadows as we walked. (check)

Arrange the rendezvous point ahead of time with Matt: the third-grade playground at the elementary school. (check)

It wasn't until we'd successfully shimmied down the fence, jogged the four blocks up the street, and seen Matt sitting there alone on the seesaw that I realized I had nothing at all to do while they giggled and kissed. I'd been so caught up in the planning portion of our escape that I didn't notice how pathetic my part in it seemed.

I twirled on the swings across the playground and out of view, once again pretending to be totally cool with it. The thing was, though, I wasn't cool with it. I felt about as important as the guy who wrote the cooking instructions for Pop-Tarts.

We probably would've stayed there for hours if I hadn't finally strode over to the jungle gym, coughing and kicking rocks as I went. Amanda poked her head out.

"What's up, Diana?"

"Can we go soon? I forgot to bring a book."

Her expectant smile turned sour. "Okay," she finally said, disappearing in the darkness. "Just five more minutes."

I wandered to the edge of the playground, thought about turning back on my own, letting her get caught out there by herself. But I wouldn't. That's what friends are for. She knew it. I knew it.

Everyone trusted me. Good old dependable Diana. Which was why most people didn't notice at first that I was in trouble.

Chapter One: Pride
1990

"So who is Jesse?" asked Ma. I sat on her bed in the darkened room. Her hair was almost gone, and she'd wrapped her head in a purple terrycloth turban knotted in front. The hair loss aged her from forty-something to nearly dead, making my breath catch every time I looked at her. Her face was like a canyon denied rain.

"He's just a guy I know." I smiled at her, not really meaning to, giving myself totally away.

"But I don't know him," said Ma. She swung her legs over the side of the bed. Last month, one leg had been operated on to remove the tumor. The scar reminded me of a shark bite. *Chomp, chomp. All gone. So long, normal life.*

"He moved here this year from Kansas City," I said. I decided not to tell her about either Jesse's brother or Jesse's driver's license. "He's a sophomore, and I'm sure his record is clean."

Ma ignored me. "Is he cute?"

"*Ma.*" I was not looking forward to a whole afternoon of this. I gave Ma a look that told her the conversation was over. She still wanted me to marry Dylan Morgenstern just because she liked his mom. What did she know about guys?

"Oh," she said, pulling out a shiny envelope, "by the way, I have something for you."

I flipped open the flap, smelling the film still tucked in beside the glossy pictures. "Thanks, Ma. I'll go put these in my room."

As I padded down the stairs, I pulled out the stack, flipping through the images of our Fourth of July picnic. Scattered, blurry fireworks barely visible in a huge background of night sky. Pa standing behind Ma, his fingers rabbit ears over her turban. And—*holy Lord*—me…from the back, in a pair of pleated, high-waisted cut-off jeans. I didn't think they looked too bad from the front, but I'd never seen them full-on from the back. I looked like a thirty-eight-year-old woman with three kids and a cheeseburger habit.

I felt the sweat start to prickle on the back of my neck, and my throat tightened. I stared closer at the photo. My arms were up in a victory sign. I clearly had no idea what I looked like.

But everyone else did.

Not again. I sank down into my desk chair, pulling out the drawer with one hand, rifling through the contents by touch. I couldn't look away from the picture. My fingers closed around the scissors, the sharp ones with orange plastic handles.

The first cut felt smooth, the blades slicing through gleaming photo paper, just the right amount of resistance. I took quite a bit off my butt and thighs, slightly less around my calves. My breathing slowed as I worked, as though my transformation were already happening.

I held up the scissors, running the sharp tip down the inside of my thigh, right where I'd shaved an easy ten pounds off the *me* in the photo. The blade drew a drop of blood. And it hurt.

"Diana!" Ma yelled from upstairs. "What's taking you so long? Come on, let's go."

I tossed the scissors and the pictures into the desk drawer.

Pa was in the field, so I'd agreed to go with Ma to get her new hair.

Wig Lady's house—a sky-blue ranch with white vinyl shutters—perched at the deep end of a cul-de-sac in the nice part of Omaha. When the thin older woman answered the door, I stared hard at her hair, trying to decide if she was modeling the merchandise.

Her white chignon sat in a tightly coiled pile on her head: wig or Clairol? Impossible to tell. She led us into her white living room—white leather couch, white-satin-covered chair, white tile floor, glass-and-bronze chandelier hanging from the ceiling on a brass chain. Little glass icicles meant to look like crystal dangled from the fixture. I balanced on the edge of the sofa and stared down at the white Persian cat lolling underneath a nearby fern.

Wig Lady—Mrs. Dupont—leaned over, her cream silk blouse sliding forward around her neck, gold necklaces clinking against the beaded cord from which her tortoise-shell glasses hung. She cleared her throat delicately. "Mrs. Keller," she began, "what was your natural hair color?"

Ma didn't even have eyelashes anymore. We both blinked.

"Brown," Ma said finally.

I laughed without meaning to. It was the right answer; it was the wrong answer. Then my throat tightened and I realized I was going to cry again, just like I did every night she was in the hospital. The cat shifted next to me, and I fixed on its soft white fur, imagined what a nice rug it might make.

Wig Lady smiled again, as though this were normal, and pulled out a thick book filled with hair swatches in every color imaginable. She opened the book to "brown," flipping the pages slowly with fingers ensnared with gold and diamonds. I wondered if she got a special car for selling wigs, like you got a pink sedan for selling Mary Kay. Was it brown? Ash blonde? Silver-blue?

"Here is our selection of brown," she said. "Stop me when I come to the right color."

We leaned forward. We stared. I couldn't remember either.

Ma looked at me, her eyes filled with tears. "Why can't I recall what color my hair was?" she whispered.

I shrugged, realizing I'd have to make the decision for her. I remembered, but couldn't remember,

14

just like everything else. Normal life, hair color, days when Ma came to pick me up from school instead of a neighbor; these details I remembered but couldn't remember. Everything changed the day Ma didn't come home from the doctor's office; the day Pa told me she was really, really sick; the day I cried until I threw up all over the couch.

I reached for my head and tugged on a handful of hair. Pulling out a bunch didn't hurt—it was only when I grabbed it strand by strand and tugged that I could really feel the pain. *My mother has cancer*. Nothing. *My mother cries at night and doesn't hug me because even the air hurts*. Ouch.

I handed the wad to Wig Lady. "Match it to this," I said, putting my arm around Ma's bony shoulders just as they began to shake, looming over her in the glare of the mirror. I kissed the top of her head where her hair should've been thick and strong and was now fine and downy as a toddler's. "Make it like mine."

****

When Pa walked in from the field, he did a double-take. Ma didn't see him at first; she had her back to him, making cookies. I sat on the couch pretending to read a book and trying to guess where Jesse might be later.

Pa's face lit up when he saw Ma's new hair. He walked up behind her slowly, reaching out his dust-streaked hand and touching her hair gently just before she felt his presence behind her. She didn't turn to look at him.

"They were two hundred dollars each, Albert." Her voice shook.

"It's okay."

"This disease is so damn expensive. I can take them back. I can take one back—I don't need two."

"It's okay."

"I just wanted to look normal again."

"It's okay."

Pa pulled her to him, wrapping his muscled forearms around her and kissing the top of her head. She turned and buried her face in his dirty denim jacket.

I tucked my nose back in my book before Pa looked up. It sort of felt like their moment, like I should be watching it on a movie instead of in my living room. *The Cancer-stricken and the Hairless*.

"You look beautiful," he said.

She looked at me, pleading. "Here, Diana," she said, pulling a cookie off the cooling rack. "Eat."

I shook my head. After the day we'd just had, I didn't want her to mother me just this minute.

"*Eat*."

****

Amanda arrived late that afternoon, overnight bag in hand. She popped her gum as she stepped out of the car. I waited for her on the sidewalk, chewing a piece of grass, wishing I could be more excited to see my oldest friend. I wasn't really in the mood for Amanda after Wig Lady—I just wanted to be alone. And I couldn't decide if I wanted to tell her about Jesse. It turned out she already knew.

She grabbed my arm, leading me toward my room. As soon as the door was closed, she dropped her bag and seized both my arms. "Tell me all about it," she said. The black eyeliner made her eyes fierce.

"About what?"

"About Jesse, moron. You showed up at Pizza Hut in his car."

So she had seen me. Had she seen him introduce himself to Pa?

"Lin said you disappeared from the football game, then Jane told me she saw you guys pull in right before your dad picked you up. Where were you all that time?"

I flopped on my bed, leaning back against the blue cotton throw pillows and staring up at the spider webs entangled with the popcorn ceiling. There must have been whole spider families up there, watching me live my life as they went about theirs. I sighed, letting her tension build: I had something Amanda wanted.

"Oh, chill out, Amanda. He just got his license, so he asked if I wanted to go for a ride. It was cool."

"Is that all?" I looked over at her. She looked like she might bust a gut. I made a face at her and waited for the steam to come out her triple-pierced ears.

"Yeah. It wasn't really that long that we were gone. I went to the snack bar first and had to wait forever. It was like the end of third quarter by the time I saw him. No big deal." I pointed my toes toward the end of the daybed, felt them curl around the brass rail. I loved the feeling of cold on the soles of my feet, almost as much as I loved torturing Amanda when she wanted information.

I didn't tell her most of it: I had just reached for my cup of pop when I felt a hand on my shoulder. I jumped slightly, sloshing Coke all over my arm. As I reached down to lick it off my wrist, I turned to see Jesse grinning at me. He was alone.

"Hey, Diana. Sorry about that." I hadn't seen him up close in a week or so. His eyelashes had grown blond at the ends from the sun. He smiled.

"Oh my God. It's fine. I wasn't expecting anyone, that's all. I'm so clumsy."

I am a moron.

I moved out away from the snack bar. I couldn't believe I had him to myself. "Who did you come with?" I asked in what I hoped was a casual tone.

"Just me."

"Did your parents bring you?" I knew his only sister was younger, like sixth-grade younger.

"No. I just got my license today."

"You are kidding me. Today is your birthday?"

"Yep." He stretched his arms out, hands clasped. I wanted to put my hand on his biceps to see if they felt the way they looked.

"Well, wow! Happy birthday. I feel like I should give you a gift. Here, have a Coke." I extended my sticky hand with the cup.

"Well, since it's from you…" He took the cup and drained it in a swig. "That's the best gift I've had all day. Well, except for the license." He looked over at the field. "Hey, we're losing."

18

"Oh, so you know how to play the Obvious Game?" I admit I was kind of surprised. I thought nobody played that game but Seth and me.

"What?" Jesse looked confused, and I flushed. *Duh, he was just talking.*

"Oh, it's this game I play with Seth. You say things that are obvious. Like, *we're losing.* You played it perfectly."

He smiled. "*I just drank a Coke.*"

"Exactly. *You're sixteen.* You can have a whole conversation like this and drive everyone insane because they have no idea what you're doing. Usually it just takes two or three sentences before they're looking at you like you're a moron."

Jesse laughed. "The Obvious Game. I like it."

I looked around. The football game was in the end of the third quarter. The night was going way too fast, especially now that Jesse was standing in front of me. I shifted my weight, tried to think of something fabulous to say. I said: "Um."

Jesse leaned toward me. "Actually, I was going to see if you wanted to go for a ride. I haven't driven around town that much. You could show me the sights. My parents only drove to the bank and to drop me at work and stuff."

I hiccupped. I always hiccupped when I was excited. I clapped my hand over my mouth. I looked around again, thinking guiltily about abandoning Lin— I'd been sitting next to her. But I only felt bad for a second. Then it passed. "What do you drive?"

19

Jesse drove a white Buick LeSabre, a big boat of a car with burgundy cloth interior. I laughed when he led me to where it was parked and showed it off to me.

"Hey, now," he said. "This car is a beautiful machine."

"Right, right," I said. "It's a lot more attractive than my car."

"What do you drive?"

"A riding lawnmower, in my yard."

"So much to know about Diana," he said and opened the door, gesturing for me to get in. I tried to hide my smile as I climbed into his car. I felt unnervingly comfortable with him.

Jesse didn't seem nervous in the least to be driving with a brand-new license as we pulled out of the high school parking lot. "Where to?" he asked.

"Um, go that way," I said, pointing. Just down the hill and around the corner was the golf course, which I knew would be empty due to the football game. The sun had just set, and the shadows were growing darker.

I motioned for Jesse to turn into the golf course parking lot while quashing my next hiccup. He did, laughing. "Ah," he said. "The fabled golf course."

"Sure, doesn't everyone want to see the golf course? Hop out. I'll show you hole sixteen."

"What's so special about hole sixteen?" he asked.

"What's not?"

It grew dark surprisingly fast on the course, and when we reached hole sixteen, the stars had already appeared, painfully bright. The closest streetlight rose from the asphalt by the clubhouse; there were no lights on the course itself. We sat on the bench beside hole sixteen and looked up at those stars…

"*Ahem.*" Amanda twirled a lock of hair between her fingers, her nails painted blood-red. I crossed my legs nervously. "You're holding out."

"No, I'm really not. Besides, my mom got wigs today." I knew I could always distract Amanda with anything involving hair, sex, or chocolate.

"She did? Where?"

"I'll show you."

Ma was out grocery shopping. Pa had disappeared with his computer. Nothing stirred in my parents' bedroom when we opened the door. Ma's extra wig sat on its dummy head on her dresser, shiny and full as her own hair had never been.

"It's freaky," said Amanda, drawn toward the disembodied head. She reached out and touched the glistening hair.

"It's human hair," I said, sitting on my parents' bed. Something about the look in Amanda's eyes made me nervous.

"Really? Where do they get it?"

"I didn't ask. It's hardly a question one asks, Amanda." I rolled my eyes at her. "Were you raised in a barn?"

She pulled the wig off the dummy head, rotating her wrist, letting the hair spin out in a circle like a shampoo commercial. "So if it's real hair, can you style it?"

"Yeah, I guess. Don't."

She walked into the master bathroom, picking up a hairbrush from the counter. She put the wig on her head. Her own hair hung out beneath it.

"Don't," I repeated.

Amanda tossed her hair, wrapping it up and stuffing it under the wig. The bob highlighted her cheekbones, her sharp jaw. She glanced back over her shoulder at me, smiling. "She won't be back for an hour. You know how they get to talking when they go to the store."

I knew she was right. It's impossible to go to a small-town grocery store without being detained by somebody. The last time I'd been there alone, Mrs. Eichelberger had cornered me about Ma for forty-five minutes. I'd made it through the conversation by studying Mrs. E's enormous nostrils, which were always flared like a hangar waiting for the flyboys to come home.

Amanda started a small braid down the side of the bob. "I can't believe how much like hair this feels."

"It is hair, Amanda. Knock it off."

"The possibilities are endless." She leaned over on the counter and dug her fingers into a pot of styling gel. She began working it through the wig, spiking the bangs. I swatted at her arm, hard, and she looked around nervously.

"You're going to get me in trouble," I said. "I am so not in the mood for trouble right now."

"Don't be silly. We can wash it out."

"I don't know how to wash a wig. She just got it. It cost two hundred dollars."

Amanda looked at the pot of gel. "Oh," she said. "Maybe I better get it out."

She ran her hands under the water, dousing the bangs, but the gel stubbornly refused to wash out. She whipped the wig off her head and filled the sink with water, shoving the whole wig in.

"Amanda! You idiot!"

I felt the bedroom door open before I heard it. Ma stood on the threshold of the darkened room, the wig's twin perched on her head. Her face was white. "What are you doing?" she asked quietly.

Amanda looked at me sharply. "Diana was just showing me your wigs. They're beautiful."

"Why is it in the sink, Amanda?" My mother clenched her fists around the gallon of milk she still carried.

"Diana said you could style them because they're made of human hair."

Ma looked at me, her face deflated, betrayed. Her mouth pinched into a small, hard line. "Get out."

Amanda looked alarmed.

"Call your mother, Amanda. You're going home."

Amanda ran out of the room. I heard her thundering down the stairs. In all the years we'd been friends, my mother had never spoken to Amanda harshly.

Ma turned and looked at me, shaking with anger. "How could you, Diana?"

I didn't answer. I couldn't get my mouth to speak. The hair was standing up on the back of my neck. My entire body vibrated with panic. "I didn't tell her to do it, Ma."

"It doesn't matter. You let her. That is my hair."

"She's hard to control, Ma," I said softly, knowing she'd never understand.

Ma turned to the hairless dummy head on her dresser. She pulled off the wig on her head and set it on the dummy, turning back to face me. She'd shaved her head. None of the downy duck fuzz remained. Without eyebrows or eyelashes, she looked alien, smaller than usual. I forced myself to look at it, to look at her.

"The world is hard to control, Diana," she said. "If it were easy, I wouldn't look like this." She grabbed my shoulders, shaking them as she stared hard at me with angry eyes. "You have to take responsibility for your part in it. You're not a little girl anymore."

Her arms dropped then, the anger flowing out of her as she sat on her bed and began to sob. I tried to hug her, but she pushed me away.

"Get out," she said, covering her face with her pillow. "Just leave."

I stood there a moment, feeling the hollow grow inside me. It lived in my gut, in the precise spot that used to glow when Ma smiled.

As I left the room, I passed Pa, who headed for the bedroom. "What happened?" he asked.

"Amanda." He grunted in response.

I didn't say goodbye to Amanda, just watched as she ran out of the house to her mother's waiting car fifteen minutes later.

Once I heard Ma and Pa go into their bedroom to talk, I ran up to the kitchen and devoured six cookies, shoving them in my mouth so fast I barely chewed. The cookies smelled like Ma, like normal, though I didn't even taste them as they went down. Afterward, they sat in my gut like the waterlogged wig in the sink—and it was too late to take either back.

Chapter Two: Appetite for Destruction

Pa came down after a while, rubbing his eyes. I could tell he didn't want to talk about it.

"Pa, it wasn't my fault. You know Amanda. She gets an idea in her head and she just does it."

He nodded, hands in the pockets of his jeans. He rocked back on his heels.

"Should I go talk to her?"

He shook his head, pulling a toothpick wrapped in cellophane from his shirt pocket. He unwrapped it slowly, twirling the toothpick between calloused fingers before placing it in his mouth. "I don't think this is the right time. Let it be. It's been a big day for her."

I opened my mouth to speak, but Pa cleared his throat, the conversation over, and just like that, Pa shut me down. Just like Amanda. Just like Ma.

Pa was talking again. "I'm going into town to pick up food for us. What do you want from Dairy Chef?"

"Chicken fingers," I said automatically, immediately regretting it when I saw the desk drawer still partly ajar.

"Okay, then."

I heard Pa's car rumble down the gravel driveway and fade into the distance. We lived close enough to town to see the water tower but too far away to read it. Pa returned what seemed like only minutes later and left the food on my desk, moving soundlessly through my room. He paused to kiss my head before he left. I sat on the carpet and opened the bag, pulling out the Styrofoam container.

I brought the container to my face, breathed in the thick smell. Grease lined the waxed paper, shiny, glinting. The fries were already starting to curl like dying flower stems. I picked one up, running it between my fingers. Oil immediately coated my fingertips.

Ma used to take me to get chicken fingers from Dairy Chef on the way to dance class when I was in middle school. She'd pat my knee and tell me about her day as we drove uptown to the glamorous studio with full-length mirrors and a former Rockette for a teacher. I wanted to be just like that teacher. I missed those trips, missed thinking I could be whatever I wanted if I just tried hard enough. Ma was trying pretty damn hard not to be sick.

I stood up and undressed in front of the full-length mirror, turning sideways. A solid roll of flesh protruded just below my belly button, refusing to disappear when I sucked in and bulging under my waistband every time I sat. My rear hung, full and round

28

and totally unlike Amanda's or Lin's high, firm, boy-like butts, butts that looked awesome in jeans.

Evidence of my chubby childhood still clung to me: in my inner thighs, in my upper arms. Even though my face had thinned out, I still saw it everywhere. Everyone told me I wasn't fat anymore, but all I could see was that kid that got laughed at for being heavier than the biggest boy during the Presidential Physical Fitness Test. *Hilarious.*

And now the fat kid was back in bad cut-offs at the Fourth of July picnic. I picked up the Styrofoam box of cold chicken fingers and limp fries and carried the food to the trash can in my bathroom, smashing the box and shoving it into the tiny green plastic bin before covering it with at least half a box of wadded-up Kleenex.

Song after song played on the radio long after the darkness fell outside my window. I stretched out under my covers, hungry. My stomach growled and grumbled, but it seemed almost like someone else's pain. When I placed my hand on my abdomen, I could feel the gurgling through my layer of blubber.

Good. If scissors won't work, maybe starving will.

There was a cookbook under my bed, I remembered, left over from when Ma first got sick and I thought I would make something. I pulled it out and turned on my lamp, flipping the pages to the ones with pictures. I skipped the ingredients and went straight to the description of mixing, baking. I imagined eating the carrot cake warm from the oven, the thick cream cheese

29

frosting melting against the heat of the spicy cake. It felt almost like I'd really eaten it.

Then instead of food, I thought about Jesse. I'd met him at the pool the day after I found out about Ma's cancer, the new kid in a town with nobody new. I'd heard about him, of course. We were on *new* like flies on ice cream in Snowden.

He'd walked up to me while I was sitting on the picnic table at the edge of the parking lot, staring at switch grass too long to mow and wondering why I'd left my house that day at all.

"Hey, are you okay?"

I wiped my eyes with the towel and raised my head. "Oh, hi. Yeah, I just felt sick all of a sudden. I had to get out of there."

Jesse sat on the table next to me, scratching his back just turned pink by sunburn. I tried not to stare at his very adult-looking triceps.

"You're Jesse, right? I'm Diana." I wondered if I should shake his hand. Truth be told, I hadn't met all that many people my age for the first time before. I kept my hands under the towel, clasped around my legs. I felt safe still wrapped in my towel. He couldn't really see me.

"I know," he said. "I guess news travels fast in this place, huh?"

I grinned. "Where are you from? New York?"

"Nah," he said, brushing again at his sunburn. "Kansas City. It's sort of the same."

I laughed, looking out at the parking lot and ignoring my worry for the moment. I wondered what time it was. Already I could hear my friends diving back into the pool, adult swim over.

"Hey, your friend Amanda told me about your mom. Is she going to be all right?" Jesse studied a piece of grass he rolled between his palms, its tip flipping left and right as though dancing.

Caught off guard, I felt the tears coming again. *Shit. Shit!* I should've known Amanda couldn't keep her mouth shut for ten minutes. She'd always been the one to share the newest gossip, no matter the cost, and I'd accepted—even before I got into her mom's car—that she would tell. I hadn't really cared if the other kids knew, because they'd know anyway as soon as their mothers went grocery shopping.

I hadn't known there would be a new kid.

But I felt so tired. Not sure what else to do, I leaned my head back down on my knees. The towel muffled my voice. "I don't know. I guess you probably think I'm really weird. I probably shouldn't have come out in public today," I muttered. "I just found out yesterday."

I felt Jesse's hand on my shoulder, sensed it an instant before he touched me, my breath drawing in abruptly. His hand rested heavier than the silken touch of Amanda or the antsy jerks of Ma. I could feel the warmth of his palm like sunlight on my bare shoulder. I felt my ear leaning toward his touch, almost as though I had nothing to do with it at all.

I looked over then, and Jesse was staring off at the pool's ancient swingset, his hand, as though forgotten, still on my shoulder. I noticed the tips of his

31

eyelashes were blond before he looked back at me, sucked in a deep breath and stood, hands on his thighs and pushing up, out of the moment.

"It's going to be okay," he said, like he knew. I wanted to believe him.

I brushed my wet hair out of my face. "I'm glad to meet you," I said, meaning it. "Even though you're not from New York and all."

He smiled. "I'll see you around, Diana," he said, raising two fingers halfway to his head.

Then he turned back toward the sunshine and the pool without looking back. When he was gone, I touched my shoulder where his hand had been and thought about his eyelashes.

****

As Ma began treatment, I replaced fear with thoughts of Jesse's brown hair, which was turning blonder every day. He got a job bagging groceries at the Jack & Jill Mart and wore white t-shirts that highlighted the shadows of his back muscles. Every time we drove through town, I scoured the streets for a sign of those white t-shirts. I imagined them as I mowed the lawn, as I combed my hair, remembering the jolt I'd felt when he touched my shoulder, that instant when I finally understood chemistry.

"I think he likes you," Amanda whispered in third period biology after he'd peeked his head back and waved after walking past our classroom down the hall.

"Was he looking at me?" I whispered, trying to speak without moving my lips. Mr. Hartman, our biology teacher, was pouring clear liquid from a large plastic

32

container into a beaker. He looked up at Amanda and me, blinking. Whenever Mr. Hartman got mad, he'd start blinking faster and faster like a playing card in a bike wheel. He blinked twice in rapid succession.

"Um, yeah." I could hear Amanda's pencil tapping impatiently on her desk behind me.

I sank down in my chair, imagining Jesse's stubby fingers in my hair. My stomach seized.

Mr. Hartman picked up the beaker again and cleared his throat for attention. I heard Seth's stage whisper from across the classroom: "*Drink it.*"

The class giggled, and I found myself smiling in spite of my wish to be cool. Twisting around in my seat, I made a face at Amanda, but she was looking out at the empty hall.

"Drink it," whispered Seth again, and I laughed into my hand as I turned away from Amanda and whatever she was not looking at anymore.

****

The next morning Ma came in early, not bothering to knock. She sat down on my bed softly, shaking my shoulder. When I opened my eyes, her face was kind. She was wearing her wig and her favorite green knit dress. She looked better than she had since she started chemo. I noticed she'd applied blush and lipstick, though there was no camouflaging her lashless eyes.

"Ma, I'm sorry. I seriously didn't tell her to do it. I tried to stop her."

"It's okay. We don't have to talk about it." She coughed into her arm, and I could tell she was just done with it. That was Ma's way. Once she decided an argument was over, there was no resurrecting it, no instant replay, no Cliff's Notes. *Done, gone, over and out.*

I sat up. "Did the wig dry out okay? Was it wash and wear?"

She laughed, almost barking. "Apparently. I called Mrs. Dupont, and she explained how to fix it. I may have to bring it in if it doesn't go back to normal."

"I'm sorry, Ma."

She reached over and squeezed my shoulder. "I guess that's why Mrs. Dupont insisted I buy two. An extra just in case your daughter's crazy friend shoves one in the sink."

I smiled and followed Ma upstairs to breakfast. My stomach, no longer immune to my hunger, gurgled at the smell of bacon in the microwave. My head hurt.

Pa sat at the table in dress pants and suspenders, the Sunday paper spread out in front of him on the table. He balanced a cinnamon roll between thumb and pinky finger to keep the frosting from dripping on the rest of his hand, taking bites without even looking at the roll. Pa brought eating drippy food to an Olympic level.

Ma swished into the kitchen for coffee, returning with more bacon and cinnamon rolls. I took one slice and rammed it in my mouth, immediately regretting it. I wanted about a thousand more.

"Hurry up and get dressed for church, Diana," Ma said, picking up the lifestyle section of the paper.

I knew better than to argue. I'd begged to sleep in a million times, and a million times I'd been led to St. Luke's Lutheran Church, all one hundred years old of it.

My entire family was super-religious. Pa insisted each Sunday on attending church. He never talked about the sermons, but he went. He sang in the choir and adjusted the sound system when it popped and echoed, even after I begged him to permanently break it when the pastor's wife sang "I Am the Tree" on Easter morning. Pa had no respect for the congregation's eardrums.

I'd look up at the lights hanging from the arched sanctuary ceiling on ten-foot chains and imagine swinging from light to light like a chimpanzee, wondering if I'd still be able to hear the pastor's droning from those heights. If I'd be closer to God.

On the drive in, Pa began humming to himself the week's choir hymn. We watched the fields fly past the window, and pretty soon Ma was humming, too. Despite myself, I started singing under my breath.

Ma cocked her ear, her eyes closed. "You have such a lovely voice, Diana," she said. "Why did you quit the choir again?"

"I don't know," I said. But I did. *It was what that kid said.*

"You know, Connie asks me all the time why you don't try out for more at school. You were so amazing in *The Sound of Music*."

****

When Ma had been too sick to come with us to church, I often wandered out to the long white vinyl couch in the hall, enjoying the otherness of being outside the sanctuary during worship, how silent the hall seemed compared to the rustle of polyester slacks and whimper of babies inside. A painting of Jesus knocking on a wooden door hung above the couch. I read the entire Bible while Pa sat with the choir.

God lived in the hall.

I was shocked at how short most of the Bible stories were. I imagine if I'd been writing the gospels, I'd have spent a little more time on that part. So much of the Bible is history and Jewish law. It's hard to take the rules about how to treat your slaves too seriously. The poetry is actually pretty good.

Seth saved a seat for me in the balcony, as he had since our parents let us sit alone if we promised to pass notes instead of whispering. Seth's mother liked my influence. My mother wanted me to have friends who didn't comment on my weight.

I'd met Seth under the ladies casual wear racks at our small-town clothing store when we were five. I hid from my mother, he from his. When I lifted the red polyester slacks to take my usual place, a small blond boy peered up at me, then moved over to make room. I sat beside him with a thump, peeved that someone had discovered my place. Seth offered me a Tootsie Roll and held a finger to his lips. I could hear his mother calling his name from three feet away, could see her feet anxiously pacing in Dr. Scholl's clogs. Twenty seconds later, she lifted a tweed skirt and hauled him out, not giving me a second look.

A few weeks later, Seth plunked down next to me at kindergarten recess, handed me another Tootsie Roll, and beat the ground with two knotty, splintered sticks, the drummer in a band that jammed only in his head. I'd been drawing unicorns with discarded classroom chalk. I hadn't yet perfected the bodies or hooves but was growing very adept with the head parts. I glanced over at him sideways under my straight-cut bangs, not lifting my head.

"What are you doing?" Seth asked, never taking his eyes off the sticks.

"Drawing, I guess. I'm not very good," I muttered, rubbing out the mistake I'd made once again on the unicorn's hoof.

He looked over without pausing his thrashing. "Looks fine to me," he said.

I always looked fine to Seth. Long after he became "Sticks" to everyone else, Seth was still Seth to me. I listened to his endless rampages against his mother and mankind, his drum solos, his anarchy. It wasn't so much that his life was bad, more that his energy had nowhere to go—it just splayed about him like Medusa's hair no matter how much his mother tried to contain it. After church, we would hide together under the stairs behind the rectory, spitting sunflower seeds and counting down the seconds until his mother's head finally exploded.

This Sunday, I squeezed in beside him, feeling the roll at my belly bulge under my straight skirt and folding my arms over it, already mad at myself for eating the bacon. The first note slid across the hymnal on my lap before the pastor finished his welcome and announcements.

What happened with you and Amanda last night?
I rolled my eyes. What did she tell people?
She ruined my mom's new wig. Ma freaked out.

37

He dropped the paper, craning to see my mother over the edge of the balcony. He wasn't the only one. The wig looked nothing like my mother's old hair. I could see old ladies sneaking glances at her when she wasn't looking. I wondered if Ma could feel their eyes. I hated them all, wished their hair would disappear before my eyes as the pastor began the Kyrie.

Seth dug for the pencil in the pew cushion. *She looks like your mom, only hotter. Or with better conditioner.*

Ugh. I don't want to talk about Ma's wig. What did Amanda say?

She really didn't say anything. Just said you wouldn't be out.

Where were you guys last night?

Just hanging at the Kwik Shop. They wouldn't let us into the strip club.

I tilted my head, smiled at Seth. He knew what I wanted to hear.

He paused, studying me from under his white-blond forelock, then added another line. *Jesse wasn't out, dude. It's cool.*

I let out a sigh. I hadn't missed him, then. Who knew where he was, but he wasn't there getting draped all over by Amanda in her tight jeans. Then I remembered. *Was Lin with Hutch?*

Seth grinned. *Yep. They watched a movie at his house. Or so they say.*

What?

I think you could say it was a date. Personally, I think she was helping him with his homework, but whatever.

WHAT? I smiled. I couldn't really believe Lin was the first of my friends to go on an actual, bona fide, fifty-cent date.

The choir walked into the sanctuary, royal blue robes rustling. Pa stood in the back row, next to Seth's dad. His mouth shaped into a little O and his chin doubled as he pulled back his head to hit the lowest notes. He looked up to spot where Seth and I always sat in the balcony and lifted his chin in a wave. I returned it, though Pa surely couldn't see my hand behind the pew.

By the end of the service, my abdomen ached from the constricting skirt and the effort of holding in my gut for an hour while the pastor droned on about holding ourselves to higher standards.

After church, Ma and Pa dawdled in the fellowship hall over coffee and doughnuts while Seth and I hung out in our usual place under the stairs by the rectory.

I sat down, smoothing my skirt beneath my thighs on the cold cement stairs. "*It's Sunday,*" I said, beginning the Obvious Game.

"*You're wearing a black skirt,*" replied Seth, pulling out his sunflower seeds.

"*Your feet are huge,*" I replied.

"So what's the story with you and Jesse?" Seth asked, drumming his fingers on his knees.

"I kissed him."

Seth nodded, reaching for another sunflower seed. "Are you guys *dating*?" He leaned on the word and faked pulling down imaginary reading glasses to stare over them at me. He sounded just like Ma would.

I laughed. "Dating? Who dates?"

"Lin and Hutch, apparently."

"Touché. Nah, I don't think so."

"But you like him? His big, handsome, strapping self?"

I ignored Seth's tone. "Of course I like him. He's smart and funny and hot. I can't figure out why he likes me."

"I keep telling you, Diana. There are tons of crazies out there. You bag on yourself too much."

I rolled my eyes. "It's hard not to when you're best friends with Amanda."

Seth paused. "Amanda's scary. She must keep a box of headless baby dolls in her closet."

I punched him. "But she's better at getting guys."

"There's a difference between being better at it and being better, Diana."

Chapter Three: Scarecrow

"I'm on the court!" Amanda stage-whispered as she sat down behind me. I could smell the spearmint gum on her breath from two feet away. She pulled my hair aside and looped it over my shoulder, leaning in to grasp both my arms, pretending to be discreet but as obvious as a nitroglycerine explosion. "Can you believe it?"

Let's see. Could I believe that the girl who'd won every popularity contest our class ever had—starting with the run for president of fourth grade—had secured one of the two coveted spots for sophomores on the homecoming court? I pinched the web between my thumb and forefinger to keep from screaming.

As Amanda continued whispering, I directed my gaze forward at my biology homework. Amanda pulled my hair back into a ponytail, kneading it through her thin fingers like dough. Then she pulled.

"Ow." I snapped, "Jesus, Amanda."

"Are you listening, Diana?"

"God. Yes. Congratulations, okay? I'm trying to do my homework."

Amanda smacked her gum, rebuffed. "Fine," she said. "I don't know why you bother so much. Grades won't mean anything after we get out of this shithole."

I turned all the way around in my seat, causing Mr. Hartman's eyelashes to flutter. I spun back around, pretending to scratch as he reached up to pinch his nose at the bridge. The man was going to give himself a coronary over high school sophomores one day. Even I could tell what a waste that would be.

"Well, they won't. Plus, you could always get hit by a bus." I heard Amanda slide a hardback textbook from her backpack and slap it on the desk. *Thwap.*

Then a skinny, spiral-bound notebook. It would probably be the blue one, which had white hearts gracing its cover that Amanda had personally worn in with the edge of her eraser and traced with pink marker. *Thwap.*

Silence.

"Will you at least come shopping with me for a dress on Saturday?" Her voice sounded small. I knew she hated to go anywhere alone, that she really did want it to be me to come with her. I sighed and looked out at the hallway just as Jesse passed by on his way to the office. He turned just as he was about to escape from my view at the edge of the door. Smiling, he held his thumb and forefinger up to his head, like a phone. I felt like there was nobody else in the room.

Call me.

I flinched as Amanda seized my hair again and yanked. I yelped, and Mr. Hartman's eyelashes flapped like shutters in a hurricane.

****

Rumors always reached me last. I don't know why. Especially when they might involve me.

Lin and I usually hung out in the balcony during gym, watching most of our class half-heartedly playing horse or lifting weights. If the coach came up, we pretended to be doing the aerobics video we always let run on the VCR shoved against the wrestling mats. It was better than actual participation, even if it was "Buns of Steel." Mine felt more like buns of aluminum, but whatever.

"You really like him, right?"

I feigned innocence. "Like who?"

Lin rolled her eyes and pushed up her glasses. "Come on. Jesse."

"Yes." I tried to catch my smile by biting down on the sides of my mouth. It didn't really work.

"Well, I thought you should know—I saw him and Amanda talking in Kwik Shop the other day. They were sitting in a booth together."

My gut contracted. I laughed, but it wasn't funny. "What am I supposed to do about that?"

"I don't know, maybe nothing. I just thought you would want to know."

"Well, if Amanda wants to go out with him, it's already over for me," I muttered, my stomach still in knots. My head felt hot.

43

Lin jerked her head back. "Why would you even say that?"

"Listen, Lin, Amanda can get any guy she wants. She got the body of a cover model when we were still playing hopscotch on the playground. You know this."

I paused, remembering last year when Amanda stole Tony Kennedy from Grace Ryan two weeks after Tony gave Grace his school jacket. Lin and I had spent the majority of one sleepover hashing over how that could possibly have happened. Surely she hadn't forgotten already?

"You don't have to roll over dead just because she looked at him." Lin snorted, like she was disgusted with me, which hurt. Lin usually didn't judge me. It was one of the things I liked most about her.

I sighed. Maybe Lin was disgusted with me. I sort of was. Why should the same people always win? I leaned over to touch my toes, pretending to be deep in thought, hoping the pose concealed my red face. Usually when Amanda moved in, I did, in fact, roll over. It was easier and less embarrassing than trying to compete. But I'd never wanted to be with anyone as badly as I wanted to be with Jesse.

I straightened up. "Did you hear what they said?"
"No."
"Did he have that Amanda look?"
Lin shrugged. "I'd tell you if I knew. He had his back to me. She saw me come in and that was it. I waved, paid for my gas, and left."

I leaned over to touch my toes again. The blood slowly drained to my eyeballs while I thought about what

44

to do. If Amanda wanted Jesse, I had to do something. But what?

"Thanks for telling me," I mumbled, turning away from Lin.

Below the balcony, down on the gym floor, kids were playing dodge ball. My friend Mark, as usual, was staging a full-out assault every time he could get his hands on the ball. He'd wrapped a white bandana around his forehead, Karate Kid-style. I watched him smash the red rubber ball into Annabeth James's back as she attempted to tuck and roll away from him. Mark shrieked with victory and dropped to the floor just in time to avoid getting tagged himself. He seemed to be the only one taking the game seriously. To them: dodge ball. To Mark: humanity's last grip on the planet Earth.

"Sure. But listen, you can't let Amanda move in this time. I can tell you really like him. What are you going to do?"

"I have no idea."

"You should talk to him, and soon." Lin began doing squats facing the VCR as the coach's steps echoed on the metal stairs leading up to the balcony. I automatically turned around and started lunging across the floor like my very buns depended on it.

"No offense, Lin, but why are you so into me getting Jesse?"

The coach poked his head around the corner, saw us squatting, and headed back down the stairs, probably to peel Mark off the basketball rim. I turned to Lin, who pushed up her glasses and straightened up.

"Because, Diana, when you talk about him, your face changes. You're sad so often since your mom got sick. I'd just like to see you happy again, you know?"

I smiled at her and resumed lunging just for the hell of it. I was sure my butt would thank me in the morning.

****

After school, I changed into sweats and walked out the door toward Logwood Street and the hill that led up to the town square. As I sped up, leaves loosened from the trees and fell, making more noise than seemed possible. I didn't even notice the LeSabre until Jesse pulled up beside me and leaned over to roll down his window.

"Hey, Diana, where to?"

"Oh, hi. I don't need a ride. I'm actually walking on purpose. For exercise. It's this new thing that's supposed to be good for you." I smiled despite myself. I had a smile default setting for Jesse, like a reflex.

"Walking on purpose? That sounds fascinating. May I join you?"

He pulled the LeSabre onto a side street and got out. Same work boots, same jeans, same white t-shirt.

"I guess you already have." I crossed my arms, pretending to be mad.

He laughed. "You don't look very excited to see me."

On the contrary.

"Are you used to women falling at your feet?" I wished I hadn't said that.

But he didn't react badly. "Oh, yes. Women the world over swoon when they see me."

Does Amanda? But I didn't say anything. I'd learned years before, appearing jealous of Amanda was extremely counterproductive in almost any situation.

I smiled and started walking again, glancing back over my shoulder to see if he'd follow me. I didn't actually know what I was doing, but I hoped he would catch up to me.

After shaking his head for a moment, he did.

"You're following me," I said softly.

He laughed and bumped against me with his shoulder. The jolt passed between us again, so strong I felt dizzy for a second. "Sometimes you sound like you're thirty years old, you know?"

"Is that bad or good?"

"It's good. I ran into Amanda at Kwik Shop the other day and—no offense, I know you're friends—but she cornered me for a half hour. That girl can talk the ears off a brass monkey without saying a damn thing."

I turned my head so he wouldn't see my expression. I asked myself if I could do it, if I could take what I wanted, just like she did. I could feel the heat traveling up my neck. Finally, I stopped: I just had to know.

"Jesse, if you want to go out with Amanda, you need to stop hanging out with me."

He stopped walking and gaped at me. "Why do you think I want to go out with Amanda? Why would I even say that if I wanted to go out with her?"

"You'd be surprised how many guys have bitched to me about Amanda in the hopes of getting more information about her." I ran my hands through my ponytail. "It's sort of par for the course."

He flinched, his face flushing. He was studying me like I was a feral dog.

I didn't want that. I wanted him to want me. I took a deep breath and decided to go for it.

"Listen, ever since we took that drive all I can do is think about you. But Lin saw you with Amanda, and I've been friends with Amanda since preschool. She gets what she wants."

He rocked back on his heels, his eyes intent. The flush was moving up his face, but he seemed unaware of it. "I've been thinking about you, too, Diana. Do you get what you want?"

I paused, considering. "Not usually."

He smiled and grabbed my hand. I felt the touch all the way up my arm. "Well then, maybe you should try a little harder." He squeezed my hand and let it go, while I stood, frozen.

I watched him walk back to the LeSabre, and I resolved to do just that. Jesse was going to be mine, no matter what it took.

****

Ma stood at the microwave, one hand pressed to her forehead backwards the way she did when she had a headache. A Tupperware tray of unseasoned, frozen green beans twirled inside the microwave, just beginning to release that smell. My stomach roiled.

"Hey, Ma, what's for dinner?"

She looked over at me. "Broiled chicken, green beans, and rolls."

I swallowed drily. I hated Ma's cooking even when she was feeling fine. For a while when I was in elementary school, Pa and I had tried to stage a cooking coup. My specialty was macaroni and cheese; his was French dip. Unfortunately, Ma got bored and took back the kitchen within a week.

I took out plates and began to set the table anyway. I liked to use things that matched, though Ma and Pa would eat off a Frisbee. In my kitchen, someday, people would use linen napkins with napkin rings and drink from goblets instead of the 1985 Care Bears tumbler collection from Pizza Hut.

"How are you feeling?" I asked from my vantage point, unable to see her face. I wanted her to lie to me.

"I guess the same," she said. "I'm really tired. I think I'm going to go to bed after supper."

"Ma?"

The microwave dinged, and without looking I pictured her sliding the tray out, sticking one finger into the dish, and shoving it back in. I heard her reset the timer and shuffle to the edge of the counter where I could see her. She looked way more tired than her shiny wig did.

"Did you ever call guys to ask them out?" I asked.

Ma's face took on energy like she'd been shot up with meth. She smiled coyly. "Of course. Does this have anything to do with homecoming?"

I sat down at the kitchen table and began shredding a white paper napkin embossed with tiny green teddy bears. "Of course."

"Do you want to ask this Jesse boy?"

"Of course."

The microwave dinged again, but she left the vegetables inside and came over to sit by me. I could smell her chemical breath, but I still leaned toward her. She shifted her chair so I could lean all the way in, draping my body over hers. I was bigger than she was, definitely stronger, but I wanted to be held.

"Is he nice?"

"Of course he's nice."

"Not all boys are nice, Diana. And I've never met his mother."

I sighed, smiling and hating myself for it. I couldn't think about Jesse without smiling—damn if I wanted her to know. She knew anyway.

"Well, I can tell from your smile that he's nice. How old is he?"

"Sixteen."

"Can he drive?" she asked after a moment. She seemed to be moving through a mental checklist.

I sat up, trying to figure out if this meant I couldn't go to homecoming with Jesse. I knew I couldn't lie, though. The news would travel fast enough. "Yes. He just got his license. Pa saw his car. Pa met him."

I invoked Pa's name to shroud how little Ma knew about Jesse. Really, how little *I* knew about Jesse. It wasn't like I'd known him my whole life, like I did everyone else. He could have moved here because he skinned puppies, and I would be none the wiser.

Ma smiled, standing to return to the oven, where the chicken breasts were quickly drying out. "If he can drive, he should ask you," she said over her shoulder. "But you should make sure you give him all the opportunity he needs. Now go get Pa."

I followed her and hugged her again, tucking my chin into the hollow of her clavicle. She might be sick and skinny, but she was still taller. "Thanks," I said.

"Don't thank me yet," said Ma, leaning over to pull out the chicken. "Once he asks, then we'll talk about whether or not you can ride in that car of his."

It took Pa three warnings to leave the computer alone, but finally we sat down to dinner. I reached for my spoon, but Pa cleared his throat. "You forgot the prayer," he said quietly.

****

Pa got called in to work. As I was staring at my book, trying to read the same page for the thirtieth time, I heard a thump. The clock read ten-forty-two pm. I sat up in bed, listening. Silence. Another thump. Pulling on my bathrobe, I padded up the stairs into my parents' bedroom. Ma sat on her bed in the lamplight, both feet flat on the floor. She looked up at me and half smiled, but the weariness dragged down the corners of her mouth.

"Lie down, Ma."

"Your father is still at work. Would you get me some water?"

I nodded. On the way to the kitchen I passed a framed photo of Ma and me in the old leather chair she'd given away to the church preschool. I was about three in the photo, serving Ma tea in a green plastic cup shaped like a frog.

I found it in the kitchen behind the Tupperware. It still had its little plastic feet to steady it. I ran the well water from the separate faucet and dropped in three ice cubes. They crackled like summer as they hit the water.

Ma sat up when I brought it to her and took a sip. "Do you remember this cup?" she asked as I held her back to steady her. I nodded, patting her hand.

We sat on the bed for a little bit. Then she handed the cup back, wiping her mouth with the back of her arm, a habit of mine she hated. I turned out the light and crawled under the covers next to her. "Do you want me to stay a while?"

"That would be nice."

An owl hooted outside in the woods, and I slid down beside her into the crook of her arm. Ma started humming the old song she always used to when I couldn't sleep, and I lifted her arm over me like a blanket. She pulled me closer to her, her breath rattling in my ear.

I heard her breathing lengthen and slow before mine did, but I don't remember falling asleep. When the alarm went off, Pa was on the couch and Ma's arm was still around me, the frog cup resting on the nightstand.

****

Snowden wasn't normal when it came to homecoming. Most schools have a dance, sure, and a homecoming king and queen, but they're crowned on the football field and immediately forgotten after the Friday-night fireworks. My school's celebration was the stuff of documentaries.

The homecoming dance didn't follow the football game. It followed a grandiose coronation ceremony for the king and queen that took place in the high school gym, attended by all the town dignitaries. As each senior's name was called, he or she had to bow or curtsy to the king and queen.

Bow or curtsy. To someone you used to watch wet their pants. The last homecoming king used to ride my bus. He could fart the ABCs.

The sad part? The parents really did believe there was honor in that piece of cardboard. So did Amanda. So did I.

I'd participated for as long as I could remember. Ma hadn't grown up in Snowden—she'd grown up in Chicago—and her patience for the proceedings was as short as mine. Also? The parade made it hard to park. Ma was really big on good parking.

I sat at my desk, staring at the darkness falling on the woods outside my window. I'd already rearranged the glass elephant collection on my windowsill and watered the struggling begonia. The phone book sat on the desk. I ran my fingers over the smooth plastic arc of the receiver, tapping, tapping. I could feel my heart pounding, could feel the broiled chicken I'd barely touched sitting like a brick in my gut.

He'd motioned to call him, but that felt like years before. Why didn't he call me? Had I freaked him out too much on the walk? I had to make the next move.

Did I have to?

I should.

I rolled my shoulders, rolled my neck, heard my back pop. The darkness made my window a mirror. I smiled at my reflection, then grabbed my cheeks and pulled, just like Seth would. I felt the familiar clench in my abdomen, the tension in my back.

I almost fell over backward when the phone rang. I stared at it, unable to pick it up. I heard Ma answer upstairs, move toward the staircase, holler at me. "Diana, the phone's for you."

"Hey, what's up?" I said to who I figured was Amanda, wishing she wasn't digging into my Jesse-calling time.

"Hi, Diana. It's Jesse."

My pulse immediately quickened. "Hey, you," I replied, trying to keep my voice steady. *Ohmygoddonotmessthisup.*

"Why didn't you call?"

I wanted him. I was going to get him. "I was waiting for you."

"Were you, now?" I could hear the smile in his voice.

"What is it that you want, Jesse?" I sucked in my breath slowly, hoping he wouldn't hear. It was now or never. I watched my alarm clock's second hand swinging around its arc.

He coughed. I plucked one of the dying begonia blossoms from my plant, twirling it between two fingers. And I waited. The second hand cleared the six and started up its hill.

"Do you want to go to homecoming with me?" he asked finally.

"Are you kidding? I'd love to go with you."

"Is it as bizarre as I've been hearing?"

"Yes. No. Maybe worse than what you've been hearing."

Jesse laughed, and I heard his voice relax. "That's great. I'm looking forward to it."

"Me too. Me too. You're going to need a tour guide, trust me."

****

Everyone stayed late at school on Thursday. Forty cans of paint lined the sidewalk, brushes at the ready. Lin and I burst through the doors the minute the last bell rang, hoping to be the first to seize paint. I got white.

"Hey, Diana," Jesse said. I jumped involuntarily.

"Hi."

"What is all this?" Jesse gestured to the paint. "What are you doing with the paint?"

I smiled at him. "We're painting the street. It's part of homecoming. It's fun, you should try it."

"Why? I don't get it."

"Why do we do anything in Snowden? Because we're bored."

He laughed, looking around for paint. "Okay, if you say so."

Amanda walked up, holding out a brush to Jesse. "Go ahead, you try." Amanda could make ordering a cheeseburger sound like a proposition. She dangled it in front of her V-neck, right where her locket disappeared into her cleavage, a move that seldom failed to register.

55

Jesse took the brush, careful not to touch her fingers, his face flushing again. She smirked, but her eyes narrowed.

I touched his arm. "Here," I said. "You can use this." I held out my paint. When he took it, he slid his fingers over mine.

"Thanks, Diana," he muttered. I loved the way he said my name so often, the way it sounded in his voice.

Jesse squatted to the street. He painted a symbol I recognized from the wall of the wrestling room. Jake hooted.

"That's it. Screw football."

Mark grabbed the paint pot from Jake, dipping his brush and slapping an "x" across Jesse's t-shirt. Jesse looked down, surprised. Then he took off toward the back parking lot.

"Get him!" yelled Mark. "He must not escape!" Mark threw off his jacket and raised his fists. "Onward!"

We ran across the grass as Jesse started up the hill behind the school. He got about halfway up before Mark caught him and poured paint over his head. Jesse howled as the paint coursed down his cheeks. "It's in my ears!" he yelled, punching at Mark, who danced away.

Coach Davis blew his whistle then from the circle drive. "Okay, everyone, that's enough. Street painting's done. Go get some rest. Tomorrow's the big game."

We weren't ready to go home. Pink streaked across the sky as we milled around the parking lot. Mark pulled out his truck keys as parents started pulling up. I saw Pa, fourth back in the line of cars, and ran over to him, nearly tripping on my untied shoelaces. "Can I stay, Pa, please?"

"What are you going to do?"

"Mark has his truck. We'll just hang out and drive around a little. Please? Everyone else is."

Pa glanced over at Mark. He'd gone to high school with Mark's dad. He sighed.

"Please?"

"Okay," he said. "But don't get caught by the police." Before I could tell if he was joking or not, he jiggled the stick shift and eased his way out of the car line.

Kids were climbing into the bed of Mark's truck when I got back. His engine idled. I ran up to the window, hopped on the truck's rail, and poked my head in the open window. Jesse sat shotgun looking out the passenger window, his expression hard to read. "Where are you going?"

"Who knows? Get in. I'm going to leave in two seconds." Mark grinned and glanced in his rearview mirror. There were at least ten kids in the bed of the truck.

Amanda leaned her head over the side from the back of the truck. "Diana, get in." She picked her way over paint-splattered bodies to the rear of the truck and held out her hand.

I had to hoist myself up to the back fender, suddenly conscious of my clumsiness. I'd never been good at climbing. I stepped on my shoelaces as I hauled myself up, my foot shooting out from under me. I had one of Amanda's hands as Mark started to pull away, and

57

for an instant, I thought we might both catapult onto the concrete. Seth grabbed my other hand and hauled on my arm. I flew into the truck bed and landed hard on his stomach.

"Ow, God, Diana! Heavy!"

My face flamed. I stared down at him in horror. "Did I hurt you with my extreme bulk?"

Seth pushed me off. "No. I just wasn't expecting it. Jeez." Then he saw my expression. "Hey, it's no big deal," he called, trying to grab my arm, but I pulled away.

I felt like an elephant. I crawled over by the wheel well as Mark pulled out on to the highway, trying to squish myself into the smallest shape possible. My hair pulled free of my ponytail and whipped around my face as he picked up speed. I don't think anyone saw the tears. It was really dark.

We drove up and down the strip for an hour, laying on the horn anytime we passed another car full of kids. Everyone was out.

Amanda crawled over by me on the second pass. "Hey, what's wrong?" she said, seeing my face in the streetlights when we turned around in the church parking lot.

"Nothing."

She hit my knee. "Come on, I'm not stupid."

"Nothing, okay? I don't want to talk about it."

"Okay, fine," she said. "Where's Jesse? Why aren't you with him? Aren't you guys going to the dance together?"

"Shhhh." I whispered, "He's in the cab. I don't want to make a big deal. I'm waiting for him to talk to me first. God, you're so embarrassing."

She grinned. "Whatever."

I felt the truck pick up speed and pulled my hair back off my face. We were pulling out of town, turning back onto the highway. It was freezing in the back of the truck, going so fast. I had no idea where we were headed.

After a few miles, Mark turned the truck off the highway onto a gravel road, jouncing us in the back onto each other. We passed under the viaduct spray-painted with names from years before and pulled up at a small country lane next to an abandoned power plant, its tower extending toward the sky. Mark parked the truck back behind the tower, out of sight, and we all piled out.

My knees were stiff from sitting in the truck for so long. I leaned over to stretch them as Seth and Hutch wandered over to a steel drum upright by a stand of trees. Seth leaned over and looked inside, nodded, and motioned to Hutch to follow him. They appeared a few minutes later carrying armloads of twigs and small branches, which they dumped into the drum. Seth lit a match and tossed it in the can.

Lin wandered over to watch. Some of the other kids started smoking and gathered around the drum. It was definitely chilly, and the fire began to crackle as they poked at it with long sticks.

Jesse emerged from behind the truck. I could barely see him, but he glowed white from the paint. He'd pulled off his t-shirt and sweatshirt and was wiping the paint from his hair with the t-shirt. I looked away so no one would see me staring at his bare chest, but I saw enough of it for my breath to catch. I still couldn't believe he'd asked me to the dance. I remembered practically crushing Seth and wrapped my arms tightly around my torso. The shame prickled the back of my neck, like ants marching. I wanted to be more confident. I wanted to be the one to talk to him first.

Jesse finished wiping what he could from his hair. The t-shirt was full of paint. He tossed it into the truck bed and pulled his sweatshirt back on, the hood catching over his head before he tugged it down. Most of the other kids were still by the fire, so I walked over to him in the shadow of the truck.

"Sorry you got soaked," I said.

He laughed. He still had streaks of white paint on his cheeks. "I think it's weirdest in my ears," he said. "I've never had that feeling before."

I stood on my toes to peer at his ears, feeling the tingle at being so close. "It looks like you got most of it," I said, holding onto the truck for support so I wouldn't have to hold onto Jesse. I wasn't sure what I'd do if I actually touched him. It was all I could do to smell him. The smell of him made my stomach flip.

He smiled and sat down near the edge of the field and patted the ground next to him. "Have a seat."

I lowered myself down. It was actually warmer on the ground amidst the broken-off cornstalks, out of the wind.

Jesse gestured up at the sky. The stars had emerged, and here away from town, the night sky looked like a planetarium.

"Are you pissed about the paint?" I asked.

He shifted. "I'm letting it go."

"Why?"

"That's how I do things now. It's easier than getting mad."

We looked up.

"We didn't have stars like this in KC," said Jesse.

"No, I suppose you had electric lights and stuff, not like here," I said. His control impressed me. Imagine just *deciding* you weren't mad—no shoulder prickles, no stomach clenches, no tight chest trying to breathe while everyone looked at you. No going home and hating yourself, hating your body, hating, hating, hating, until you wondered why anyone ever spoke to you at all.

"Well, it was bigger, and there was different stuff to do, but it's not so bad here once you get used to it. It's new to me still. I don't know what I think, I guess. Is that okay?" He answered like he'd done it a thousand times before. I knew the feeling. He smiled at me, leaning back on his arms. I fought the urge to put my head on his chest.

"Okay? Well, sure." I swallowed, wanting to push forward anyway. "Was it hard? To get used to it? I mean, do you miss Kansas City?"

"Well, sure. But Diana...my big brother died there."

I nodded, remembering what he'd told me at hole sixteen on the golf course. I knew he understood what was happening with Ma. He'd gone through it too, and he'd been even younger, and it was his brother. Different, maybe, but the same, too. More the same than anything I could share with Lin or Amanda or Seth. They could talk to me, but they couldn't understand. Not like Jesse could, not like he *did*.

Jesse cleared his throat. "After Justin died, it just wasn't the same. Everywhere we went, it seemed like there were memories. My mom wanted to be closer to her family in Omaha, and this seemed like a good place for my sister and me to go to school. So here we are, in paradise."

"Yeah, paradise." I leaned back, trying to imagine moving as a sophomore in high school. Moving at all, ever. A brother dying. Having a brother. Having someone else at home besides Ma and Pa to talk to about the hospital, the doctors, the wigs.

"I was ready for a change, Diana. Anything could happen here, and something already happened there that I can't undo. Here I can just be normal. No drama. It will get normal again someday, Diana."

Jesse leaned back. He didn't look at me when he asked about Ma.

I didn't mind it as much coming from him. "She's mad a lot. Over random stuff, like groceries."

He nodded. And waited.

"She keeps comparing herself to Job."

"Job?"

"The guy in the Bible who gets tested by God."

He laughed, covering his mouth. "I'm sorry," he said. "That's not funny."

But I found myself laughing, too. It *was* funny, in a bizarre sort of way. He couldn't possibly know how serious Ma was when she did it—she really did feel she was being tested by God, which sort of blew my mind. Surely God had better things to do.

"How was it when your brother got sick?"

"Well, I was really young. I don't think I realized how serious it was until it was too late. I was jealous of how much attention he got. My parents were gone a lot. I wish I would've been nicer to him. I didn't understand what was going on, why everyone was ignoring me. But I was also really worried about him—he'd always been my strong big brother, and all of a sudden he looked like this skinny wreck."

Jesse inhaled deeply and looked up at the sky again. I wondered if he was trying not to cry. That's what I did when I was trying not to cry. But I had to ask anyway. "Did you know he was going to die?" I looked up, too, almost holding my breath.

He inhaled again deeply, not saying anything. Seconds passed, and I was sure he was mad at me for asking. Then he nodded, some sort of spell broken. He leaned over and brushed my arm lightly with his shoulder. "What do you want to know?"

"What will I do if she dies?" I asked, feeling my lower lip start to tremble. I blinked back tears, keeping my eyes up. He placed his hand over mine as we sat facing the night sky, not looking at each other. Some conversations have to be had with your eyes averted.

"Everything is different now. You said they caught it early, right?"

I nodded. "Well, they caught it. I don't know if things are different."

"Stop being such a *dick!*"

63

Both Jesse and I whipped around to see Seth yelling at Mark, and the intensity went out of our conversation just like that. I felt okay again. I took a deep breath, relieved.

Jesse put his arm around me, drawing me in, and I turned and leaned into the warmth of his sweatshirt. I could smell the acrid paint, but underneath that, I could smell his skin. I inhaled deeply before pushing away.

"I've lived in the same house my whole life," I said, sitting up. "What's it like to move?"

"It teaches you what you miss when it's gone," he said, smiling.

"I…" I turned but didn't finish my sentence, because Jesse was right there, his breath hot on my cheek.

Chapter Four: True Colors

Amanda's brother, Derek, dropped us off at the mall at ten a.m., right as the gray-clad security guards fumbled with the locks on the glass doors. I wondered if they understood what was coming their way: homecoming season.

Amanda grabbed my hand and led me past kiosks selling gold chain by the foot and fiber-optic lilies and ceramic reindeer to the back of the mall. I always dreaded the formal dress section of Dillard's, which at ten-oh-five was already teeming with impatient teenagers and their weary mothers. The sequins in that section could float a cruise ship to Alaska.

Amanda and I headed for the racks. I pulled out only plain black dresses, my eyes skipping over anything with color or embellishment like weeds in a garden. Amanda reached for the reds, the oranges, the blues, nearly grooming her plumage as she searched. I yawned.

After twenty minutes of pawing through crepe and tulle, we headed for the dressing rooms. We both shoved ourselves into the largest room at the end, the one with the little bench.

I'd brought my body armor. I had girdle-like panties with a control top and a bustier that—without the girdle pants—would squeeze my belly fat out into a neat little doughnut sitting on my hips. Together, the combination had the effect of chain mail. I felt like Wonder Woman's slightly overweight sister, only without, you know, super powers.

In the dressing room, I wiggled out of my clothes, facing the wall, and stuffed myself into my fat gear while Amanda slipped off everything but a pair of satin panties and stood before the mirror, admiring the little heart of white skin on her left hipbone that she used to gauge her tanning bed progress.

She picked up the first dress, a tight sheath of sequins that poofed into a mermaid-like fin at the bottom. It was blood red, and the color stood out in sharp contrast to her tanned skin. She leaned over and dug through her purse, producing a ponytail holder. "I'm wearing my hair up this year. Are you?"

I looked in the mirror, meaning to study my hair, but all I saw were my thighs compressed into shiny sausages by the underwear. "I haven't thought about it. Do you think it makes that big a difference?"

Amanda knitted her eyebrows at me. "Of course it matters, Diana. Have I taught you nothing?"

I laughed. "You've taught me nothing."

"Whatever. What do you think?" She pulled her hair up off her face, her clavicles popping against the straps of the dress. She turned to the side, svelte, perfect.

"It's amazing." I meant it. She looked glorious. Sometimes it was hard not to feel bad for Amanda for never getting her own TV show. She'd grow out of this perfection here in Snowden without anyone important ever seeing it. Amanda really needed Hollywood, not southwestern Iowa.

"Yeah," she said, turning slowly and raising her hands to the ceiling like Marilyn Monroe. "It really is."

We tried on more than forty dresses. Amanda ended up buying the red one she'd tried on first.

My dress went all the way to the floor. I felt much more comfortable with my legs safely stowed. When I plunked down on the dressing-room bench to check out my seated reflection, the undergarments bent me in half uncomfortably.

My money barely covered the cost of the dress with nothing left for shoes, but I figured with my feet covered I could wear some normal pumps. Amanda wanted to head to the shoe store to get custom-dyed heels to match her dress.

As I waited, I imagined the death-by-chocolate-cake recipe from the cookbook under my bed. I pictured digging a fork into it, the chocolate syrup inside oozing out like a river.

****

"Hi, Diana, what're you doing?" Lin came up quickly behind where I stood just past the football field bleachers. The homecoming game had already begun.

I put my hands in my back pockets and tried to look casual. "Just hanging out. Ready to go in?"

Lin took off her glasses and began cleaning them with her t-shirt. "Are you okay?" she asked. "How is your mom?"

"She's fine. She started chemo. It's going to be okay." I didn't want to talk about my mother. I wanted to go find Jesse.

Lin seemed to understand. She poked my arm, still freckled from the summer sunshine. "Come on," she said. "Let's go sit down. I see Sticks and Hutch."

I looked around. They were sitting at the edge of the bottom row with the band. Seth had his black beret off and was tossing it in the air, catching it on the edge of his drumsticks. He saw me and spun one around his fingers, the drumstick dancing like a baton between skinny fingers with chewed cuticles. I waved and Lin and I headed in his direction.

"Do I look okay?" whispered Lin.

I turned around. I didn't think Lin cared about stuff like that. I looked at her, and then at Seth and Hutch. "Why?" I felt the corners of my mouth tug up even though I was trying not to smile.

She looked down at her Keds, which were missing the laces. "Hutch asked me out again for tonight after the game."

"What?" I grabbed her hand and pulled her toward the bathrooms. "Why didn't you tell me? You are actually getting serious with him, aren't you? That's great."

"Please don't make a scene," she implored, her cheeks flushing. "I don't want everyone to stare at me."

"It's fine," I said. "They'll think it's just me being weird again, anyway." I grinned at her, making my patented crazy Michelle Pfeiffer fish face.

"Oh, stop it. I don't think you're weird," she said.

I studied her, standing there in her gold Snowden t-shirt and tapered jeans. I knew she didn't think I was weird. And I appreciated it. "Thanks."

We scooped around behind the bleachers as if that were our plan all along and emerged on the other side closest to Seth and Hutch. I scanned the cheerleaders, looking for Amanda. She stood in the center of the back row, tall and slim, her dark ponytail topped with perfectly tied black-and-gold ribbons that whipped in the breeze. She was popping gum, which I knew she wasn't supposed to do, but Amanda never cared what she was supposed to do. I waved, but she didn't see me. She was laughing and turning her head to watch the game in a way that showed she knew half the boys in the front row were envisioning exactly what she looked like under her uniform. And she liked it.

"Hey, girl, what're you up to?" asked Seth, leaning over to talk to me, blond hair falling in his eyes. He smelled like cinnamon gum. Everything was fine, the weirdness from the other night gone.

"About five-seven," I joked. "Did you do your recon?"

Without looking away, Seth spun his drumstick and brought it down on the head of his snare drum with a sharp rap that my eyes involuntarily followed. Then his shoulders relaxed, and he set down the sticks. "Of course

I did. He's at nine o'clock, currently paralyzed with lust for you."

"What do you think I should do?"

"Since when do you ask me for man advice?"

"I don't know. Maybe since you got so fucking tall."

Seth stretched his legs, smoothing his jeans. I could tell he was trying not to smile. "I am filling out nicely. I say you go talk to him." But he stared at me a little too long, until I fidgeted.

I looked up at Jesse in the bleachers, surrounded by what seemed intimidatingly like half the wrestling team. I imagined them poofing away, vaporized by some convenient force that removed them from the scene without, you know, really hurting them. Like a video game. Where are the delete buttons in real life?

Lin sat down by Hutch, who played cymbals in the band. She laughed at something he said, tucking a shiny piece of hair behind one of her small ears. I touched her arm. "Hey, I'm going to get something to drink," I said.

She grinned. "Good luck with that," she said.

I felt naked by myself. I decided to take the front way and say hi to Amanda, make it look like I'd ventured across the bleachers for that reason and not to give myself more time to think about how to get Jesse's attention without having to walk up to him.

The wrestling coach stood at the edge of the cinder track that circled the football field. "Hey, Diana," he called as I passed.

"Hey, Coach," I answered, dreading the next question.

"How's your mom?"

"She's sick," I said. "You know what? She's sick." And I kept walking, my eyes turned to the ground.

We lost the homecoming game.

****

I looked for Jesse at Pizza Hut, but he wasn't there. I barely heard anything Amanda and Lin said as they drew detailed outlines of their dresses on napkins and described how many hours it would take to get ready.

Lin and I met in seventh grade when she was the last new kid in Snowden I could remember. She taught me geometry during freshman year study hall, her voice thick with sarcasm as she described how the geometry teacher raised his voice when talking to her as though she didn't understand English despite being born in Connecticut.

"So Jesse's a wrestler, huh?" asked Lin, finally turning to me. It was an obvious question designed to get me to spill on our relationship, whatever it was.

"Yeah," I answered as noncommittally as possible. Like I wanted to tell them I was hopelessly in a crush with Jesse.

Amanda pushed aside the napkin drawing and fixed me with black-lined eyes. "Which weight class?" she asked. Amanda cheered for wrestling, too.

"I don't know. Why?"

She laughed, pushing her straw up and down in the red plastic glass. "He could go up or down. It's hard to tell how much he weighs, but it's a little high of

71

middle. Which is the toughest place to be in our conference. Get ready to kiss that boy goodbye."

I seized my own glass and took a pull of Diet Coke, pissed but considering. "I don't know that I've particularly kissed him *hello* yet. We're just going to the dance," I said, immediately regretting it. What if he heard I'd said that? What if he thought I didn't really like him?

Amanda smacked my arm. "Oh, we *know* you've kissed him hello," she said.

I felt my cheeks burn. "Just because it's actually rare for me."

"So back to wrestling," said Amanda. She wasn't going to let this one go. I hoped it was just simple curiosity. Amanda loved nothing more than being in everyone's business.

Lin spoke up. "Hutch says Jesse told him he used to wrestle in Kansas City, but it's more competitive here than it was there."

I turned to her, one eyebrow raised. This was news to me.

"I guess he was pretty good there, but he doesn't know how he'll be here."

I leaned in. "What else did Hutch say about Jesse?"

Lin shrugged and pushed up her glasses. "You know, he's cute and nice, but I get the feeling that he just wasn't all hot shit in Kansas City. I think he was just a regular guy." She smiled at me. "Not in a bad way, just maybe in a nice way."

72

Who cared whether he wasn't a big deal in Kansas City? All that mattered to me was Snowden. I pushed my uneaten pizza away.

"Aren't you going to eat that?" asked Amanda. She was already digging her fingers into the cheese of my pizza slice. Like I'd ever consider eating it after that.

"No, you can have it," I said, feeling my inner thigh and resolving never to eat pizza again.

****

The next morning, Ma woke me up with breakfast on a tray. "Are you excited for tonight?" she asked, looking sleepy in a red turban.

I struggled to sit up. "What's all this? Am I dreaming? Am I finally a princess?"

"You might as well eat now. I know you'll forget later." Ma cracked her knuckles and wiped a finger along the brass rail of my daybed, checking for dust.

I picked up a strip of bacon and sighed, ignoring her silent request that I clean more often. "I wish it were time for the dance now. I don't know if I can stand to wait."

Ma laughed, twirling my hair with her long fingers. "I remember those days," she said. "I remember those days."

"Really?"

"What? You think your old mother is so ancient? I went with Andy Higgins. He was six feet tall, dark hair, freckles. Star basketball player."

I gawked at her. "You really remember all this." It wasn't a question, more a statement of fact for my own benefit. It always escaped me that Ma had a life before she had me.

"Oh yes," she smiled, patting my hand. "I wore a long pink dress with ruffles." She laughed. "It was the style in those days, of course."

I thought of my sleek black sheath. "Thank God it's not the style now. I might die."

She eyed me. "Yes, I think you might."

"Did you kiss this Mr. Andy Higgins?" I asked.

She swatted my thigh with her newspaper and left the room without telling.

I spent the morning on the phone with Amanda, who was taking a poll of all our friends to see if she should really wear her hair up or down.

I decided to do my hair up. My dress wasn't very fancy, and my hair wasn't very good, so I'd bought a jewel-y barrette and figured I could do sort of a French twist thing. The French twist and liquid eyeliner proved more work than I'd intended, so when Ma came down the stairs at four-thirty with snacks, I was still in my sausage suit in the bathroom, frowning at my hair and trying not to smudge the liquid eyeliner by crying. I ignored the food, and she didn't say anything.

"Diana, put on your dress. I want to take pictures before that boy arrives."

Terror.

"Ma, you're not going to make me take pictures with him, are you? I actually might die of embarrassment. Like literally keel over, and it would be in these undergarments."

"I want to. You're my only daughter. It's your first homecoming date." Her face looked so young, like a child's. Eyelash-less.

I looked at her again. She'd brushed her wig in a different way and was wearing a silk blouse and black pants. I knew she wasn't going to coronation. She'd dressed up for me. I hugged her, turning my face carefully to avoid smearing make-up on her blouse. "Of course you can take a picture. But just one."

Ma came in while I was staring at my butt in the mirror. She immediately started crying. "Oh, Diana. Oh, Diana," she kept saying.

I grinned. "Thanks, Ma."

Pa knocked. "Can I please come in now?" He stepped onto my shag carpet and held up the good camera, the Nikon. I tilted my head the way I'd practiced in the mirror and swiveled my hips to what I thought was their best angle.

Jesse pulled up in the driveway while we watched from our hiding place in Ma's bedroom. Ma smiled at me. "Do you want me to get the door?"

My stomach lurched. It would be unbecoming to barf, I decided. "No, I'll get it."

I watched Jesse get out of the LeSabre. He was wearing a black suit. It emphasized his broad shoulders and slim waist, making him look taller.

The doorbell rang.

Oh. My. God.

I opened the door, smiling involuntarily. Jesse grinned, holding out a plastic box containing a red rose wrist corsage. His cheeks, freshly shaved, looked soft and

75

clean. I wanted to reach out and brush my fingers along them, feel his skin under my fingertips.

I'd never had a corsage before. I'd forgotten to get him a boutonnière. "Oh, God, I forgot your flower!"

Jesse just smiled. "Can I come in?"

I could hear Ma and Pa coming down the stairs. I stepped back, embarrassed, and he walked across the threshold. He leaned down and kissed my cheek just before Ma and Pa opened the staircase door. As he did, I caught my reflection in the hall mirror. My eyes—Ma's eyes, my best feature—looked blue as an ocean. They looked pretty.

Chapter Five: Can't Hold Back

Jesse's car glistened. He opened the door for me, waving to Ma and Pa standing together in the front window. Pa held Ma around the waist, and I could tell she was tired. I grinned at them nervously as Jesse walked around the front of the car.

He got in, started the engine. "You look great, Diana." He reached over and touched my hair. I could smell him again, the scent of him that drove me crazy. I wondered if I smelled like that to him, if we were just destined to seek each other out, if that happened with some people, like magnets.

"You don't look so bad yourself," I said, touching his arm right above the elbow's bend. We both jerked a little when my hand met his jacket. "And your car looks amazing."

"My car isn't amazing. My car is clean."

"Exactly. Obviously."

He laughed. I loved the sound of his laugh. And we drove down the driveway together for the first time.

****

The gym was a million degrees hot. Moms in sweater sets crowded the wooden bleachers next to squirming toddlers and the student body of Snowden Community High School. The traditional black velvet backdrop hung in front of the thrones, and the seniors were assembled, shifting nervously on folding chairs. The lights fell as the court filed in, taking their places. Amanda stood next to Grace Ryan, who had made the mistake of also wearing a red dress. Amanda's wrist was completely covered in a huge corsage of red and pink roses.

As the senior class members were called up in alphabetical order, I looked over at Jesse. He was clearly dumbfounded. He leaned over to me. "This is insane," he whispered. I could smell breath mints, but I felt his breath in my ear more. I resisted leaning toward his mouth.

I laughed, too loud. "It's always been this way. Amanda's mom was homecoming queen in her day. The bowing and curtsying is definitely the worst part."

Jesse shook his head. "I can't think of a better way to make people feel like shit."

For the next hour, I pretended to watch the coronation, concentrating instead on the feeling of Jesse's leg next to mine. The gym was crowded, and we were smashed next to each other on the bleachers. I felt the heat of his leg through his suit pants, through my dress, even through my magic girdle, as close as though we were skin to skin. The scent of Jesse got lost in the perfume of flowers all around me, but I felt I could follow his warmth like a heat-seeking missile.

After the coronation, we headed over to the lunchroom for the dance. Jesse's hand took my elbow as we ascended the stairs. Balloons covered the ceiling and walls, the lights low. My shoes pinched my toes as we waited to file past the court. I could see Amanda and her date, John, talking, Amanda's head turned to show her best side for the clicking cameras of parents dropping off their kids. She'd worn her hair down, curled loose and swingy above the glittering sequins of her dress.

As we approached, she smiled at me, her future-queen smile. Then she looked at Jesse, up and down. I saw him blush even in the dim light. Amanda could make any guy feel naked just by looking at him. I tightened my hands into fists in the semi-darkness.

"Hi, guys." Amanda grabbed me. "Accompany me to the little girls' room?" Once inside, she reached into her small silver clutch for lip gloss. "Are you ready to party?" she asked.

"Of course," I said. Amanda was making me nervous already.

She reached back into her purse and produced an airline bottle of Jack Daniel's. She uncapped it and took a swig, grimacing. "John got these. Do you want some?"

I looked around the packed restroom. There were parents in here. She was batshit crazy. "I actually prefer scotch."

"Suit yourself." Amanda drained the rest of the bottle, wiping her chin with one manicured hand. "Let's go."

****

The music slowed. Jesse stepped into the circle and took my hand, startling me. I began babbling awkwardly. "Are you having fun?" I asked. "Is this too over-the-top? I mean, they had dances in Kansas City, right?"

"We had dances, but nothing like that coronation. In KC, the king and queen were lucky to get a standing ovation on the football field, not thrones in the gym. That's just bizarre."

"Yeah, I never thought about how odd that must seem to someone who didn't grow up here."

"Well, I live here now," he said. "I guess I'd better get used to it. I think I can—you're here, and I'm definitely getting used to you."

I leaned in, catching his scent again, trying to identify what it was that smelled so good, so *Jesse*. My voice dropped, and I laughed more confidently than I felt. "Maybe someday you'll be king."

He actually shuddered. "God, I hope not. I'm going for normal, remember?" He pulled me a little closer, and I wrapped my arms tighter around his neck, struggling to keep my hands from shaking.

"Well," I said, as I inhaled his scent again, "I don't think you'll have any control over it, either way."

"Oh, sure I will," said Jesse. "It's pretty easy to avoid popularity. I'm very good at it." He smiled.

I laughed. "I find that hard to believe."

He looked down at me, turning serious. He was so tall. "You've only known Snowden, Diana. It's amazing how much things can change from one town to the next, when you're still the same person."

The song ended, and the DJ gestured to the karaoke machine. "Hey, who's going to step up first?" he asked.

Lin's voice was in my ear. "You should sing." She pushed me toward the machine.

I sucked in a startled breath. "I can't."

Seth appeared by my right arm. "Of course you can, Diana. Sing for us. Like you used to."

I looked over at Jesse, saw his surprised expression. "Can you sing?" he asked.

"She can sing," said Lin, smiling. "Come on, Diana. I'll go with you."

Lin pulled me toward the spotlight. I grasped her arm. "I don't do this anymore," I whispered angrily.

"You're going to," she said. She tugged my arm. "Everyone's looking. You have to now." I looked beyond her shoulder to see them, all my childhood friends, looking at me. Lin smoothed her short dress with one tiny hand. "We want to sing 'Respect,'" she told the DJ.

Before I could protest, the music started. And I did it—I sang, with Lin whirling about me doing all the back-up parts. As I held the last note, Lin bowed deep and the kids erupted in applause. Mark stepped onto the stage and started singing the theme song from *The Jeffersons*, and I sheepishly sidled over to Jesse.

"You don't belong here, you know," he whispered.

****

81

Amanda and John appeared again about a half hour before the end of the dance. Amanda was wasted. She'd taken off the red satin pumps and dangled them from one finger. Her wrist corsage hung like a dead animal from its stretchy silver elastic. Her hair hung limply around her sweaty forehead, and she staggered toward me with wild eyes. "Diana! Whazzzzup?"

"Dude, you've got to tone it down. I can totally smell you coming."

She laughed, breathing fumes all over me. "John boy here was just sharing his stash, right, John boy?"

John didn't seem as drunk as Amanda, but he'd definitely had his share. "Come on, baby," he slurred, patting Amanda's butt. "Let's dance."

The song wasn't slow, but they didn't seem to care. Amanda rested her head on John's shoulder as they staggered around the dance floor.

After the dance, Jesse drove us all to Denny's. Amanda passed out in the backseat, John's hand on her thigh. Lin and Hutch had squeezed in beside them and were whispering and laughing. The front seat felt like a different world. Jesse laid his arm across the back of my seat like he had on the golf course bench and told stories about dances in Kansas City all the way to Denny's and back.

"How many dances have you been to?" he asked.

"Um, well, there were the junior high dances in the gym. I went to pretty much all of those. And then homecoming last year. I went with Lin. She was my date. Right, Lin?" I hollered.

"Sure!" she yelled back, but I could tell she had no idea what I was talking about. She was laughing at something Hutch whispered in her ear.

"How about you?"

"Well, we had a homecoming dance, also in the gym, and a spring formal. You were supposed to rent a tux, like prom or something, and the rich kids rented limos."

"Limos? I don't think we even have limos in Snowden."

"Yeah, that's actually one thing I like about Snowden. Everyone's pretty much in the same boat. Limited access is limited access, right?"

I shook my head. "I can't believe you like that. I think it sucks."

He glanced at me sideways. "Ah, but think about it. Would you really want some people to have limos and hotel parties and their own swimming pools?"

I frowned. I'd never considered it, hadn't imagined it, kids with stuff like that. Adults didn't even have that stuff in Snowden. "I see your point."

When we got to Denny's, Amanda revived long enough to eat half a pancake, then slept all the way back to John's car. I worried as I watched their taillights pull away. I could never decide whether I felt like Amanda's sidekick or her pissed-off mother.

Jesse looked at the clock. "We've still got an hour before you have to be home," he drawled quietly. "Do you want to hit hole sixteen?"

My feet ached, so I pulled off my heels and left them in the car. The night air was cold, and Jesse pulled off his suit jacket and handed it to me. It smelled of him around my shoulders. We picked our way through the dew until my dress hem was soaked. Hole sixteen seemed a mile away, but I didn't care. I wanted the night to last forever.

Jesse looked at my feet, my dress, then leaned over and picked me up as though I were as thin as Amanda. I struggled for a minute—all I could think about was my weight, him throwing out his back, but he laughed and bounced me once to show he wasn't going to drop me. His forearms felt like iron beneath me as I realized he was up to carrying me. "I don't like to brag, Diana, but I can bench press more than you probably weigh," he whispered in my ear.

"You must bench press a lot," I whispered back. I knew I weighed more than he thought, more than any of my tiny friends.

He carried me to the bench and sat me down, leaning over as he did. The moon behind him outlined his jaw line covered in new stubble. I reached up and touched his cheek. His jaw flexed when my fingers stroked his temple, that shock still there. Jesse seemed so much older than a sophomore, so much older than sixteen. I felt older when I was with him.

"You don't know how beautiful you are," he said gruffly.

My stomach tightened. "I don't think I'm beautiful."

He sat next to me. "Are you serious?"

I looked down at my thighs, feeling as though I could see through the dress to my body armor, suddenly

84

miserable. My eyes were starting to itch around the corners, a sure sign I was going to cry. I hated myself then for ruining the moment, for being fat. I should be fascinating, not a train wreck.

He reached for my arm, and I pulled back, surprised, when he touched me. He left his fingers there. "What's going on, Diana?"

"I haven't had many dates in Snowden, I guess."

Jesse looked genuinely surprised. Then he gestured for me to continue.

"I was a really fat kid, okay?"

"Define 'really fat.'"

"I weighed one hundred pounds when I was four feet tall."

Jesse sat back, studying me as though I were a young heifer, no doubt trying to see the fat fourth-grader.

"I don't know why I'm even telling you this and ruining the fact you didn't even know."

"What does it matter? You're not fat now."

"But I am," I said, and as I said it, I realized how unattractive this whole conversation probably sounded to Jesse. But at the same time, I desperately wanted him to tell me it wasn't true. "And they were so mean—the other kids—until just a few years ago. It's hard to explain. It's hard for me to trust them now, except for Amanda, Seth, and Lin. And you…because you're new. I do trust you."

"Diana, I'm going to play the Obvious Game now: *You are beautiful*."

And then he was there, mouth hot, breath heavy, fingers in my hair. Lifting my dew-drenched feet, he pulled me around to lie on the bench, leaning over me, not resting his weight on me but hovering above. I gasped, and he kissed me deeper, lowering himself down slowly until I felt his body touch mine from chest to knees. Felt him want me.

I wished I could see what he saw.

****

As we pulled up the driveway, Jesse removed his hand from my knee, adjusting his bowtie. I could see Pa silhouetted in the picture window, waiting. As I peered through the window, Pa lowered the shade. Their bedroom window was dark and silent.

We sat in the driveway a minute. I kept an eye on the lowered shade as Jesse took my hands. "Jesse, I…"

He traced the inside of my wrist with a finger, and that current traveled through me again. "Diana, I really like you," he said, his voice low.

My stomach lurched. I waited for the other shoe to drop. Waited for the "but."

"Let's do this," he said, still staring at the wilted corsage on my wrist.

"Do what?" My voice squeaked.

"Let's be together."

"Are you sure you want to do that?" It came out wrong, different than I wanted it to. "I mean, God, I'd love that, but are you sure you want to be with *me?*"

He looked up, touched my hair. "Why not you?"

I unconsciously glanced at my thighs, wrapped in polyester and spandex under the black dress.

"Is there something else I should know?"

"No," I said quickly. "I'm just… My mom…"

"Oh, right. You're a mess." He smiled.

"She's mad a lot. Which makes me mad a lot."

He nodded. "I was mad once. I understand. Maybe I can help you forget about being mad. Let me help you find normal."

He leaned in and kissed me softly, and I forgot to watch the window. I wanted to disappear inside of him. When he kissed me, I forgot about everything but him.

"Diana, I told you. I get that. I've been there. I like that you're real, that you're not hung up on fashion or something. I respect that. When we talk, it's like we've known each other forever. I felt like I already knew you the first time we met."

The porch light came on. Pa was signaling I'd been in the driveway long enough.

"Okay," I said, squeezing his hand, unable to wrench my eyes away from his as I reached behind me for the car door. "Okay. We're together."

Chapter Six: Hysteria

The oncology ward's waiting room appeared identical to any other waiting room in any other wing of the hospital, except everyone there seemed to be bald. Most of the women wore terrycloth turbans in bright jewel tones or wrapped handkerchiefs around their heads, tying them in neat little knots at the napes of their necks. I immediately sensed there was something else different about them, but it took me ten minutes to realize they didn't have eyebrows or eyelashes. This lack of detail left their faces vulnerable, infantile, puffy. I tried to picture which hairstyles Wig Lady would choose for each, especially if she decided to get loose with natural color. I decided the woman next to Ma would look good with a blue chin-length bob. It would complement her eyes, which were huge and pretty when she smiled at me.

Ma gripped the aluminum arms of the green vinyl chair fiercely. I patted her arm and stood, told her I needed to use the bathroom, and almost ran down the hall to the pay phone. After digging for a few minutes in my purse, I found change and called Jesse. He picked up on the second ring.

"Hi. It's Diana."

He laughed. "I know. I recognize your voice."

I paused, playing with the metal phone cord. I wasn't sure what to say. I just knew I needed to talk to him; he made things easier to handle.

"It's loud wherever you are."

"I'm in the oncology ward. It's chemo day."

"Oh." He inhaled loudly. "Are you okay?"

"I think so."

"Take a deep breath."

I obeyed, feeling stupid.

"Take another one."

"Jesse…"

"Take another one. When people get stressed out, they take really shallow breaths. I read about it in one of my mom's magazines."

I inhaled again, held it a minute, and let it come shuddering back out. "Why were you reading your mom's magazines?"

"I was in the can."

I shrieked with laughter that was too loud, but I felt some of the tension seep out of me.

"The chemo helps."

"I know, but it makes her sick. She throws up and doesn't eat and looks like hell."

"That's temporary."

"What if it's not?"

A nurse rushed past, her sneakers squeaking on the tile floor.

"Another breath."

I inhaled again, listening to his voice.

"Tell me a joke. One of your little sister Janey's."

"What did the teddy bear say when he was offered seconds?"

"What?"

"I couldn't. I'm stuffed."

****

When I got back, Ma looked up from her magazine. "Everything come out all right?" she asked.

Just then a nurse appeared. "Mrs. Keller?"

Ma stood slowly, looked back at me. "Do you want to come with me?" she asked.

I looked around at all the turbans. I didn't really want to be left with them, blue bobs or not. "Yeah, sure, I guess. I wouldn't want you to have all that fun without me."

She nodded, not really listening.

We walked down a noisy hallway littered with hospital miscellany: gurneys, IV holders, nurses, small children dragging their feet and whining. The chemo room contained ten or so chairs with IVs hooked up to them. Ma sat in a tan one. I averted my eyes while the nurse inserted the needle.

"What now?" I asked, looking up at the nurse. She still had her eyelashes. Her nametag said "Mary."

"Well, you both just sit here until that bag is empty," said Mary, sliding her pen into the front pocket of her scrubs. "Easy."

I looked at Ma. She'd closed her eyes and leaned back in the chair. Her knuckles were white against its arms.

"Yeah," I said, picking up a magazine. It was the fall issue of *Cooking Light*. The cover showed a picture of deep dish apple pie. I could almost smell it. I imagined smashing it on top of Mary's head, the filling plopping to her shoulders and then sliding down to the floor. *Floop.*

I grinned at her. "Easy."

****

Jesse had wrestling practice every day after school, and I begged Pa to come get me late so I could hang around and wait for Jesse to emerge from the squat wrestling room behind the football bleachers.

It was really hard to hang around that area casually, so I took up jogging to not look like such a needy puppy. I ran up and down the bleachers, starting with one set and building to twenty as the season wore on. One afternoon as the streetlights around the edge of the track were clicking on, Jesse burst out of the wrestling room and jogged up to meet me on the bleachers. I was only on my nineteenth cycle, but I slowed when I saw him sitting on the edge of the bleachers.

We both stretched as our breaths puffed out in hot bursts from exertion.

"Let's play the game. *You have two shoes*," I said.

He looked over at me. "*Your sweats are black.*"

"*You're smelly after you work out.*"

"*You're painfully honest.*" He laughed and reached for his feet.

92

"What were you like as a kid?" I asked, studying his stubby hands as he reached for his tennis shoes and stretched.

"Sad," he said.

I looked over at him, adjusting my ear warmers. I motioned for him to continue.

"My brother.... He was just...gone. Everyone was upset. I didn't even know how to be upset. I was nine."

I looked down at my knees and leaned toward my feet, afraid if I reached for him I'd break the spell that had him talking about it.

"After that, I got in trouble a lot. I was really angry."

I nodded, understanding the anger.

"I started wrestling in middle school. It gave me something to channel that anger into. I was pretty good in Kansas City."

"Did your friends help?"

He turned to me. "I didn't have a lot of friends in high school, Diana. I freaked people out. After Justin died, I was an asshole all through elementary school and junior high. I made fun of people, I played tricks, I stole stuff, I got in fights. By the time I wasn't mad anymore, my old friends had already moved on—they wanted nothing to do with me. That's why I was happy to move and why I don't want to be mad anymore."

I reached out for his hand. He grasped mine, squeezed, let go.

"I decided to start over here, to be the person I would've been if Justin hadn't died. See, there's stuff

93

about me you didn't know, either. Does it make you like me any less?"

"No. Oddly enough, it makes me like you more."

****

As I jogged more and more laps around that cinder track, I started to lose weight. When I went to see Doc Fontane about a spider bite, he pointed out I was two inches taller but sixteen pounds lighter than at my August physical. It was the first time I'd ever lost weight in my life. I was shocked; I hadn't really believed it possible.

At night in my room, I'd take off my clothes and analyze my progress. My legs were getting more muscular, less tree-trunk-like, but a thin layer of flab still covered my tummy, and my arms had no shape.

One night in disgust I went hunting through my closet for something to use for arm weights. I found a pair of heavy brass bookends shaped like elephants. Eagerly I grabbed them and did bicep curls the way I'd seen people do on TV. I didn't know how many sets to do, so I did ten sets of ten. By the end, the sweat stood out on my upper lip, and my arms burned with exertion.

I dropped to the floor and did sit-ups with my feet in the air, the thigh fat pooling at my hips from gravity. The burning felt good, was a good way to punish myself for that layer of flab. I did five hundred sit-ups that night, but after a few weeks I was doing one thousand every day.

After my sit-ups, I'd pull out from under my bed, one at a time, the stack of cookbooks I'd pilfered from the kitchen. Cookbooks, Harry & David catalogs, women's magazines—I wanted pictures of food, the kind of food I wouldn't let myself eat. All I wanted to do was look at the pictures and imagine how the food would taste. It was almost like eating it, plates and plates of dangerous food: tacos, lasagna, green bean casserole. I stared at the photos until I fell asleep, hungry.

Jesse watched me admiringly one night as I finished my tenth set of bleacher runs. "You're getting really good, Diana," he said when I plopped down next to him on the bleachers.

"Thanks. I have to keep up with you, you big stud."

He laughed, the hood of his pullover sweatshirt falling from his head. He was dropping a weight class, and his cheekbones stood out in a way they hadn't before. He never ate at Pizza Hut when we went there on the weekends, just sat sipping water through a straw and leaning away as far as he could from the bubbling cheese.

Now he leaned forward, slid his hands down my back and up under the waist of my sweatshirt. I sucked in my stomach like always, but it was growing less necessary. My newfound abdominal muscles pretty much kept my stomach in one position all the time. He kissed me. He tasted salty.

I crawled up onto his lap, less conscious than I used to be of my weight on his legs, more conscious than I used to be of the rise in his sweats. "Is that a banana in your pocket or are you just happy to see me?" I whispered in his ear. "Where did you get a banana so big? This must be imported."

"Don't you be starting something you can't finish," he drawled, running his hands over my hips. I

95

wanted very much to finish it, make the bleachers disappear, but I knew Pa would be showing up at any moment, and if he saw me in Jesse's lap, I'd never see the inside of that LeSabre again.

"I'll finish it someday," I said, lifting myself off his lap.

"When?" he said, still leaning over.

"What?"

"When?" he looked up, his expression earnest. "Are you serious?"

I bent to tie my shoe. I didn't really know if I was serious or not.

Chapter Seven: Nothing's Shocking

Snowden High School offered two choices for lunch: government-cheese-coated grease from the cafeteria line, or the salad bar which featured wilted iceberg lettuce, chopped ham, and croutons. I started eating salad. I also started watching other people eat instead of doing so myself.

My salads were always the same. I'd start with a thick layer of iceberg lettuce, and then add two teaspoons of chopped ham spread wide so it looked like there was more. No croutons. No dressing. If there were carrots, I'd take handfuls of them, because eating carrots—eating salad, really—took forever, and if I chewed each bite slowly, nobody would question why I didn't have time to finish by the time we dumped our lunch trays. Plus, people don't really notice what you're doing half the time anyway. They're too busy worrying about themselves.

The way I looked changed. A lot. As the weight came off, adults complimented me. After twenty pounds, the other girls looked at me with envy. Boys who had never looked at me except to copy my homework started bumping me in the halls the way they'd always done to Amanda. Lin was the only one who didn't seem to notice—she spent lunch inhaling tater tots without a second glance and talking about Hutch.

Lin and Hutch spent all their time together. She mooned over what to get Hutch for Christmas, more than a month away. Gold chain? Drakkar cologne? A sweater? She wore his class ring on her finger, wrapped in pink knitting yarn to make it fit around her tiny finger, the ring so big and bulky she could barely wrap her hand around her fork as she ate.

Jesse and I never ate when we went out. On Friday nights, we went to the movies during dinnertime and made out in the back of the theater, his hands running up and down my ribs, which were starting to protrude. I wanted to inhale him to quell the hunger pangs. The deeper I kissed him, the less I felt anything but my desire.

We were at the movies the first time he slid down the zipper of my jeans. He groaned softly into my ear. Suddenly someone stood in the front of the theater, and in an instant his hand was back on the armrest and my shirt was pulled down over my zipper as though someone else had rearranged us. A middle-aged woman shuffled past us up the aisle toward the theater doors, barely giving us a glance. Everything was normal.

Except I was panting and clutching the armrests as though my life depended on them to keep me from floating into outer space.

****

Jesse wrestled at one hundred fifty-eight pounds. He'd started out at one-sixty-seven, but he lost too many matches against those kids. Jesse won most of his wrestling matches at the lower weight class, but the weight loss was difficult for him to maintain. He spent his lunch periods running in the gym with the other wrestlers, a silent line of rustling bodies in illegal plastic suits. You weren't supposed to use them because of dehydration, but Mr. Mitchell, the guidance counselor and assistant wrestling coach, always watched them from the door between the cafeteria and the gym. Probably to make sure nobody passed out. I knew it was the way things were for Snowden wrestlers, but I couldn't help but see Mr. Mitchell as some crazy circus master training the tigers while he sat on his fat ass.

The weekend before Thanksgiving, Jesse had a big meet. I sat in the bleachers with Ma and Pa. Jesse looked beautiful. His muscles stood out from his bones, a spider web of veins resting on top of them. I could see his vertebrae through his singlet, and his eyes, normally deep-set, seemed hooded underneath his headpiece.

When the whistle blew, Jesse circled his opponent like a cat, crouched low, looking for the opening only he ever saw. I could never figure out what he was doing, despite my better-than-average understanding of the half nelson. It always seemed to me that one moment they were circling and the next Jesse had some guy down, both of them rolling and twisting to escape. Getting pinned is the harshest punishment in sports, the most undisputable.

Amanda perched on the edge of the mat in her cheerleading uniform, her dark hair in a perky ponytail tied with black-and-gold ribbons. As she cheered, she pounded the mat with manicured fingers. I didn't like the way she called Jesse's name when she encouraged him, didn't like the admiring glances she gave him when his ass was in her face on the mat. Didn't like how much you could see showing through that black singlet.

It couldn't be helped. I couldn't stare anywhere else, either. But still: Jesse was mine. In my mind, I assigned Amanda an ash blonde, feathered shag wig. I could almost see it brushing the shoulders of her uniform, clashing with the gold of her sweater. It made it easier to watch her cheering for Jesse, anyway.

Jesse defeated his opponent easily, and Ma sighed with relief, standing and smoothing her pants. "So, do we leave now?"

"No, Ma, he has to wrestle like three more times if he keeps winning. This is an all-day meet. Aren't you glad I don't wrestle?" I laughed at my own joke.

"Oh," said Ma. She looked at Pa, who was reading a computer magazine. He'd glanced up to watch Jesse, then dropped his eyes right back down without moving his head. Ma was bored out of her skull, I could tell.

"You don't have to stay, Ma. Seriously. I completely realize this is four hours of mind-numbing boredom punctuated by a two minutes of blood-pounding action," I said. "I can get a ride home from Jesse when it's over. It'll go until like five, then we usually go get pizza."

100

Ma leaned in toward Pa. She nuzzled his shoulder with her nose. "We could go to the movies," she said.

Pa looked up, surprised. He'd clearly been planning to read his computer magazine on the bleachers all day. He cocked his head. "Why, sure."

Ma smiled. Pa looked at me, still dizzy from the fog of broken focus. "Are you sure you're okay here? Do you want to come with us?"

I feigned shock. "And miss all this? No, seriously, I want to see Jesse wrestle. And Amanda's here. You guys go and have fun. I'll get a ride. I'll be home on time."

Ma tugged Pa's arm. "Come on, Al. I feel good today. Let's go have some fun."

They stood and filed out of the bleachers. I watched them walk out the double door under the red exit sign, holding hands. They were cute when they held hands.

My stomach growled. I hadn't eaten since the single slice of dry toast I inhaled each morning for breakfast. I looked at the clock: noon. I ignored my hunger and turned back to the program to see when Jesse would wrestle again. I'd have a pretzel at three, I decided. That should carry me through until I got home at eleven. Seeing all those wrestlers gave me confidence. If they could do it, so could I. And I could do it better.

Jesse's next opponent looked tougher: a short, compact junior from Red Oak. The kid had dark hair and dark eyes, and he didn't look skinny at all. He looked thick and muscular, like a bulldog. Jesse towered over him by several inches, but his arms and legs were thinner than the other guy's. I sat on my hands and leaned forward. I could feel kids around me staring at me, but I looked only at Jesse.

He didn't look worried. The referee blew the whistle, and they started their dance, batting at each other's bent knees. The circling continued much longer than usual as each looked for not just any opening, but the perfect opening. It was clear once they were really down, it would go fast.

The other kid lunged at Jesse, catching him behind his right ankle. Jesse dropped to one knee but quickly spun out of the hold. It went on like this—the other kid grabbing Jesse, Jesse rolling out—until finally the other kid had one of Jesse's shoulder blades on the floor. The tendons stood out on Jesse's neck as he strained his other shoulder toward the ceiling, eyes focused upward.

Everyone was screaming, but the clock just kept ticking its digital red seconds away. Then Jesse's foot shifted and his polyester singlet slid on the mat, breaking his focus. I heard one of the cheerleaders shriek as the kid drove Jesse's other shoulder blade to the ground and held it there. The referee crouched with his chin touching the ground as his open palm slapped the mat three times, counting down the pin. He blew the whistle, and the fight went out of Jesse, who slumped flat, panting. I felt my own body sag on the bleachers as I finally exhaled, channeling his disappointment.

Lin, who'd appeared beside me with Hutch during the match, patted my back. "Hey, that sucks," she said, handing me a Twizzler. "We were watching from the door." Hutch waved, then placed his hand on Lin's knee. I took the Twizzler and stared at it, slick and ropy. It immediately began to melt, staining my palm red.

"Yeah." I sighed. "I guess he's out of the meet. It does suck."

Jesse was on his feet. The referee raised the other kid's arm, and Jesse turned on his heel and jogged off the mat. He was out of the meet hours earlier than I'd expected.

"What are you doing now?" asked Lin.

"I don't know. My parents just left, and I appear to be without a ride until the meet's over. I guess I'll watch more hot wrestling action."

"Do you want to come hang out with us? Hutch's parents are out until late. We can watch movies and make spaghetti or something. Jesse can come over when he's done."

I looked back at the mat. Going to Hutch's and watching movies sounded so much better than watching high school boys roll around on the mat barely moving. Plus, I'd been wanting to hang out with Lin for weeks. I pulled a piece of paper out of my purse and wrote a note to Jesse telling him I'd be at Hutch's if he wanted to come by.

As we passed the wrestling team on the way out, I handed the note to Jake at the end of the row. He palmed it and nodded at me.

Hutch drove a Ford Escort, two-door. I squished myself in the back seat. "Where have you guys been all day?" I asked.

"We went to the mall," said Lin.

I met Hutch's gaze in the rearview mirror. "You went to the mall?"

Hutch held my gaze even as he pulled out of the crowded high school parking lot. "Yes, of course. There was a notable annual craft show going on there."

Lin started laughing. "It really was amazing."

I tried to picture Lin and Hutch inspecting an Iowan craft show. The plastic baby dolls with crocheted clothing. The knitted Kleenex box covers. The appliqued Christmas sweatshirts. I groaned but smiled.

"The best part? There was this table at the very end with a whole stack of bumper stickers that said *I Love Wooden Miniatures*. But the 'love' was totally a red heart. So we took a bunch of them." Lin was laughing almost too hard to talk. "And when we left the mall, Hutch put them on every single pick-up truck he could find."

Hutch grinned. "I wish I could've seen their expressions when they came out."

I snorted. "You're kidding me. You really did that?"

Hutch eyed me in the rearview mirror. "Come on, Diana. After all this time, do you really doubt my powers?"

I leaned back, still laughing. No, I didn't. Not at all.

****

Hutch and Lin headed back to Hutch's bedroom when we got to his house. I saw a stack of movies on the TV and popped one in while I waited for Jesse. I was getting really hungry when Jesse walked in without

104

knocking, his face hidden by his sweatshirt hood. He silently plopped down beside me on the couch.

I looked over at him, but I still couldn't see his face. I reached out for his arm, but he pulled away. "Not yet," he muttered.

Surprised, I turned back to the movie, inching my way across the couch to the other end. I heard him taking deep breaths.

"What're you watching?" he asked after a few minutes.

"Molly Ringwald."

"Has she gotten any more interesting?"

"Nope." I turned to face him. "Lin and Hutch haven't come out of his bedroom since we got here. Are you hungry?"

"I'm starving. I'm always starving. Sometimes I fucking hate wrestling."

"When's your next weigh-in?"

"A week."

"Want to eat? I'm thinking eating would improve upon your cheery disposition."

"Yes."

We went into the kitchen and rummaged through the cupboards. We found all sorts of junk food, but nothing that really looked good.

"Lin talked about making spaghetti. I think she was kidding, but we could actually do it." I eyed Jesse. If he ate, then I would, too. "What do you think?" I didn't know what I wanted him to say.

He looked interested. He rubbed his hands together, his hood sliding down off his head as he visibly relaxed. "I make excellent spaghetti," he said. "Please be seated."

I flipped on the under-cabinet lights, and the kitchen glowed as we hunted through cupboards for bowls, pots, pasta, and sauce. The smell of food roused Lin and Hutch from the depths of the house, and by seven o'clock we were sitting around in the darkened dining room, eating and talking. It felt so safe and normal, like how it must feel to be an adult.

The full moon shined through the sliding glass door, illuminating Hutch's face as he talked about his parents' impending divorce. I told them about how sick Ma had been, about Amanda messing up Ma's wig. Lin squeezed my hand under the table, and when I looked over at her, her eyes glistened. I smiled at her that smile you make when you're not sure what else to do.

"The moon is out," I told Jesse, to change the subject.

"The moon is full. Do you want to go admire it?" he asked.

We stepped outside to take it in, round and orange and just above the horizon. I knew by eleven it would be high in the sky, tiny and white, but at that moment it perched above the fields, the harvest moon I remembered from elementary school, the one that always seemed close enough to reach.

"It's beautiful," said Jesse.

"Pa taught me all the constellations when I was in second grade."

He lifted my hand to his lips, kissed it. "What do you wish for?" he asked.

I paused. "Man-made things—neon signs and museums. Civilization," I answered. "It would be nice to not have to drive thirty miles to find a pair of jeans not cut for my mother."

He nodded, rubbing his full belly. "Why don't you sing like you used to, Diana?"

I sucked in my breath. "What do you mean?"

He looked out over the backyard. "Sticks said you used to play the lead in all the musicals, then one day you just stopped."

"He didn't hear what I heard."

Jesse reached out for my arm, but I pulled away. "What did you hear?"

"You know what they say about the fat lady?"

"Someone said that about you?"

I reached down to my shoes, feeling for the ground, wanting to feel the ground. I couldn't believe I was going to tell him. "Some little kid said it was really over because the fat lady sang. He was talking about me. I was twelve."

"Diana…"

"I know this is probably hard for you to imagine. You're perfect. But here…here you just are what they say you are. I stopped singing so I couldn't be *her* anymore. At least not in public."

Jesse reached over for my hand. I pulled away. He touched my shoulder in that one special spot, then my hair. "You are so special," he said. "You are amazing."

I wanted so badly to believe him.

Cold, I slipped back inside, motioning for Jesse to follow me. Hutch and Lin had disappeared again. Jesse slid the door shut and pulled me onto the couch, lifting my shirt to expose my newly hardened stomach and palming it with one stubby hand. I felt his callused fingers brush the skin of my abdomen as he leaned down.

He kissed me gently, then more urgently, almost inquisitively, as his lips parted and drew away. I reached for him, and he held my arms above my head with one hand, running the other up and down my torso until I shivered in anticipation.

I looked up at the ceiling, thinking I should stop him, but my breath was rasping in my chest and my thighs were on fire. I realized I wasn't going to stop him. I didn't want to stop him.

He rested only part of his weight on me, like he'd done that night at the golf course. His hands raked through my hair as he leaned on his elbows. "Do you want to?"

All I saw were his brown eyes looking at me so intently. All I felt was my need. I leaned up and kissed him instead of answering. I didn't care about anything in that moment but Jesse.

****

Afterward, I couldn't tear my eyes away from his as a slow moment passed, his breathing gradually slowing as the movie played on in the background.

I reached over for my jeans and leaned back gingerly on the couch, not a virgin anymore. My mind reeled.

Jesse collected the newspaper carefully in his thick hands. He looked up and saw the tears in my eyes. "Hey, are you okay? Didn't you like it?"

"I love you," I said, instead of explaining.

He seized my knees in his palms and lowered his forehead to rest it on them, not looking at me. "I loved you before I knew I loved you," he said quietly.

The moon shined through the glass door onto the dinner table.

Chapter Eight: Just Like the First Time

I worried that my parents would immediately notice the change—that they'd know I'd had sex—like it would waft out of my pores after I showered. Instead, they treated me normally, like the child they'd always had. The sex was just another one of my secrets. I'd spent so many years trying to keep secrets from my parents, then suddenly, when I sort of wanted to tell them, it was too hard. *Good morning, Ma. I'm not a virgin anymore. Sorry you have cancer, but your daughter's chastity belt shrunk in the wash.*

Ma hummed as she bustled around the kitchen on Thanksgiving morning, her wig swinging as she pulled open the oven door a thousand times. She constantly reset the four timers placed strategically around the kitchen, even when they didn't ding. Ma couldn't cook a meal without at least two timers. I'd always helped her prepare, but I was trying to steer a wide berth around the food.

The pounds started to come off slower than I thought they would after my initial loss, despite the stairs and salads. Still, by Thanksgiving I was down thirty pounds on the old yellow scales I kept hidden under my bed. My jeans had started hanging off me, so I cinched them tighter and stole Pa's college sweatshirts from his closet.

One day at lunchtime, Mr. Mitchell stopped me on the way back from the salad bar. "Hi, Diana. I see you're having salad again," he said, smiling like adults smile when they think they're being sneaky.

I looked down at my tray, smiling sneakily. "Why yes, it appears that I am. As you know, the cafeteria offers salads now."

"Don't you think you should try something else once in a while? Maybe mix in a sandwich?" He smiled widely, and I noted he should've had braces as a child. Unfortunate.

I really, really hated it when people tried to tell me what to do. I paused, thinking, then let my gaze wander over to the open door to the gym. I saw Jesse jog by in his plastic suit. Apparently it was fine for the wrestlers to lose weight, but not me.

I looked slowly back at Mr. Mitchell. "No. This is actually working for me. I guess you have to do what works for you. Like, you know, plastic jogging suits. Salads somehow seem so much…safer." I looked back at the cafeteria door again.

Mr. Mitchell turned and walked away without another word.

112

Furious, I ditched my lunch and went to the library. I found a big book of quotations. There were a ton on hypocrisy. I took out a piece of paper and wrote Mr. Mitchell my first note:

"Clean your finger before you point at my spots." –Benjamin Franklin (1706-1790).

I folded the note and stuffed it in my backpack. On my way out of school, I checked Mr. Mitchell's door. It was locked. I slid the note under the door, feeling lighter than ever, imagining the look on his face when he read it. He'd never be able to prove it was me.

Dinner took on an almost religious ritual. I started eating right at five when the news came on and chewed each bite thirty times, trying to stretch the experience out until six. If I stopped eating before six, I was climbing the walls with hunger before bedtime. I fiddled with the start and end times of my dinners until I could make it all night on only a Lean Cuisine and an apple, which I ate in the bathtub while I perused my cookbooks. I ate the entire apple, including the core and seeds. It didn't taste anything like the cornbread with maple glaze I was reading about, but the fear of eating the cornbread made me cling to the apple stem until I snapped it in half.

The only problem I saw with such a long meal was that the food got cold. I ate so little food that it seemed unfair for anything cooked to be less than piping hot. I usually ended up popping the Lean Cuisine back in the microwave four or five times over the course of dinner. Ma sat on the couch and watched the news, complaining I never ate with them anymore.

On weekends I didn't eat dinner until after I got home from hanging out with Jesse. By then I'd be nearly faint with hunger, my fingers shaking as I microwaved my dinner. I ate standing up in the kitchen with the lights out, leafing through the living section of the newspaper, staring at the recipes. Eating the same thing every day made me feel safe, even though I went to bed every night hungry, tracing my fingers over my newly emerged hipbones as I waited to fall asleep.

One of the four timers went off. I don't know why Ma worried so much about timing all the food perfectly. She always forgot the rolls—no matter how many timers she set—and one dish was usually cold by the time the rest came out of the oven.

When her timers failed her, Ma tried to convince us to eat the dishes one at a time. Pa and I had no patience for this practice. Pa liked to mix all his food together into a giant, jumbled mess, and I liked to see exactly what was coming so I could determine which foods would be safe to eat and in what amount. Nothing panicked me more than being forced to eat more than I'd planned.

Thanksgiving dinner wasn't too tough to resist, because I never liked creamed anything. Thanksgiving is mostly creamy. Sitting at the Thanksgiving table, we prayed hard for the cancer to die—though I don't think those were Pa's exact words. I spent the prayer staring at the juices dripping off my food and pooling at the center of the plate in a viscous puddle. I could no more imagine putting that in my mouth than looking across the table to see Ma sitting there with a full head of her old hair.

"So what would you like for Christmas, Diana?" Ma asked as she popped up to turn off the final timer, which dictated the pie. She'd remembered the rolls and actually removed her jalapeño-printed apron to eat.

I stared at the filigreed handle of my fork. I'd set the table. I loved the good china, all white with delicate real gold rimming the plates and glasses. I hadn't given Christmas a single thought. The months I'd filled with Jesse had flown by in a flurry of cinder-track workouts and late-night phone calls. I spent all my time on my diet and him. Lin was always with Hutch. Amanda's new boyfriend, Randy, played center on the basketball team and barely spoke to any sophomores. I often saw her on my way home from school, smoking cigarettes with him and his friends on the sidewalk just beyond school property.

All I wanted was to exercise and not eat and hang out with Jesse.

One afternoon when I'd walked in from school, Ma had asked why I never had Amanda over anymore.

"I don't know," I'd mumbled. "I've been busy, and she's been hanging out with seniors, anyway."

Ma peered at me over the edge of her newspaper. "Did you guys have a fight?"

"No. We're fine."

"You're not spending too much time with Jesse, are you?"

My mouth went dry. "No. I told you, everything's fine. She's got a new boyfriend, too."

Ma's eyes had dropped back down to the paper. "Never dump your friends for a boy, Diana," she'd said.

I chewed my first bite of turkey only fifteen times so Ma wouldn't think I was avoiding her question while I thought. What *did* I want for Christmas?

"Um, I don't know. World peace?"

"You're going to be sixteen in a few months," Ma said, reaching over with her bony fingers to pat my hand. "My baby's growing up. You must want something good."

Pa smiled at me, looking up finally from the giant pile of food he'd mixed together on his plate. Mashed potatoes balanced on the rim, completely covering the gold and threatening to spill over the edge onto the linen tablecloth I'd found in the basement and ironed for dinner. "You want some power tools?" he asked.

I laughed.

"Well, you think about it," Ma said. "It's been a hard year, and we should celebrate getting through it."

Ma picked up the timer she'd brought with her to the table. It was shaped like a frog, green with yellow spots and a jaunty pink tongue. Her next doctor appointment was scheduled for the week before Christmas, and I worried the cancer wasn't gone.

If I let my mind go there, I'd start panicking, and I didn't want to panic on Thanksgiving. I imagined Pa with a Beatles bowl-cut wig and relaxed a little. It would actually look kind of good on him. He had a square jaw that would balance out the style nicely.

Ma turned the timer around to face Pa. "Guess what, Al? I remembered the rolls," she made the frog say.

Outside the sliding glass door, the tree in back bent, then straightened, then bent again in what was

116

surely an icy wind. The trees had dropped their leaves, and the grass was brown and dead.

"Are Grandma and Grandpa coming for Christmas?" I asked.

Pa wiped his mouth, swallowing loudly. "So far, so good," he replied.

"When will they be here?"

As we talked, I pushed my food around on my plate, occasionally taking a bite and chewing it thirty times. I ate two teaspoons of plain mashed potatoes and a third of my piece of turkey while Ma and Pa filled their plates a second time. When they went to the kitchen, I pulled off half a dinner roll and put it near Pa's water glass, figuring he wouldn't notice it wasn't his. I carefully covered my untouched green bean casserole with the other half of the roll then picked at the turkey through the second half of dinner.

The pie was harder to avoid. Ma knew I loved warm apple pie, and this one was my favorite recipe, the recipe I stared at most often in the Betty Crocker cookbook. My stomach wailed with insistence at the perfume of cinnamon wafting from the stove.

I put my hands under the table, encircling one upper thigh with my fingers. As long as I could make a circle around my thigh with fingers and thumbs touching, everything was okay. My fingers overlapped.

I stared hard at the pie as Ma carried it proudly in from the stove. *Maybe just a bite. Just one bite.*

She scooped me a huge piece without even asking if I wanted it and set the plate under my nose, impossible to ignore. I was so hungry, had been hungry for months.

All of a sudden I was *hungry,* and also mad that Amanda and Lin and my other friends could eat like pigs and still be skinnier than I was. That I had to work so hard, make so many sacrifices just to look like them. They didn't jog around the track. They didn't run the bleachers. They didn't have to—they could be skinny just by existing.

The rules were different for me. The rules said I couldn't have pie, not even on Thanksgiving.

Pa laid a slice of American cheese on top of his pie and began scooping it up in huge forkfuls. Ma poured herself more coffee and dug into her piece, pausing every few bites to dab at her mouth with her napkin. She looked tired. We always ate pie after Thanksgiving dinner before we went into the living room to watch movies together. I wasn't sure she'd make it to the movie part. Ma looked like she needed a nap.

I used the tip of my fork to open the crust. Steam poured out, scented with fruit and spices. I lost control, shoving forkfuls of pie in my mouth as quickly as I could, the hot apples scalding my tongue as I hurried to get it in before I could change my mind.

As soon as I pushed back from the table, I panicked. I frantically tallied in my mind the number of calories in a slice of apple pie. Hundreds. I usually ate eight or nine hundred calories a day, and I'd just inhaled at least half of my daily allotment in eight bites. I reached down to encircle my thigh again and convinced myself my fingers were no longer touching. I felt the crash of self-loathing wash over me, and I almost cried out with the pain of it.

I carried my plate over to the counter, staring at the dirty dishes everywhere. Ma came up behind me, and I could tell she was thinking the same thing. Her eyes had dark circles under them, and she seemed to be losing energy with every step.

"Why don't you go lie down, Ma?" I said. "Pa and I will get this. Thanks for making dinner."

She smiled gratefully at me and leaned down to kiss the top of my head. "Thanks, Diana. I think I will."

Pa leaned back, toothpick in mouth, hands resting on his flannel-shirt-covered belly. He looked over at me. "I suppose you need some help, then," he said.

"Why don't you clear the table then go watch TV? I really don't mind," I replied, piling the pans on the counter. Maybe after I washed the dishes I could go downstairs and work out on the jogging trampoline. It wouldn't be perfect, but better than sitting on the couch getting huge.

It was a mistake, I told myself as I scrubbed the pots as fast as I could and stacked the plates in the dishwasher, already calculating how much of the pie I could burn off. *A mistake I will never make again.*

RITA ARENS----THE OBVIOUS GAME

Chapter Nine: Use Your Illusion

Ma believed in wearing things out or using them up. As a result, she usually looked slightly threadbare, and I usually looked almost right, but not quite—like fake Oreos. I was shocked when Ma insisted we spend the first Saturday in December shopping for Christmas dresses.

"Do you want to go first?" she asked, her eyes darting around the store. She rubbed her index finger against her thumb nervously.

"Nah, you go first."

We headed to the old-lady section, and Ma reached out to touch a dress lovingly before turning over the price tag. She actually gasped. "We better get out of here," she stage-whispered. "This is the wrong section."

"No, it's not," I whispered back. "You need a pretty dress to go with that shiny wig. Now try something on."

It was like forcing a toddler to try on clothing. She balked and resisted as I picked out seven dresses in black, red, or gold. "Come on, Ma," I said, "you're being ridiculous, seriously. Put on the fancy dress already. I want to see you."

I balanced on an overstuffed chair covered in mauve silk pillows in the dressing area, watching Ma's feet slowly lift and lower.

"Oh, Diana, I don't know," came Ma's voice.

"Come on, Ma. It's going to be great. At least that's what Amanda always says."

The door opened, and Ma came out in the first dress, a red knit. It clung in all the wrong places, making her look both lumpy and frail at the same time. I laughed before I could catch myself. Ma shook her head at me, knitting the skin where her eyebrows should've been, then she slowly smiled at her reflection. "I told you it was bad."

"It's like the designer asked himself how a dress could cling in all the wrong places. Not your problem. Try on the next one."

The fifth dress—black silk with a fitted waist and flared skirt—floated around her. Ma twirled in front of the mirror. She looked beautiful. Black usually made her look washed out, but she'd applied red lipstick before she came out, and she looked graceful and dramatic.

"If only it weren't so expensive," she said, never taking her eyes off her reflection.

"Fuck it, Ma." I'd never used that word in front of her before. I waited for her to murder me.

It didn't happen. Ma preened before the mirror, smoothing her wig and the dress where it flared around her hips. The boat neck showed off her clavicles, not where her breastbone protruded.

"Fuck it," she murmured, fingers calm.

We went to the juniors section next, Ma's dress hung and wrapped in a big white plastic bag tied at the bottom. She slung it over her shoulder proudly as we walked.

I knew I wanted a sweater dress, hopefully black, simple. I pawed through the racks while Ma rested on the chair by the dressing room, dress lying carefully over her lap.

Finally, I found four or five that I liked and carried them over. "I'll come out and show you," I told Ma. "You stay here."

Inside the dressing room, I pulled out my body armor and slid into the girdle. It didn't feel right. It was too big.

I slid on the first dress and realized I'd gone down at least five sizes since homecoming. I could grab handfuls of material on either side of my waist. To my relief, a clerk's feet appeared, and she asked if she could get me anything.

I hung the dress over the other side of the door. "Can you get me this in a smaller size?" I asked quietly, not wanting Ma to hear.

"Sure, I'll look."

I stood in the dressing room in my underwear while I waited for her to come back, panicking. I'd been schlepping around in layers and layers all winter, hiding. My stomach was flat, my butt high. But my chest looked concave, and I could see my breastbone and all my ribs. The next size the clerk brought fit.

"Diana?" called Ma. "Can I see it?"

I opened the door. Ma's eyes widened as she saw me.

"Diana, you've lost *too* much weight." She reached her hand out, running her fingers over my clavicles where they peeped out of the V-neck.

I looked down. I could see my hipbones poking out through the fabric as hers had. It was okay for me: I wasn't sick.

"I could just be growing. People grow. You've always told me the doctor said when I was born that I'd be five-foot-nine."

She eyed me up and down, lips pursed. "Well, make sure you don't lose any more." Her index finger returned to her thumb and rubbed as she touched my clavicle again, as though it were made of glass.

"Can I have this dress? Pretty please, with cream and sugar and *bacon* on top?"

She stared at me hard, worried lines forming at the edges of her eyes.

"I swear, Ma, I'm not trying to lose weight. I'm just growing."

"Okay, Diana." She picked up her keys, jingling them thoughtfully. "You know your father doesn't need anything else to worry about."

I was already back in the dressing room pulling on my clothes, and I barely heard what she said. All I could see was the size tag hanging from the sleeve of the dress.

As we walked out of Dillard's, I heard my name. Ma and I turned to see Amanda standing in the entrance of Claire's with Jennifer and Karen, her new friends—both seniors. I smiled and waved as my stomach knotted.

"I'll be right back," I told Ma, who immediately sank into a chair by the frozen yogurt stand. "Hey, Amanda," I said, walking over as casually as I could. "What're you guys up to?"

Jennifer laughed as though I'd just said the stupidest thing ever. "Duh, Diana. We're shopping."

I turned away from Jennifer and focused on Amanda. "What're you doing tonight?" I hadn't hung out with Amanda in weeks.

Amanda looked surprised at my tone. She glanced over my shoulder, from Jennifer and Karen, browsing six-packs of cheap silver earrings, to my mother, who clutched her dress like a lifeline. "We're going cruising. We've got a hook-up. Do you want to come?"

Karen looked over sharply. Knowing she didn't want me along made me *want* to come along. In my mind, Karen was now wearing an Annie wig, coiled orange curls inches from her inner eyelid eyeliner. The image was so great I stared a minute too long before turning back to Amanda.

"Sure," I said. "Where should I meet you?"

"Kwik Shop," she said. She waved at Ma. "Hi, Mrs. Keller. You look great," she called, grinning broadly. "See if you can stay at my grandma's. I'll show you a good time," she whispered to me.

"Okay." I looked over my shoulder at Jennifer and Karen. "Are they staying, too?" I whispered.

"No," she said. "I miss you. It'll be just you and me."

I missed her back, even though she was standing right there. I wanted to hang out with her, I really did. "I'll ask right now. See you at Kwik Shop at seven," I said, brushing past the sunglasses rack. "Come on, Ma, let's go home," I said. "I need to get ready. Can I stay with Amanda tonight?"

Ma's eyebrows shot up. "I thought you and Amanda didn't really get along anymore," she said.

"Well, I miss her."

Ma put her arm around me, partly in a hug, partly for support. "Ah, yes," she said. "I remember being a teenaged girl."

We drove home in silence, looking for things to see on the side of the road. I was beginning to think I didn't owe Amanda anything anymore.

Chapter Ten: Bat Out of Hell

The Honda tires rattled on the rough parking lot pavement when Ma dropped me off at Kwik Shop. I didn't see Amanda anywhere. A mob of twenty or so freshmen hung around the railroad ties outside, talking and laughing, their breaths coming out in steamy wisps as they sipped hot chocolate from Styrofoam cups.

I walked to the back and locked myself in the graffiti-covered bathroom. My hair, never my best feature, had grown limper in recent months. I tried to puff it up, imagined myself with an amazing mermaid-hair wig. Hot. I was white-hot.

When I went back out into the aisles, I saw Amanda sitting with Jennifer and Karen at the booths in the rear by the hot dogs. She looked like a queen with her handmaids.

"Diana." She gave me a hug. I waved to the other girls, who barely acknowledged my presence.

Jennifer smoothed her acid-washed jeans and got up, twirling her keys. At least ten individual rings clipped together held two keys, a rainbow-printed foam flip-flop,

127

a miniature Iowa driver's license with her name on it, a tiny stuffed reindeer, a pair of dice held together on thin copper wires, a woven-leather thong with beads wrapped at the end, a plastic cocker spaniel, a pair of itsy-bitsy handcuffs, a rhinestone letter J, a black-and-gold pom pom, and finally a Tiffany lock with a tiny key dangling next to it.

I followed the girls to Jennifer's white Grand Am. I slid in the back next to Karen. Amanda took shotgun. Jennifer put one of her two keys in the ignition and revved the engine at the freshmen on the railroad ties, who looked at her with wide eyes and squirmed as she pulled away.

I didn't ask where we were going. Amanda said there was a hook-up, which could only mean she'd already lined up a buyer. Her outstretched hand appeared between the front seats, and I put a rumpled ten in her palm. Karen did the same. We drove down the strip to the edge of town and pulled into a country lane, the engine idling. I smoothed my hair and watched the grass on the side of the highway blow.

"Where's Randy?" asked Karen.

"He's out with his friends. Maybe we'll see him later," replied Amanda, laughing and reapplying lip gloss in the visor mirror. Jennifer put the car in park and flipped through the cassette tapes she kept in a huge blue case. She popped one in.

A few minutes later, a silver Mitsubishi pulled down the lane and killed its lights. I groaned.

Jennifer rolled down her window as Davey Willis got out of his car and strutted toward the Grand Am. "Did you get it?"

"Of course, darling. Anything for you," he said, leaning his head through the window. "Hello, ladies."

Jennifer ripped the paper bag out of his hands and pulled out a bottle of peach schnapps. It was a big bottle. She handed him the money and started to roll up the window. Davey pulled back, looking hurt.

"You girls need someone to party with?"

"No, thanks," Amanda chirped brightly, giving him one of her widest smiles. "You have a good night, Davey."

After the Mitsubishi's tail lights vanished, Jennifer drove farther out of town to Buzz Road. The gravel path wound in a wide circle, unpaved and rutted but wide enough. Jennifer set the cruise control at thirty-five miles an hour—the slowest possible setting—and Amanda twisted the metal cap off the bottle of schnapps. The sickly sweet smell cut the night air, making me dizzy, sort of excited.

"Cheers!" she cried and took a huge swig, wiping her chin delicately before passing the bottle to Jennifer, who tipped it without taking her eyes off the road.

Amanda pulled out the tape case and stared intently, as though her choice of background music could influence the rotation of the earth. Karen took a very small sip of the schnapps. She smiled secretly at me as she held out the bottle. Our fingers touched as I took it from her. Her hand felt sticky.

I'd never drunk anything alcoholic in my life except communion wine, but I thought the sacrament couldn't possibly count as booze. I tilted the bottle back until I felt the liquid touch my lips. It stung, and I started coughing and spilled it on my jeans. Karen snatched it away and laughed.

"Good God, Diana. Haven't you ever had a drink before?"

I met Amanda's eyes in the rearview mirror. She knew damn well I'd never had a drink before. She winked at me.

"Only at the Playboy mansion," I said, raising one eyebrow. "What, why?"

"So tell me, Diana," said Karen, leaning forward after passing me the bottle again. Her fingers were still sticky. "Are you and Jesse lovers?"

I ignored her and took another drink. This time I knew what to expect and didn't cough. When I lowered the bottle, I felt the schnapps burning its way into my near-empty stomach. After only two gulps I felt hot, really hot, and I squirmed out of my coat as we passed a dead maple tree for the third time. My body felt good, relaxed, warm. I looked down at my legs and realized they were splayed all over the back seat, not positioned for the best angle. I sat like a skinny person.

I was a skinny person, the skinniest person in the car. *Hell's bells and cockle shells.*

"Diana? Did you hear Karen? I want to know, too." Amanda leaned over the edge of the front seat, her face nearer to mine than expected. She exhaled peach all over me.

"Well," I said, fascinated by my own voice, as though another person were talking. "I need another drink to answer that question."

Karen hooted and passed me the bottle again. I took a longer pull this time.

"Yes," I said.

Amanda's face dropped, then brightened. The expression flickered so fast only I saw it. But it was there. "Our little Diana is all grown up!" she screamed, rolling down the window. "Diana is a woman!"

We drove around until the bottle was empty, then headed back into town to look for Randy. We found him with a bunch of guys from the basketball team parked in the grocery store parking lot, the place where we turned around to cruise up the strip again. Amanda hopped out and trotted over to Randy, brushing up against him. He ran his hand over her hair and let it slide down to her lower back, where it hung just above her tailbone. She winked at me again, but her hair had fallen, and her eyes looked wild. Jennifer and Karen piled out of the car to go flirt with Randy's friends, one of whom I'd had a crush on in middle school, Brad Hampshire. As I stared at him, I suddenly saw two Brads, which couldn't possibly be right, yet...yes, clearly: two Brads. The plural of Brad. Brad squared.

I knew I should get out of the car, but it was spinning too hard for me to think of leaving it. I was sure if I opened the door I'd fall out like a pile of cordwood. I put my hands on the front seat to steady myself, feeling sick, really sick.

Really sick.

I looked at my watch. It was after eleven. Surely Jennifer would need to drop us off at Amanda's grandma's house soon. If I could just make it until then, everything would be okay. It suddenly made sense for me to count backwards from one thousand to pass the time faster. I kind of wanted to do it by fives but knew that would be ridiculous.

Karen came back to the car and knocked on the window. I rolled it down, burping uncertainly.

"Hey, what are you doing in there?" she asked, giggling and grabbing for my arm. On the last pass around the dirt road, she'd decided we were friends. I reached for her arm and hit the door lock instead. I decided to pretend like I'd done it on purpose. Karen didn't notice, because she was busy checking out her reflection in the side mirror and glancing back at both Brads.

"Um, Karen? I don't really feel that good. I think I'm just going to stay here."

"Really? Okay. Just don't puke in Jennifer's car. She'll kill you."

"Okay," I said weakly, rolling up the window. "I'll be sure to puke outside." That made so much sense to me. Puke outside, no problem, if it happened, though I really hoped it wouldn't, because Randy and Paul and both Brads would see me doing it, and I still had a modicum of pride.

I leaned my forehead against the cold window glass, and it felt amazing. I pressed my entire cheek up against it, breathing against the car's revolutions, willing them to stop. It was the best car window I ever felt in my entire life.

****

When I woke up, we were outside Amanda's grandmother's house. Jennifer was laughing and shouting for us to get out, that she was late. I looked at my watch. One-fifteen a.m. Oops.

Amanda's grandma lived on the edge of town. Amanda stayed with her any time she knew she was going to blow her curfew. Her grandma—a tiny, nearly deaf woman with blue-tinted hair that she had set each Tuesday—wore housedresses and camel-colored orthopedic shoes and made cookies every afternoon even if there was no one around to eat them. When Amanda stayed over, her grandma just went to bed and never knew when Amanda got home. Amanda grabbed my arm and pulled me inside. She dropped her coat in the front entryway and stomped loudly into the kitchen.

"Amanda!" I hissed. "Shouldn't we be quiet? What if your grandma hears us?"

Amanda laughed, and when she turned I could see a hickey blooming on her neck. I pointed dumbly.

"You totally have a hickey."

Amanda looked in the hall mirror and laughed. "Grandma!" she yelled. "I have a hickey, and we're two hours late! Come and get me!"

"Amanda! Dude, shut up!"

She spun around in circles. "Diana, you know Grandma's deaf once she takes off her hearing aids." She opened the freezer and pulled out a box of frozen Girl Scout Thin Mints, ripped a few out and hurled them

133

against the refrigerator door. They sounded like rifle shots as they bounced off, but the upstairs level remained silent. I watched them bounce across the floor, amazed at the resilience of Thin Mints. They didn't even chip. You could use Thin Mints to build things. Tall things.

Amanda is throwing Thin Mints at the refrigerator, I thought, wishing that Seth or Jesse was there to appreciate all the Obvious Game possibilities operating at that moment. Alas, all I had was Amanda, who appeared to be trying to find the last batch of real cookies her grandma made, with no luck.

I pulled a box of melba toast from the pantry and ate a few slices, hoping to settle my roiling stomach with as few calories as possible. I'd had maybe five shots all night long, which I figured to be about five hundred calories. I'd have to jog extra to make up for it.

When I looked up, Amanda was stalking her grandmother's yellow cat, weaving across the green linoleum. The cat sat licking its toes, oblivious to her. Suddenly, Amanda seized the cat by the back of its neck and in three steps was across the kitchen and stuffing the cat in the microwave.

"Amanda! What the hell?" I yelled, not caring if her grandma woke up now. Amanda was really pissing me off, and I was suddenly exhausted.

Amanda whirled. "What? I never liked this old cat, anyway." She had the microwave closed, and I could see and hear the cat inside yowling frantically. She pushed the buttons. "One minute should do it."

RITA ARENS----THE OBVIOUS GAME

I lunged across the kitchen at her, not caring about anything but the cat. She laughed and held up a finger dramatically to push "start."

I swept her knees.

She hit the floor chin-first, too drunk to put up her arms to catch her fall. I left her there on the floor, groaning and laughing, as I opened the microwave door. The cat leaped past me and scooted under the couch, hissing. I didn't blame him, not one bit. If I could hiss, I would totally hiss at Amanda, too. Honestly. Cats don't go in the microwave. Everyone knows that.

Amanda was lying on the floor holding her chin. "It hurts," she moaned, still giggling. I tried to hiss, but alas, all that came out was a cough. Damn.

I took a bag of frozen peas out of the freezer and held it out to her. She lay there on the Thin-Mint-strewn floor, still laughing, her lip gloss smeared across her face. "You know I wasn't really going to do it," she said.

"Did I? Sometimes it's like you are three years old. God."

That made her laugh even harder. "Okay, Mom."

I tried to hiss again. Nothing. Giving up, I didn't even take my clothes off before I fell into the spare bed and passed out.

****

I woke up before Amanda, who lay snoring next to me in bed, her hair a rat's nest of tangles. Her eye make-up was smeared all over the dainty white embroidered pillowcase. I stared at the pink plastic phone in the guest room, trying to think who could take me home. I couldn't call Jesse—he was visiting relatives in

Omaha all weekend. My throat hurt from the hissing attempts.

Then I remembered I'd told the girls about us…about Jesse and me.

But maybe they wouldn't remember. They'd all kept drinking long after I passed out against the world's best car window—at least two hours had gone by while they did who knows what. I didn't even know if we'd gone anywhere.

I picked up the phone, staring out the window, wishing I had my own car. I dialed Seth's number. He picked up on the first ring. "Seth," I said.

"Diana," he said.

He waited.

"Diana," he repeated.

"I have a really huge favor to ask," I said.

"What's up?"

"I'm at Amanda's grandma's house."

"Right-o."

"Amanda tried to microwave the cat last night."

There was a short pause. "I'm on my way," he said.

I shuffled down the stairs and leaned over to give the tiny woman sitting on the couch watching TV a hug. "Thanks for letting me stay, Grandma," I said, inhaling her old-lady lilac scent. The cat sat in her lap, ignoring me, safe with the old woman.

"That's fine, Diana," said Amanda's grandma. "Just make sure next time you pick up your cookies after you eat them."

Chapter Eleven: Head Games

Seth drove straight to the Perkins on Exit 44 just outside Snowden. A low fog covered the ground, and I leaned back in the seat and put my feet up on the dash. "Thanks for picking me up."

He grinned and ran his hand through his hair. "I was looking for a reason to get out of going to church. So seriously, Diana, what the hell?"

I sighed, smoothing my jeans. "We got drunk, I passed out, and when we got home, Amanda stuffed her grandma's damn yellow cat in the microwave. She would've fried it if I hadn't totally knocked her down and left her lying on the kitchen floor."

Seth whistled. "Her grandma really is deaf, isn't she?"

"Did you hear the part about the cat?"

"Do you think she really would've done it?"

"I think she was drunk enough to not get what she was doing."

Seth blanched. "That's just sick, man."

A wooden wishing well filled with cheap plastic crap stood right in the middle of the lobby waiting area, oddly placed so you had to walk around it to reach the door. When I was a kid, the best part of Perkins was that wishing well. We slid into a booth by the window.

"Sorry I bugged you," I said when the waitress had brought coffee. "I had to get out of there before Amanda woke up. What've you been up to?"

"I've been around, you know, fighting back my fans. I've been seeing less and less of you." He looked pointedly at my hands. I looked down to see the veins standing out, ropy against my pale hands. My fingers were actually tinged with blue. I folded them on my lap.

"I know," I said. It was pointless to deny anything to Seth—we'd known each other too long.

"*You're skinny*," he said. "And yes, I'm playing."

"I've lost a little weight. *It's snowing*."

"A little?" he raised one eyebrow as my oatmeal arrived. He'd ordered three eggs, sunny side up. Gag.

"I don't want to play. Anyway, you've always been skinny without trying. It's different for me. I lost a few pounds," I said, curling my hair around my finger. I liked how slick it felt when I pulled it tight and rubbed it with my thumb.

"A few pounds? Is half your body a few pounds by your standards?" He paused, chewing thoughtfully. "Don't bullshit a bullshitter, Diana. You called me, remember?"

"You don't understand," I said, taking a defensive bite of oatmeal. It was bland, tasteless. No milk. No brown sugar. No raisins.

138

Seth put down his toast and leaned forward. "What I don't get, Diana, is why you think it matters. I really, really don't get that."

I picked up my spoon and made it walk around the table. And I told him. "Imagine I'm your mother. Every ten minutes I interrupt you from whatever you are doing and tell you to clean your room. You clean it. It's clean. It's spotless. You could serve the Queen Mother off your floor. Ten minutes later, I walk back in and tell you to clean it again.

"'It's clean,' you say. 'I just cleaned it.' 'Clean it again,' I say. 'You missed a spot.' So you get down on your hands and knees and scrub the floor with your toothbrush. Ten minutes later, I walk back in and tell you to clean it again. This repeats, over and over, until the room is so clean it's starting to come apart at the seams with the scrubbing, but still I continue to walk in and tell you to clean it. You show me the floorboards coming up. I don't care. I tell you to clean it again.

"After a while, the floorboards do come up, and underneath them, you imagine you see dirt. You know I'm coming back to tell you to clean it again, so you begin to scrub. You scrub and scrub. And I tell you to do it again. You fall asleep in the middle of the floor. First thing in the morning, you wake up and examine every inch of the room. It is spotless. I walk into your room before you've even gotten up. And I tell you to clean it again."

I took a deep breath. "That's what it's like inside my head."

Seth stared at me, his mouth open.

139

"Anyway," I said, wanting to change the subject. "I asked you first. How are you?"

Seth leaned back in the booth. His feet appeared on the seat next to me. He always wore Vans with white athletic socks. Today's shoes were black with red ollie pads. "Diana, I think I'm in trouble."

I put my spoon down. "What?"

He looked down at his ragged cuticles. "I slept with Vanessa," he said.

I thumped my head against the wall, for effect. Vanessa was Amanda's cousin. She was a senior and played flute in the marching band and had been hot for Seth ever since he was old enough to be hot. "Why?"

He dipped the toast in the egg again, stirring it, smearing yolk around the plate. Then he dropped the toast and ran his hands through his forelock, smoothing it as it flopped back into place. "I have no idea," he said. "We were at a party, and she was really coming on to me and, you know, I'd had some drinks…"

"But you swore up and down never, never, never, no matter how much she threw herself at you, you would never give in. Never."

"I know. I know! I can't believe it either."

"You totally let her do you, anyway."

"Yeah."

"So, that sucks, but it's not that big of a deal, right?"

He covered his eyes then pulled down on his cheeks so the whites showed down to the blood vessels of his inner lids. I hated it when he did that. He was still pulling when he looked at me, not joking at all.

Then it registered. My spoon clattered to the table. "You did *not* get her pregnant."

"Yeah, I might've."

Now it was my turn to cover my face with my hands. "How do you know?"

"She called me last night and told me she's two weeks late. I don't know whether to believe her or not."

I leaned back. I would never lie about a pregnancy, but who knew about Vanessa? She still claimed she'd been a runner-up for "Star Search" when she lived in Michigan.

"Okay, well, if she's lying, this will all go away pretty quickly. But if she's telling the truth, you do have a problem."

We both turned to the window. The snowflakes had started to stick everywhere. I could see cars spinning and skidding when they approached the stoplights. I looked back at Seth.

"What did you say when she told you?"

"I asked her to name the baby after you. What do you think I did? I asked her what she wanted to do. I told her I could give her money."

I squeezed Seth's foot through the canvas of his shoe; our eyes locked. He barely had a job. He was a sophomore in high school. He'd just started driving. Suddenly I missed Ma, wanted to crawl into her lap and let her fix me, fix Seth, fix herself. It was starting to dawn on me that nothing is really fixed, ever. It just changes.

"Then," he said, "she hung up."

"And that was last night?"

141

"Yeah," he said, slapping his hand on the table and signaling the waitress for the check. "That was last night. And this is today."

I looked out at the snow again. I could see Seth's red Corolla with the Zildjian bumper sticker already covered in a coat of white. "Yup," I said, rising from the booth. "This is today."

As we passed the wishing well on the way out, I dropped a dollar amidst the plastic wrappers.

****

When I walked in our front door, gospel music rang from the speakers. Ma's head, covered in a yellow terrycloth turban, bent over our photo albums. I dropped my coat on the floor and walked over to her, peering over her shoulder. She'd opened the large brown leather-bound album to the Christmas when I was three years old. In the top photo, I'd just received a tiny tool belt filled with plastic wrenches. In the second, I was wearing the belt and attempting to repair Pa's knee. I put my arm around Ma's shoulders and squeezed. She placed her hand over mine and squeezed back.

"Did you have fun last night?" she asked.

"Yeah. I don't know. Amanda's weird these days."

Ma nodded her head, not really listening. "I think Amanda's been weird her whole life."

"Where's Pa?"

"He's Christmas shopping," she said, looking up with a smile. "What are you doing tonight?"

"I don't know. It's Sunday."

Ma put the photo album down and looked at me, her eyes shining. "Would you and Jesse like to help us decorate the Christmas tree? It's snowing."

I thought about it. Jesse had never been in my house except to pick me up. I pictured us all gathered together, sipping hot chocolate and hanging ornaments. I really wanted Ma and Pa to like him. I thought maybe that's what you did, when you were someone's girlfriend. You decorated a tree together. Sort of nerdy. Sort of nice.

"I remember the Christmas you were seven years old," she said. "We gave you a pink bike with white tires. Do you remember that?"

"Yeah. It had pink and silver streamers on the handlebars."

Ma was staring out the window. "I bought a white wicker bike basket with pink plastic flowers for it. I think I was most excited about the bike basket."

"Do you still get excited for Christmas?" I asked.

She looked at me, scratched her head. "This year I'm excited I'm *here* at Christmas," she said.

I immediately felt angry. I hated it when she insinuated she might die. It made me throw-a-chair-through-a-window angry. I knew it wasn't fair, but still.

"I can call him," I said. She picked up the photo album again, nodding at the subject change as though my voice didn't ring with annoyance.

As I stood up, I saw her brush her cheek with the back of her hand, and—mad as I was—it seemed very important for Jesse to come over.

143

"I'll call him right now," I said, taking the stairs down to my room as quickly as I ran the bleachers by the cinder track.

****

Ma was bustling around the kitchen making popcorn when we heard the crackle of tires on the gravel driveway. I ran over to the window and saw Pa's headlights.

"Sorry I'm late, guys," he said. "Hi, Jesse." Pa's face broke into a self-conscious smile. I realized he hadn't known Jesse would be here.

At nine-thirty, Ma excused herself to the bedroom. "Good night, Jesse," she said, touching him lightly on the shoulder. "Thanks for coming over tonight. It meant a lot to me to decorate the tree. I like rituals."

"No problem, Mrs. Keller," Jesse said. "I like them too."

Pa settled in his chair and flipped on the news, and Jesse and I went downstairs to watch TV.

"That was fun," said Jesse, tracing his finger up and down my forearm. It gave me tingles to feel him there. I wanted to kiss him, but the sound of Pa shifting in his chair upstairs made me too nervous.

Jesse leaned in to me. I could smell his cologne clinging to his sweater. He smelled so good, but then I remembered. He tried to kiss me, but I turned my cheek.

"What's wrong?" he asked, pulling back.

"I had breakfast with Seth this morning. He thinks he might have gotten Vanessa pregnant."

Jesse whistled low. "Seriously?"

144

I nodded. "She's been hot for him for years. I guess he caved at a party a few weeks ago. He's an idiot. Of course he didn't have a rubber."

"Is she going to get an abortion?"

I got angry again. It happened so fast, just like with Ma.

"Should she? Is that *your* immediate solution to the problem?" I held my temples in my hands. The anger boiled up in me, starting in my neck and spilling down my arms into my hands. If I'd wanted to, I could've pulled a tree up by the roots. I felt crazy.

Jesse didn't notice the edge in my voice. He seemed to be turning the problem over in his head. "Well, there's either keep it or not keep it, I guess. She's, what, a senior?"

"Would it be different if she were a sophomore?"

Now he heard the edge, looked at me in surprise. "Is there something you need to tell me, Diana?" He grabbed my arm.

"No," I mumbled. "Not yet."

"What?"

"I'm scared, Jesse. It scared me. That could happen to us."

"It won't happen to us. I'm very careful."

"How do you know that?"

Jesse got up, circling the jogging trampoline in the middle of the basement as though it were an opponent, looking for an opportunity. "This is really the last thing I want to talk about right now, Diana. We just decorated a damn Christmas tree. Like normal people."

Now his voice held its own edge, which completely broke me. I hugged my knees tighter, berating myself for getting into a position in which I should have to worry.

Chapter Twelve: Faith

That night I found Ma sitting up in bed in her shadowy room, shredding tear-soaked tissues. She was crying.

I sat down on the edge of the bed. "Are you okay, Ma?" I asked. I didn't really want to know the answer, but that's what you do, you ask.

"Diana, I just don't understand why God would let this happen to me. I've been good. I've prayed. I've tithed. I just don't understand. I'm angry at God."

I hadn't realized that was an option, not in this house. Ma usually reacted to life as though God interfered to the level of traffic jams.

"Do you want a hug?" I asked after a few minutes passed. I watched her reach for more tissues to shred in her ever-growing pile.

"No. I want to sit here and be mad." She looked at me with different eyes than I'd seen before, not the eyes of my mother who always knew what to do in every crisis. These eyes were wild, provocative, unleashed. They scared me.

The phone rang. I answered. Seth's mom's voice was tight on the other end of the line. "When did you see Seth last?" she asked. I could hear her hard-soled shoes pacing on the hardwood floors of their living room.

"Gosh, probably noon yesterday," I said. "He dropped me off right after breakfast. Why?"

"He hasn't come home. I don't know where he is, Diana."

I looked at the clock. It was almost nine. I tried to think where he could be. "Have you called Hutch?"

"Of course. I called him first. You were the last one to see him. Think, Diana."

I recoiled at her admonition, then closed my eyes and thought about where Seth might be. I knew he was upset about Vanessa. I knew he had a car. In thirty hours, he really could have gone anywhere.

"I'll find him," I said. The line went dead and I stared at the phone until it made the fast beep. Ma ignored me.

I lined up the soggy Kleenex along the green stripe of her bedspread. Her eyes were still streaming with tears, her mouth a tight line. "Are you done?" I asked. I knew I was taking a risk, but I needed her help. I didn't know what to do with Ma the crying wreck. I needed Ma who killed snakes with a shovel.

Ma looked taken aback, as though I'd punched her in the throat. "What?"

"Seth's missing."

She swallowed, her face immediately morphing back from victim to mother.

"I think I know where he is, but I need you to drive me."

Pa was out. It was her or nothing. She knew that. I was being unfair. I knew that, too.

She leaned back, covered her face with her hands. "I really need to have tonight to be about me, Diana," she said.

I reached over and pulled her hands down off her face. "Ma," I said, "I need your help. Please." I held her hands, rubbing the knuckles. They were rough, her hands cold. "Please."

She held her position a few seconds as I held my breath.

"I'm sorry," I said.

"Don't be," she said, pulling her hands away. "You didn't do anything wrong. It is what it is. Let's go."

She was up and out of the bed faster than I thought possible, pulling on sweatshirt, jeans, clogs. She grabbed the car keys on the counter in one shaking hand and pointed to the door.

As we turned out of the driveway, I motioned toward the highway. "We need to go to Omaha," I said. It wasn't far—that's where the hospital was—but far enough I'd waited to tell her for fear she wouldn't agree if she realized this wasn't going to be a fast trip. "The city of wicked delights," I added, trying to make her smile.

She wasn't having any of it. "What's going on? Why did he run away?" she asked as we pulled onto the blacktop.

I sucked in a deep breath, feeling my diaphragm contract. She was driving me there. I owed her an explanation. "He thinks he got someone pregnant."

Ma sighed. "Who?"

"Amanda's cousin, Vanessa."

Ma laughed. First just a little gurgle, then a rattling guffaw. She tried to compose herself only to start giggling again.

Confused and thinking she might finally be losing it, I studied the emergency brake in case I needed to pull it if she snapped.

Ma looked over at me and descended again into uncontrolled laughter at the sight of my panicked expression.

"Ma?"

"I'm sorry, Diana, but really…" She struggled for breath, grasping the steering wheel with one hand and wiping her eyes with the other.

"What?" I demanded.

"I thought he had better taste."

Then I was laughing, too. At Seth. At the cancer. At Job.

****

We found a parking spot and walked four blocks to the used bookstore and record shop. Whenever Seth and I went in there, a creepy bearded guy sitting in the front window with a one-eyed cat would offer us coffee. I never had the nerve to take him up on it, but Seth always confidently went to the back of the store where a row of chipped mugs hung from pegs.

I liked to look at the old books. Seth would disappear down the stairs to the basement where they kept records, posters, and sheet music.

I told Ma all of this as we trudged through the night into the store. We passed the old guy. I squeezed her hand and Ma stared down the cat as I flew down the wooden stairs. Maybe Ma's holiness made the cat nervous.

Seth sat in an olive velour armchair reading the liner notes of a Sex Pistols album. He didn't look up as I approached. "Why are you here?" he asked.

"Are you mad at me?" Silence. "I was worried about you."

He sighed. "Don't mother me, Diana. I'm not ready to go home yet."

"What are you doing here?" I asked.

"I am drinking coffee."

"You are being an ass."

He ran his hand through his hair. "Did my mom call you?"

I sat down on the arm of the chair and took the album out of his hands. "Of course. You're missing."

He ran his hands over his face, pulling down on his cheeks in frustration. "I don't know what I'm going to do."

I sighed. Who does? "Listen, Seth, are you going home soon or what? Your mom is freaking out, and I made Ma drive me here, and she's sick."

"Oh, shit. I'm sorry."

"So now you have to name the baby after *her* instead." He laughed a little, so I thought we could probably leave. I grabbed his forearm, and he met my gaze. "She's sick, and I need to go home, but I can't go home unless I know you're going home, too."

Seth nodded and set down the coffee cup. I slid off the armchair and realized how cold I was.

"Don't do that, okay?"

"Do what, Diana?

I grabbed his hand, pulled him out of the chair. "Don't scare me like that."

He smiled. "You worry too much."

"Yeah," I said, smiling back. "But you'd be surprised at all the crazies in the world." I held his hand a minute longer, rubbing his knuckles like I'd rubbed Ma's, then dropped it and walked away. This time I didn't look back.

I left him down there so he wouldn't have to talk to Ma. When I got back upstairs, she was still staring at the cat.

"This cat bears a striking resemblance to my great-aunt Maude. Was he down there?" asked Ma. She looked tired.

"He was."

"Is he going home?"

"He is."

"So we can go home?"

"Yes. Did Great-aunt Maude have one eye?"

"Yes."

"Really? You never told me that."

"It just never came up in conversation." She looked at her watch.

"Thanks, Ma."

"Any time."

We sat in the car with the engine idling until we saw Seth jog down the sidewalk to his Corolla and pull out, turning toward Snowden. I wondered as we turned off toward our house if I'd told Ma the truth.

Chapter Thirteen: Cuts Like a Knife

The snow began again the day Grandma and Grandpa arrived, their green Ford pick-up rumbling up the drive. I watched it approach, nearly dancing with excitement. Grandma and Grandpa made Christmas real.

Grandpa hopped out of the truck—so agile for his eighty-two years—and walked around the front of the truck, his eyes on Grandma through the windshield.

Grandma had wrapped one of her plastic rain bonnets over her blue-gray set hair, and it glinted in the pale winter light. I threw the front door open and stood shivering in my socks at the front door as Grandpa led Grandma down the walk. Grandma held out her arms. "Come here, child," she said, and I ran to her.

Pa joined Grandpa outside to help unload the truck. They stood in the drive talking, the old man gesturing at the fields and Pa nodding.

Ma coughed into her arm as she leaned down to hug Grandma. "Hello, Adele," she said. "How was your drive?"

Grandma removed her thick glasses and took a plain cotton hanky out of her small leather purse. "Oh, fine, fine," she said, blinking in the light of the living room.

I curled up beside her on the couch, breathing in her lilac scent. I knew she tucked sachets into her nylons' drawer. I threw my socks on the floor.

Pa and Grandpa were now circling the perimeter of the house and walking into the cornfield beyond.

"How's school, Diana?" Grandma asked, her glasses now perched back firmly on her nose. Her glasses magnified her pale gray eyes.

"It's good, I guess."

Grandma reached into her purse, brought out a cherry cough drop, and handed it to Ma without even looking at her. Ma took it and put it in her mouth just as another wave of coughing overcame her. She sank into a nearby chair and put her hand to her chest. In my excitement I hadn't noticed how much Ma was coughing, but Grandma seemed to sense it without even seeing it happen.

Ma paused her coughing and went to pour coffee. She returned with two steaming cups and placed Grandma's on the small antique table beside the sofa. She took her own cup and sank back into the chair, blowing steam in waves from the cup. "Diana has a boyfriend, Adele," she said, smiling.

Grandma turned to me. "A boyfriend?" she asked, peering at me through her glasses. "Tell me about him."

I felt my face heating up. "His name is Jesse, and he's from Kansas City."

"A big-city boy, hm?" she asked.

"We met this summer when he moved here, and then he took me to the homecoming dance," I continued, wondering if Grandma—who seemed to see everything—could tell I'd lost my virginity.

Grandma studied Ma, who had pulled a blanket over her body and sat staring out the window at Pa and Grandpa kneeling in the field behind the house, digging in the soil with their hands. "Do you like him, Eva?" she asked.

Ma turned, distracted. "Oh, yes. He's quite the gentleman for being sixteen." She smiled at me. "He seems to make Diana very happy, and that makes me happy."

"Make sure he treats you well, Diana," Grandma said. "If you demand that a man treats you well, he will." Ma coughed again, and Grandma looked at her sternly. "Eva, you sound horrible," she said. "Have you been to the doctor?"

Ma put her hand to her forehead. "You know, it really just started to be bad today. If I'm not feeling better in the morning, I'll go," she said.

Grandma frowned. "Tomorrow is Christmas Eve. It'll be impossible to get in. I think we should go now."

Ma shook her head, wig swinging around her chin. "You just got here. This is not the way I want you to spend your visit," she said.

Grandma held her hand out to me, and I pulled her off the couch. "You know as well as I do that I come to see you, not to be entertained," she said, drawing up her tiny frame. "Diana, get my son. Your mother needs to

157

see the doctor before the whole world closes down for Christmas."

I pulled on my shoes and went outside. Pa and Grandpa were immersed in a conversation about soil quality. I tugged on Pa's sleeve, and he batted me away like a fly. I tugged his sleeve again, reduced to an insistent child in my grandfather's presence. "Pa," I said, "Grandma says you have to take Ma to the doctor. She won't stop coughing, and tomorrow is Christmas Eve."

Grandpa stopped talking and placed his hand on my shoulder. He looked concerned. "How has Evelyn been?" he asked Pa.

Pa looked down, glanced at me. I could tell he didn't want to talk in front of me, still trying to shield me from Ma's cancer. I knew it was bad, but I guess none of us ever wanted to see the truth when she got worse. Pa pulled his car keys out of his pocket. "It comes and goes," he said to his father. "The cough just started yesterday, but she has almost no immunity. We'd probably better take her."

Grandpa kept his hand on my shoulder. "We don't all need to go and make it a huge spectacle. Why don't you and Adele take her? I'll stay here with Diana. I haven't seen my girl in months."

I smiled involuntarily.

"Okay," said Pa, zipping up his coat again. "We shouldn't be gone too long."

Grandpa and I watched them place Grandma in the front seat of the Honda and stuff Ma in the back, then pull down the long driveway. "Well," said Grandpa, "I guess we better have some dinner waiting for them when they get back."

"Grandpa, it's flu season, and there's only one doctor. They're going to be gone for hours. That's why Ma didn't want to go."

He smoothed his flannel shirt and stretched. "Well," he said, "I guess we better make something that takes a while."

We rummaged through the cabinets, the refrigerator, and the deep freeze until Grandpa found the ingredients for chili. I put on Manheim Steamroller and turned on the Christmas tree lights. We didn't talk much as we chopped peppers and browned hamburger meat, but by the time the chili simmered in the huge Dutch oven, my stress had slid away and I was ready to face whatever news might walk back through the door with Ma.

Grandpa and I warmed apple cider and sat on the couch, watching the tree ornaments sway when the heat kicked on. Grandpa leaned back and put his feet up on the ottoman. "Why is it so hot in here?" he asked.

"Ma gets cold," I said, tucking my feet under me.

"Looks like you might get cold too," he said, not looking at me, just watching the tree lights blink.

"Oh, sometimes. It can be cold in here."

"You're looking a little peaked yourself, Diana. Things getting to you? You eating enough?" He turned, then, head back like a turtle peering out of his shell. I should've known better. Grandpa saw things on the side of the road that escaped even Pa.

159

"It's been hard, Grandpa," I said, feeling my face scrunch up. I put my head in my hands and cried, ugly cried, with red face and sobs. I leaned into Grandpa's flannel shirt, and he rested his arm over my heaving shoulders and held me close, saying nothing, as the music played and the light faded. Eventually I stopped, but still he said nothing, just stroking my hair and sipping his cider.

"It's not just Ma." My breath came in snuffling gasps and hiccups.

He waited.

"I don't even know if I like Amanda anymore."

Grandpa sat there.

"Seth ran away, and Jesse and I had a fight, and it's so cold and dark right now—everything just seems so hard. Hard to go out, sad to stay in…. Everything sucks right now. I can't figure out how to have fun anymore. I see my friends having fun, and it's like I've forgotten how to do it."

I paused, wallowing. "I hate the way I look. And Ma is so sick she doesn't seem to notice anything. Pa never did. No offense, I know he's your son."

Grandpa laughed. "He's my son, but you're right, he's not the best with noticing what's going on with other people. Why do you hate the way you look?"

I sucked in my breath. As always, Grandpa had grabbed the real problem out of the pile I threw on his lap. I had to be careful how much to say.

"I don't know. I just always have." I pulled away from him and flopped my head on the other end of the couch, pulling the blanket over my legs before he could study my body. "What should I do?" I asked, hating the whine I heard in my voice.

Grandpa looked startled. "Do?" he replied. "There's nothing to *do* but survive it. So you take care of yourself. Your mom needs you."

"Sometimes it seems like too much at once." I chewed my bottom lip and turned my head. If I looked at Grandpa, I'd start crying again. "I don't want to take care of myself. I just want Ma back."

"Of course you do."

"I want the hard part to be over." I wished he had the power to make that happen: make the hard part end, just *poof,* just like that.

"You'll have hard times, Diana. This won't be the last one, and you'll never know how long they're going to last. The flip side is that the good times come back again. I know it's hard to understand now—you're fifteen and you haven't had that many times, period. My worst stretch of bad times lasted longer than you've been alive. But it's cyclical. You have bad and then good and then sometimes good some more before it turns bad again. During the good times, you rejoice. During the bad times, you survive. When the good times come again, they're like water in the desert. That's when you realize good times are in fact simply the absence of bad."

Grandpa patted my hand. "You don't like me reminding you you're only fifteen, do you?"

I shook my head, but I could feel myself smiling.

He turned his head back to face forward, and I could see him forcing back his own smile, trying to be serious. "Well," he said, "I'll stop reminding you you're young if you'll stop reminding yourself about the bad times. Deal?"

"Deal," I said, burrowing further under the blanket.

****

When they returned, the chili was bubbling. Grandpa had set the table while I'd slept on the couch, and Pa deposited Ma into the nearest chair. "Well, that took long enough," Ma said, looking embarrassed. I hauled myself off the couch and hurried over.

"Well?" asked Grandpa, polishing a sunshine-yellow plastic soup ladle with a dishtowel.

Pa cleared his throat. "Evelyn has pneumonia, but they think they caught it quickly enough. They gave her some strong antibiotics, but she needs to take it easy this Christmas. We may have to skip church."

I could tell that pained Pa. He loved taking his parents to church with him. Ma and I had bought new dresses and everything. Now none of it was going to happen. I felt angry, but when Ma began to cough again, looking so pale, I immediately felt guilty instead. What was wrong with me? It was Christmas.

Grandma settled herself in her chair. "It is what it is," she said. "And we will be just fine. My goodness, Edward," she said. "You've made some fine chili, I can smell it. Diana, why don't you bring it out? I'm starved half to death."

We sat under the dining room light fixture, bathed in a sort of spotlight as the rest of the house fell dark around us. I felt like I had when eating around the table with Lin and Hutch and Jesse, like it was just us in the whole world.

Ma had taken some codeine cough syrup, and as soon as she finished she stood. "I think I'd better go to bed," she said. "I'm sorry, but this cough syrup is really intense."

Grandma nodded. "Of course you will," she said. "Tomorrow is Christmas Eve, and we're going to have a lovely time."

As Ma tottered off toward the bedroom, I remembered we hadn't yet made up the guest bedroom for Grandma and Grandpa. I rushed after her and whispered, "Ma, you rest. I'll take care of getting things ready for them."

Ma leaned on me with relief. "Thank you, Diana. I really appreciate your help. I'm sorry about this."

"Sorry about what? You can't help it that you're sick."

Ma looked at me wearily, then climbed into bed fully dressed. "Neither can you, and I can't help thinking about that," she said.

I went to my room and called Jesse. I didn't want another day to end without talking to him. "I'm sorry about the other night," I said as soon as he answered the phone. "I'm really sorry."

"So am I," he said gruffly. I pictured his fingers playing with the phone cord, the way he always did.

"Ma's got pneumonia, so our normal plans have sort of gone out the window. My grandparents are here."

"Really? I was going to see if I could come over and give you your Christmas present. Damn."

My stomach leaped. He'd bought me a Christmas present? I'd gotten him a gold chain. "Do you want to come by? You could meet them."

He laughed. "Meet your grandparents? Not that that's intimidating or anything."

I laughed too, relieved to laugh, to not feel sad. "They're from Nebraska. They're not that scary. Only half the state is armed."

Jesse sighed. "We've got family stuff all night, but I could probably swing by right after lunch tomorrow. Would that be okay? I'd like to see you."

"That would be more than okay."

"I'll see you tomorrow then," said Jesse. "I love you, Diana."

My stomach flipped as it always did when he said that. We'd made it through our first fight. And he loved me. "I love you, too."

"Good night."

****

Ma looked a lot better the next morning. She stood at the stove wearing her green silk turban, flipping pancakes. She hated pancakes and only made them because Grandma loved them. Ma had even bought blueberry syrup just for their visit. Ma hated sweet breakfast food, preferring to take down an entire package of bacon when the mood struck her. Ma: bacon warrior, defender of protein breakfasts.

"Can Jesse come by after lunch to exchange presents and meet Grandma and Grandpa?" I asked.

"Good morning to you, too, Diana," said Ma, coughing into her elbow, careful to avoid the pancakes.

"Of course he can come by. Then your grandmother will stop asking me about him." She winked at Grandma, who was sitting at the kitchen table piecing a quilt from the plastic bag of material she'd brought in from the truck. A yellow legal pad sat at her elbow, and I could see her drawings and careful calculations.

"What kind of quilt are you making, Grandma?" I asked.

Grandma looked up, her gray eyes enormous. "I'm making a cancer quilt," she said.

I looked at Ma, surprised. "Why would you do that?"

Ma smiled. "I asked her to," she said, turning back to the pancakes.

I didn't get it. "Why?"

Ma flipped another pancake and took the griddle off the heat. "I don't want to forget this time," she said. "It's hard to explain. I want to conquer it, but I don't want to forget it."

I looked at the squares Grandma had laid on the table. There weren't any pictures in the fabric. Dark grays swirled with hot reds and flat black, the colors jumbled and fading into each other, sometimes in a graduated rainbow of grays and sometimes a harsh transition between red and black.

Jesse arrived shortly after a lunch I'd mostly thrown in the trash as I walked to and from the kitchen and the table, serving. Grandma had put on a soft blue sweater that changed the color of her eyes in preparation for Jesse's visit. Ma wore her wig, shiny and swinging.

165

When I answered the door, I could hardly see Jesse. He was carrying a huge bouquet of flowers—roses, lilies, hydrangea—at least forty flowers bursting from a pink cut-glass vase. I stepped back in surprise, touched. They were so beautiful.

Jesse peered around from behind the flowers. "Aren't you going to invite me in?" he asked, grinning.

"Oh, my God," I said. "They're amazing. They're beautiful. Hydrangeas in December, like that happens. I love it. Come in."

He walked in and set the flowers down on the end table by the door. He wrapped me in his arms and kissed my cheek, smelling of winter wind. "Merry Christmas, Diana," he said. I pressed myself into his chest as he leaned his head down to kiss the top of mine.

I relaxed into his grip. "I'm so sorry, Jesse," I said quietly. I could smell him, and that made everything okay for the moment.

He reached down and cupped my face in his hands. "It's harder than that to get rid of me." He kissed me, and I leaned into him, wanting to disappear in his arms.

When we got upstairs, Pa and Grandpa stood. I had taken the flowers and set them down on the breakfast bar where they unfolded even more, at least three feet across. Grandpa and Pa shook Jesse's hand, and I rushed over to introduce Grandpa, forcing myself to rip my eyes away from the bouquet.

Then Jesse walked over to the couch and leaned down to shake Grandma's hand. She took his gently and patted it. "The flowers are just what this house needs today, young man," she said. "Excellent choice."

Ma smiled. "Thanks for coming by," she said. "I know it's Christmas. What is your family doing tonight?"

"We always have a family celebration with my aunt and uncle and cousins from Omaha," he said. "It's sort of a zoo."

"Zoos can be good," said Ma. She touched the flowers. "Zoos can be good."

"I can't stay long, I'm afraid," Jesse said, stuffing his hands in his pockets. "I sort of slipped out."

"No problem," said Pa. "It's good to see you. Diana, why don't you walk him down?"

I remembered the chain. I grabbed it from under the tree and followed Jesse down the stairs. When we got to the basement, we went into the rec room.

"I love the flowers," I said. "I sort of killed my begonia. Maybe I'm better with cut flowers?"

"The vase is really the present," he said. "I saw it and just thought it might cheer you up when things get ugly. Keep it full."

"I'll try," I said. I held out the box. "I got you something. I don't know if you'll like it. It wasn't on *Cosmo*'s list of top ten things to get your man. Then again, everything on the list cost waaaay more than my allowance."

With his thick fingers he ripped the paper I'd so carefully wrapped around the box. As he lifted out the chain, I looked hard at his face, trying to gauge his reaction. He seemed genuinely surprised and pleased.

167

"Can you put it on me?" he asked. "I'm no good with little clasps."

I walked around behind him and fastened the chain around his neck. It hung just low enough to be hidden by his undershirt. "I wanted to give you something you could have with you all the time," I said. "But if you don't like it, please don't wear it just to avoid hurting my feelings. I have given many, many bad gifts in my lifetime."

Jesse reached up and touched it. It wasn't that long—he couldn't see it without looking in a mirror. "It feels nice," he said. "I love it." He twisted around to face me. "It's going to be okay, Diana. But you have to stop freaking out about what's going on with other people. Seth's problem is Seth's problem. Amanda's problems are Amanda's problems. Remember that. The minute you start worrying about other people's problems too much, you can drown in them."

"I get it. *It's Christmas.*" I shifted to the Obvious Game, because I didn't want to hear what he had to say.

"Yes. It's Christmas," he said, kissing me again.

****

I woke up from my nap to the sound of hushed voices.

Pa and Grandma were standing in the middle of the kitchen, talking quietly. Grandpa was outside warming up the car. Ma sat on the couch, wrapped in blankets and soaked in sweat. Her eyes looked glassy. She didn't respond when I sat beside her, just leaned over and coughed until she bent in half.

I ran over to Pa. "What's going on?"

He put his arm around me like I was a small child. "She got worse all of a sudden, Diana. The antibiotics aren't working fast enough. I think we're going to have to take her to the hospital."

I couldn't help myself. "On Christmas?"

Pa looked over my head at Ma. "I'm afraid so, kiddo."

"Well, I want to come this time. You're not going to leave me at home like a little kid." I reached over to the huge bouquet of flowers and plucked a red rose from the bunch. I snapped it in half and tucked the bloom behind my ear. "We're all going to be together on Christmas."

And so we drove, me in the backseat with a shivering Ma, Pa driving, and Grandma and Grandpa following in their pick-up, to the emergency room. As we drove, I quietly sang "Amazing Grace." Ma held my hand the whole way to the hospital.

And we left her there.

Chapter Fourteen: Double Vision

The first week, Ma stayed in the oncology ward's intensive care unit. Pa and I delivered her a new toothbrush and underwear in a Ziploc baggie, the kind she usually used for grapes. The side was imprinted with a place to write the date of the leftovers inside. Her toothbrush wasn't going to be a leftover. I willed this toothbrush to live forever.

Because I realized she might die.

To reach Ma's room, we had to pass through two doors and an airlock, don paper clothes over our own, wear masks. The airlock made it real. The baby-blue shoe covers wouldn't have lasted a minute outside, the paper quickly dissolving under melting snow.

For the first time in her life, Ma watched a lot of TV. Her newfound love for daytime television gave us something to talk about other than the IV lines and her queasy stomach. We both liked the soaps. It was interesting to watch other people cry on cue over nothing sad at all.

Ma told me she liked the one with Kelly Ripa. Kelly Ripa made Ma happy: Kelly was super good at crying on demand. And also at being chipper.

After that visit to the ICU, Pa drove home slowly. I snuck looks at him the whole way home. He didn't seem to notice. His face stayed forward, but his eyes flicked off to the ditches, searching for something to see. I thought about when I'd handed Ma the underwear, the feeling of cotton enclosed in the baggie, how the plastic slid back and forth between my thumb and forefinger. Her underwear was a specimen ready for identification: cancer patient's panties, circa 1990.

"She'll be fine, Diana," Pa said as we drove.

"How do you know?" I sniffed, on the verge of crying again.

"'Farmer's Almanac.'"

"*Pa!*"

"What?" He reached over and patted my hand. "It's not written anywhere that she'll *not* be okay, either."

I sat in my room after we got home, staring out the window at the woods outside. It was the paper shoes that got to me, as if the slightest speck of dust could take down the woman who cleaned sinks with a toothbrush and cooked ham balls for twenty every Easter.

And then, I was howling—the sound a dog might make.

Moments later, Pa flung open the door, concern on his face. "Diana, what's wrong?" he asked.

"She could *die*," I moaned when I caught my breath.

He shuffled over, worn leather moccasins catching on the blue shag carpet. "Well, that's true. But I don't think she will."

"I do."

He gathered me up in his arms, the way he used to do when I was a little girl. He had an iron grip. I relaxed into it.

"What if she dies, Pa? What will we do?"

He sat for a while, not answering, just rocking me back and forth. Finally I stopped crying.

The phone rang, and Pa answered it. He mouthed "Jesse," but I shook my head. I just flopped back on the bed and listened to Pa telling Jesse I didn't feel well.

I stared at the ceiling and felt Pa looking at me.

"Well, good night, then," he said, bending down to kiss my cheek.

****

Grandma and Grandpa stayed the whole week school was out. We played Scrabble for hours, ending one round and immediately beginning the next, chaining games like a smoker lighting a fresh cigarette from the butt of the previous one.

During Grandma's pick—a Bible round of Scrabble—I won using "Peter." "Grandma?"

"What is it, Diana?"

"Why couldn't Peter walk on the water anymore after he looked down?"

"He never needed to be able to," she said. "Jesus was just making a point."

I cleared the board, putting the pieces back in their little sack. "I don't get it."

"That's why it's called faith," she said, smiling over at me. "It's not that obvious."

After lunch on Sunday, Grandma picked up her rain bonnet, her sign it was time to leave. Pa carried their suitcases out to the truck. I clung to Grandma when I hugged her goodbye.

"Can't you stay?" I asked her shoulder.

"Oh, honey, we need to get home. And you need to get back to normal. School's starting again. You'll be busy. Your mother will be home soon, you know."

I didn't reply.

Grandma cupped my chin in her hand, leveling her gray gaze at me sternly. "Buck up, Diana," she said. "This, too, shall pass."

Their truck rattled down the gravel driveway like a dog shaking off water. Pa disappeared into the house and returned holding out the phone to me. "It's Amanda," he said, rolling his eyes.

"Hey," I said into the phone.

"Are your grandparents still there?" she asked. I could hear her popping her gum.

"No, they just left. Nebraska calls." I gulped, wishing they were still there. *This, too, shall pass.*

"Good. Mark's hooking up the sled."

Every winter, Mark hitched a chain to the back of his pick-up truck and pulled his toboggan along any road icy or snowy enough to handle it. It was just one of those things we did in a town with nothing to do: terrace-jumping in our cars, drinking on back roads, climbing into pens with bulls to see if they would charge.

"I don't know, Amanda. I don't have a ride."

"Don't be ridiculous. You need to get out. Get Jesse to drive you."

"I don't even know what he's doing right now. I haven't talked to him in days."

"Jesus, Diana. Don't you ever want to have fun anymore?"

I did. I really did.

I eyed Pa, who was pretending not to listen. He motioned to the car, pantomimed driving. Clearly he had no idea what I was talking about. No father grins and agrees to let his fifteen-year-old daughter ride a piece of wood across cement and ice at high speed.

"Pa says he'll bring me. Where are we meeting?"

"The school parking lot. And you need a check-up from the neck up, Diana." She popped her gum again and hung up.

****

When Pa dropped me off at the school parking lot, I saw the LeSabre by Mark's truck. I waved goodbye to Pa and walked over to it, looking for Jesse. He was sitting in the car, listening to the radio, drumming his fingers on the wheel.

I knocked on the window. He looked up and smiled with only his mouth. I walked around and opened the passenger door. "May I join you, sir?" I asked.

"Of course."

"What's wrong?"

"Why would anything be wrong?"

"Why didn't you call me to come sledding?"

"Why didn't you talk to me the other night?"

175

I felt my face getting hot. "I don't know," I said. But I did. I just wanted to be alone with my fear. I didn't *want* to buck up. I didn't *want* a check-up from the neck up. I didn't even *want* to be happy, and Jesse made me happy. Something was horribly wrong, and I *wanted* to know why—but we'd probably never know why she got sick. Ma was wrong. God didn't let it happen to her; it just happened. Sometimes the parking lot happened to be full for no damn reason at all.

I shut the door and walked over to Mark's truck. He sat in the cab with his fingers up against the heat vents even though the window was down. "Hey, Diana. What's up?"

"I want to go first."

Jesse walked up and heard me. He threw his hands in the air in frustration. "What the hell, Diana? It's really dangerous."

I glanced at him sideways without turning my head, then looked back at Mark, then down at my coveralls. "I'm accepting the challenge. Will you go slow? I've never done it before."

Mark laughed, his freckles dark against his bright red cheeks. "Of course."

Jesse grabbed my shoulder, digging his fingers in a little too hard. "Diana, seriously, you shouldn't."

I rolled my eyes, tired of people telling me what to do. "I'm fine. I did this once professionally."

Jesse sighed.

"Placed third," I said, hoping to make him smile. It didn't work.

176

Mark called to the other kids. "Hop in. Diana's going to ride."

As I climbed into the bed of Mark's truck, I grabbed Jesse's hand. "I need to do this. Please understand."

He ripped his hand away from mine, staring straight ahead as the truck picked up speed and headed for the back roads outside Snowden.

****

My toboggan traversed the packed ice faster than I'd thought it would. Much faster. Straining against the white pick-up's hitch, the thick chain attached to my sled whipped, a pendulum. Ice shards showered off the rails behind me as I gripped the birch handle tighter and strained to dig my boots into the boards.

Mark swore he'd top out at ten miles per hour, but we were easily going at least twenty-five. I shrieked as my friends shouted from the bed of the truck for Mark to slow the hell down before I flew off.

The brake lights flashed. I felt relief until I realized the brakes were in preparation for a turn that should've been gentle—would've been gentle—were the toboggan not attached thirty feet behind the truck by a three-inch chain. The toboggan slid gracefully across the ice-covered asphalt until it hit the roadside gravel and I flipped off, hitting the drifted snow of the roadside ditch with a hard thud.

I'd seen it coming soon enough to tuck my head and roll, coming to rest flat on my back. My first breath wouldn't come. Finally the air forced itself out of my uncooperative lungs, and I sucked in.

177

Jesse arrived first at my side. "Don't move," he commanded, running gloved hands over my arms and legs. "Can you feel this?" I could. His hands barely registered through my insulated coveralls, but I felt them. Even when I was mad at him, I could always feel Jesse's touch.

I ignored him and sat up, brushing the beard of snow from my face. Apparently, I didn't have any spinal injuries. Which was good, because they would have stopped me from killing Mark.

Already my arms and legs throbbed. Everything seemed to work, but my shins were blooming yellow-and-green bruises when I pulled up the leg of my coveralls to assess the damage.

Riding the toboggan had seemed like it would be easy, exciting, different. Instead—just like everything else in my life—it had been terrifying.

"I'm fine," I said, rising slowly to my feet. "And I'm going to murder Mark now. Please excuse me while I select my method."

Mark pulled the pick-up around, chain and toboggan clattering behind him like a pair of newlyweds' tin cans. His face white, he pulled to a stop.

Jesse turned to me, his face like stone. "You scared me," he said quietly. "Damn it, Diana."

"I know. It's part of my charm."

His gloved hand gripped my elbow.

"I *know*," I repeated. "God, chill out. I'm fine, Jesse."

178

Jesse turned around, his eyes still on me, then seized the driver's side door of the truck and pulled it open.

Mark scowled. "What the fuck are you doing? It's cold out there. I give her at least an eight-point-five. I did notice she didn't dismount properly."

Jesse grabbed Mark's heavy winter coat and pulled him out of the truck. Mark wobbled, staring at Jesse in shock. Jesse leaned over and whispered something to him, still grasping Mark's coat.

"Okay, fine, I'm sorry. I wasn't going that fast." Jesse's fist around Mark's arm slowly unclenched, and Jesse backed away. Mark looked at me like I was a strange bird, then crawled back into the cab. "Sorry, Diana. Get in," he said in a low voice. "So much for your luge career." I flipped him the bird, my legs throbbing. The kids in the back of the truck hooted.

Jesse walked back over to me. "When did you get so angry all the time?"

I turned to him, brushing snow from my pants, suddenly calm and wondering what Jesse had said to Mark to make him look at me like that. "I thought you remembered angry," I said and slowly raised my arms over my head, a wrestler celebrating the pin.

****

The phone didn't ring. Two days later, feeling contrite, I called Jesse and asked him to come get me. I wanted to wrap myself in his body. I wanted to stop being mad.

Jesse pulled up a half-hour later in the LeSabre. I got in the car and seized his thigh, not caring if Pa was watching. "I need you."

He looked at me oddly, didn't answer, just drove. We went to his house. His parents had taken Jesse's younger sister Janey to a movie. Jesse parked down the street in the shadows so the neighbors wouldn't know we were there alone. Cutting through the backyard, Jesse led me into the house. He'd barely shut the door before I was against him, my breath on his neck, wanting to distract myself from my hunger, my anger.

I pulled Jesse toward his basement room. He plopped unceremoniously on the bed and tipped back like an executive with feet on the desk. Confused, I climbed on top of him, pushing my nose against his chin and rubbing up against him like a cat. His body responded, but his hands stayed behind his head. Finally, I paused and pulled back, straddling his chest and resting my full weight just below his ribcage, where it might hurt. I felt rejected, unattractive. Fat.

"What's wrong?" I asked, blinking back tears. Jesse had never responded to me with such indifference before.

He adjusted his hands behind his head, avoiding my eyes. "I don't understand you, Diana. One minute you're lecturing me about abortions and the next you're trying to jump me."

I looked down at my hands.

"You've changed."

The anger returned. "From what? Someone who let you do the leading?" I immediately regretted saying it.

180

Jesse had never insisted on leading. I'd just hung back and followed. He looked at my hands, too.

"You've gotten really thin, Diana," he said after a second or two had passed. In the silence, I became aware of the buzz of his overhead light, so faint I hadn't noticed it before. "I hardly have to say what's obvious: you're starving."

I closed my eyes. "I've lost weight, but so have you," I countered. "What's the difference?" Not him, too. My mouth went dry with fear and anger, my body stiffening. I crossed my arms over my chest, opening my mouth to say something, but I wasn't sure what it would be.

"Mr. Mitchell called me in last week," he said. "He was asking about you, why you're so thin. I didn't know what to tell him. I was embarrassed I hadn't noticed it more." He paused.

"Because you didn't know I was actually supposed to be fat?"

"Because I didn't want to focus on it. You're scaring me, and I'm sick of being scared."

The next pause was longer, and I thought the buzz from the light might actually be growing louder. I tried to hear other sounds, but the whole world seemed to be filled with that buzz. Then Jesse spoke again.

"I guess I've been looking the other way because I know you're going through a hard time with your mom, and I understand that, but people are starting to talk. They say you have a problem. They say you're sick. It's like Justin all over again."

He met my gaze for the first time since beginning his speech. The intensity of his stare made me look away first.

"Do you have a problem?" he asked. "Can you stop this and just be normal again?"

My hands began tracing my ribs beneath my folded arms, checking to make sure they were still there. That the dreams I had nightly about gorging on pizza and French fries were just dreams, even though I woke from them most mornings terrified and beaded with cold sweat.

I stared down at the brown and tan stripes of his duvet cover, the corduroy buttons at its edge. Jesse rested his hands on my hips, thumbs balancing against my jutting pelvic bones. His fingers traced over my ribs, washboarding like a gravel road.

Keeping his eyes on mine, he traced my clavicles and stopped at my jawbones. Then he took my hands, pushing up my sweater sleeves and stretching my arms out as though to check a junkie for track marks, tracing his fingers up and down the ropy veins standing out on the backs of my hands. I glanced down at my hands that now looked so much like Grandma's and felt betrayed. Jesse had always made me feel beautiful. I pictured myself turning skeletal and disgusting under his questioning gaze.

I felt bile rising in the back of my throat and took deep breaths, concentrating on the buzzing of the light as I begged the food I usually wanted up to stay down. I longed to throw my arms around his neck, feel his hands on my back. He didn't understand that I had to do what I was doing. That the rules were different for me.

"I have a lot of problems. So do you. So does Amanda. Nobody else gets shit for their problems. Why is everyone so into mine?"

"Diana, you're *starving*. That's a different kind of problem."

"So are you."

"But I'm going to stop doing it as soon as wrestling season is over. It's not like I'm enjoying it. I hate it. You don't have any good reason to diet."

That was too much. "My reasons are just as good as yours. Maybe better. Why do you think you know what's best for me?" He snorted, his mouth twisted in a scowl. "You don't even know me."

Jesse sat up, piling me off his lap and onto the bed. "Really? Me? The one person who could possibly understand what you're going through? You're really going to go there?"

I glared at him, mad and terrified of what I was doing but totally unable to stop. Oh, God, I wanted to stop. It was like I was paralyzed, just watching it happen. I was going to lose him.

The buzz of the light came back out from wherever it had been hiding as we argued. This time it became intolerable. I leaned down and began lacing my running shoes, which I'd worn ever since the bones of my feet began to rub uncomfortably against all my other shoes.

Jesse reached out to rub my back, and at first I let him, wanting so badly to be caressed. But as soon as his hand crossed my vertebrae, I pulled back as if burned. I didn't trust he was touching me to comfort me. He just wanted to see how many other bones he could feel, so he could tell me he was right and I was wrong. The voice in my head said he was out to stop me, that stopping me would ruin everything.

"Diana," he began, but as the seconds stretched into a minute, I realized he had nothing else to say.

I stood, smoothing my sweater down over my thighs. "Can you take me home?" I asked, as though he were a friend's parent, as though I hadn't lost my virginity to him, as though I didn't love him so much I thought my heart might shatter right there in his bedroom.

He swooped off the bed and whisked the car keys off the dresser in one motion, brushing past me and heading to the basement door without making eye contact. I followed, half trotting, half walking as I tried to keep up with his long strides.

"Jesse!" I hissed as we cut through the neighbor's yard, our feet leaving tracks in the snow. "Are you going to slow down and wait for me?"

He spun around, his eyes sad. "I *have* been waiting for you. You just don't get it."

****

Jesse didn't call that night or the next day. At least fifteen times each night, I picked up the phone to make sure there was still a dial tone, that the phone wasn't broken. I wanted to call him, but just as I raised a finger to dial, I remembered him running his fingers up my ribcage, accusing me. No one could take away this one thing I could control. I didn't know what would happen if anyone took that away. I missed us, the old us. The *us* of hole sixteen.

On Wednesday, Mr. Mitchell appeared in the doorframe during study hall. He whispered to the teacher, who caught my eye and motioned that I should run along. I followed him, a bulldog-looking man with bowed legs and a bald spot, back to his office. I wondered if he knew I was the one writing him the notes. When we got there, Mr. Mitchell motioned for me to sit and pulled closed the windowed steel door.

"How are you, Diana?" he asked.

"Lovely," I said, edgy. I waited for the same talk he'd given Jesse.

"How's your mom?"

"She's in the hospital, actually," I said, as nonchalantly as possible. "She has complications from pneumonia." I picked up a rubber band ball from his desk and began pushing on it, squeezing it. The rubbery resistance felt good in my hands. "She's become a huge fan of Kelly Ripa. Do you like 'All My Children'?"

"I'm a little concerned about you," he said, balancing a pen between his open palms, a tightrope for a mouse.

"I guess you haven't seen it," I said. "But I'm fine."

He put the pen down and leaned forward, hands palm-down on the desk. "We've noticed you've dropped quite a bit of weight. Are you on a diet?"

I glared again, my face getting hot. I wondered if he was referring to the royal "we" or if he'd been talking about me with every teacher in the school. "You have? That's interesting. I've sort of been wondering myself about tapeworm," I said.

He leaned back in his chair and clasped his hands behind his bald spot. I could see him chewing the insides of his cheeks.

I squeezed the rubber band ball. "Wrestlers drop weight, in a week," I said. "Why is it different for me?" We both knew I'd seen the plastic suits. I knew it was wrong, unsafe, illegal.

"Well, they're supervised," he said.

I raised my eyebrows. "Are they? Because it seems a tish dangerous to me. That's probably why dropping weight so fast is against the rules." We stared at each other until I placed the rubber band ball carefully back on his desk, patting it to make sure it didn't roll off. "Of course, I'd never say anything. What you do with your team is up to you. Just saying. People should be able to make their own decisions and all."

"Just make sure you're taking care of yourself, Diana," he said. "When families are in crisis, it's easy to let your health slip."

"I'll take that under consideration," I replied, standing. "Thanks for your concern, Mr. Mitchell. Can I go back to class now?"

He nodded.

The steel door felt like it weighed a thousand pounds as I pushed it open and walked back out into the hall.

When I got back to study hall, Amanda was chewing her hair with anticipation. I felt the note poking between my shoulder blades seconds after I sat back down.

What was that all about?

He wanted to ask me about Ma.

Oh, God. Sympathy from Mr. Mitchell, the world's saddest sam.

I need to get drunk.

I could hear Amanda squealing under her breath. Getting drunk was her new favorite thing to do. She'd been staying with her grandma more and more, hanging out with Jennifer, Karen, and Randy almost every night, calling Davey more and more. I had no doubt she was drinking on school nights now.

When?

Saturday. Pa will be at the hospital and Jesse has an away meet. But I'm not staying at your grandma's. I'll need a ride home.

I couldn't bear the thought of facing that damn cat again. I didn't want to have to sleep near Amanda, babysit her or worry about what she might do after I passed out. I just wanted to be numb.

I pulled out my notebook and wrote Mr. Mitchell another note:

"The injury we do and the one we suffer are not weighed on the same scales." –Aesop

I wanted to add "you motherfucker" but I decided it would really distract from the message. The whole scales thing was perfect, though. *Yay, Aesop.*

The days dragged. Every night after school, Pa and I climbed into the Honda and drove to the hospital, only to go through twenty minutes of preparation to get twenty minutes with Ma.

My discussions with her always centered around the very important issues of "All My Children," and they were legion. I'd started buying *Soap Opera Digest* when Pa took me to Kwik Shop just to keep up. I studied it harder than trigonometry. Nothing seemed more important than "All My Children," like maybe Kelly Ripa could save Ma from falling into the pit of despair.

The cancer quilt Grandma had finished and mailed lay folded at the foot of Ma's hospital bed, gray and black and red.

****

Jennifer stood in the school parking lot, kicking snow clods with her black boots. Her key ring swung back and forth like a hypnotist's watch as she popped her gum. "Where the hell is Amanda?" she asked when I approached. We didn't talk much, but after the last time we'd hung out, she accepted me when I came around, probably because Amanda listened to me better than she did anyone else. Despite her prickly side, I kind of liked Jennifer.

"She'll be here. She's calling Davey."

"I can only imagine what he's doing right now."

"What do you think Davey does in his free time?"

"Plays with action figures. Jerks off to 'Teen Beat.' Plays basketball with an over-the-door hoop. Writes fan letters to Madonna."

I smiled at her, and she smiled back. Amanda finally showed up, trailed by Randy who had his hands in her back pockets and was letting her drag him along like a puppy. We all climbed into Jennifer's car and headed out to meet Davey, who had two bottles with him this time: the peach schnapps and a bottle of Everclear.

After paying Davey and shooing him away from the farm ditch where we'd parked behind a leafless grove of trees, Amanda pushed the Everclear through the gap in the seats. I was in front this time so Amanda and Randy could sit together in the back.

"You know, Diana," she said, "this stuff tastes like shit, but it'll do the job." I took the bottle from her, looked at the label. *Grain alcohol*, it said. *180 proof.*

"What does 'proof' mean?" I asked. The liquid in the bottle was completely clear. "Proof you'll get wasted? Proof it's awesome?"

"It tells you how much alcohol is in it," said Amanda, lighting a cigarette—her newest vice. Jennifer looked annoyed.

"Dude, roll down the window. My parents will kill me if they smell smoke in the car."

Amanda rolled down the window an inch and the wisps of smoke began flowing out the cracked window as though pulled by ghosts in the strengthening wind. "Oh, whatever, Jennifer. Don't be such a stick in the mud. Diana, you divide the proof number in half, and that's the percentage of alcohol."

I looked at the bottle again. Ninety percent alcohol. Well, then. *Hello, oblivion.*

I unscrewed the top and almost retched at the smell. "*This smells terrible*," I said, realizing a moment too late nobody in the car knew the Obvious Game. I

189

missed Jesse, wondered what he would say if he were here. Probably nothing good.

"It tastes like shit, Diana," said Jennifer. "You have to hold your nose, like this."

She plugged her nose with two ring-encircled fingers and threw back a swallow. When she pulled the bottle away, her eyes watered and two hot circles of pink flushed her cheeks. She shook her head, groaning. "Oh, man, that's horrible."

"Why would I drink it, then?" They were clearly insane.

"Because it feels awesome," said Amanda, expertly tapping her cigarette out the window. "Just hold your nose and don't take too much in one swallow."

Jennifer flipped on the radio and pushed a cassette into the player. I tipped the bottle to my lips. I guess I was crazy too.

"Hold your nose!" screamed Jennifer, reaching over to plug it for me. Her fingers smelled like liquor and spearmint gum.

I couldn't take too much. The Everclear burned going down, and my throat involuntarily closed. I pushed Jennifer's hands away from my face and handed the bottle over to her, wiping my mouth. I had to roll down the window and gulp the cold air, trying to let the swirling snow rid my mouth of the taste.

Jennifer laughed and started the car. "Hang on, sister," she said.

I don't remember how many shots I took of the Everclear. I felt fine for the first hour, then all of a sudden the world turned, and it was a struggle to stay upright.

I looked back to Amanda for help, but she was making out with Randy in the backseat. I leaned toward Jennifer. "I can't feel my mouth," I said. "I caan't fill mih muth."

"Be careful," she said. "You have to pace yourself, or it'll get ugly." She looked more closely at my eyes. "Oh, shit. It's going to get ugly for you. I'd better take you home."

Jennifer didn't seem too bad off. I couldn't remember how much she'd had to drink, but I trusted her to drive more than I trusted myself to sit up. Suddenly I just wanted to be home, as though home might make it safe to shift my position. I was so drunk that I was afraid to move. Seriously. This happens? *Why does anyone drink hard liquor?*

"Jennifer, pull over," I commanded. She didn't argue and slid quickly to a stop on the side of the gravel road. She reached over and opened the door for me, holding me by the sweater so I wouldn't fall out of the car as I puked all over the snow. The cold air felt like a gift against my face.

When we pulled into my driveway, Amanda sat up. "Good God, Diana, you've got puke in your hair." She pulled a tissue out of her purse and tried to clean it out. "You're white. You look the Count from Sesame Street." She screamed with laughter.

"You'd better go," I said to Jennifer. "I've got a key."

I'd barely cleared the headlights of the car before I heard Jennifer pull away. I fumbled for my key, dropping it twice in the snow before I could make it stay in my hands. I grabbed handfuls of snow and rubbed them against my burning face. It felt so good to have that cold snow on my skin. Cold snow was the best thing in life. Finally I got the key into the lock and opened the door, falling through it as soon as it opened. I looked up at the stairwell door from my position on the floor. For the first time, I wondered if it was real wood. This question was *fascinating*.

"Diana?" Ma called from upstairs.

She'd come home.

I thought maybe I could fool them just long enough to get myself to bed. Surely they wouldn't notice my limbs were no longer attached? Because, really, if I could pull that off, I deserved to be Homecoming Queen 1991.

"Can you come upstairs?" Ma called.

Hellza. I navigated myself to the door at the base of the staircase. Turning the handle seemed beyond me, since I couldn't tell where my hands were. Which, you know, were an important detail. The whole thing suddenly bored me.

I climbed the stairs slowly, pitching forward twice and sliding down a few steps at the landing before I made it upstairs. I paused, one hand on the banister, and eyeballed the distance between where I stood and the couch where Ma and Pa sat wearing shocked expressions. I tried to walk forward but quickly lost my balance, reaching out to steady myself on the Christmas tree we'd never gotten around to taking down. It was lightweight and fake, and when I grabbed it, it immediately toppled over on top of me, sending ornaments shooting across the carpet and pinging off the walls. I lay on the ground at my parents' feet, mesmerized by the blinking lights of the tree.

"I'm home," I said, breaking into helpless laughter. And then I blacked out.

Chapter Fifteen: Disintegration

I woke up for the first time retching violently into the toilet. Next, I woke up on the floor of my bathroom, Ma holding an enamel bowl under my chin. "The toilet is clogged," she said, smoothing my sweaty hair off my forehead. I nodded and eased my way back onto the floor. The last time I remember puking, green bile came up, burning my throat and mouth. I wanted to brush my teeth, but I didn't have the strength to move.

What must've been hours later, Pa burst into my room and slammed the door. I had to pull myself hand-over-hand up the brass rails of my daybed to sit, my stomach muscles aching with every movement. My head pounded as he pulled back my shade, letting in the harsh winter sunlight. It caught the remains of Jesse's flowers, still in their pink vase. I turned away.

"What the hell was that, Diana?" Pa stood before me, fists clenched. I'd never seen him so mad. For the first time in my life, I was scared of my father. I felt my face crumple like a toddler's. My head hurt so badly, my stomach hurt, everything hurt. I put my head in my hands and wailed.

Pa waited, his face white with anger, for my cries to subside into heaving snuffles. All the crying had made my stomach hurt worse, but I felt better, like I'd scraped the mud out of a deep cut.

Pa stood so still I thought he might fall over. He wasn't a pacer, wasn't a nervous man. He had no tics. He never tapped a foot impatiently, never whistled with anticipation. He waited. I was quite sure he'd never before looked at me like I was a traitor.

I swallowed. My throat felt gritty, raw. I desperately needed to brush my teeth. I tasted vomit and Everclear, which made my gut involuntarily contract. Pa didn't move, even while I struggled not to dry heave.

"I'm sorry," I began. Pa raised a hand, palm flat, the way you might down a dog.

"The part that bothers me most," he said, palm still up, "is that your mother spent her first night home from the hospital cleaning up your vomit. She barely got any sleep. She needs to get better, and even in her condition her first thought was of you."

I hadn't felt guilty before, just scared. I remembered Ma's face in the bathroom the night before, the fear and concern in her bloodshot eyes. "I'm sorry."

"Diana," he said, finally lowering himself onto my desk chair, "*sorry* is not going to be enough."

My face began to crumple again, but there were no tears left. I felt there was no liquid at all left in my body.

Pa wasn't watching me. He seized the back of the chair, slammed his palm down against it. "She wanted to take you to the hospital to have your stomach pumped. We probably should have."

I stared at my comforter, spotted with dried puke. "Why didn't you?" When I looked up, I could see Pa's eyes glistening.

"If you'd thrown up any more bile, we would have. When you finally got to that point, you stopped and slept. I've been checking on you every half hour. You look alive to me." He stood, finished with me. "We don't need any more hospitals right now."

"Pa?"

He strode out the door, and I thought that was it, but he returned a minute later with a pitcher of water and a glass. He poured a few ounces into the glass and handed it to me. "Drink this. I want to see if it stays down."

I took the glass, thinking I could live my whole life without ever seeing clear liquids again. I took a deep breath and tested a sip of water. My stomach turned over but held steady. I waited, Pa staring a hole through me. When a few seconds passed with no heaving, I took a long swallow. This time my stomach didn't protest. Pa held out his hand for the glass, and I gratefully gave it to him.

"We'll talk more later," he said. "If you'd been normal drunk, you'd be out shoveling snow right now. The only reason you aren't is that I need to make sure you're okay before I make you want to die."

I looked up, surprised. Slapping the chair seemed to have drained some of the anger out of Pa. He didn't smile, but we both knew he'd made the sort of joke Ma would never get. "Yes, sir," I whispered.

His mouth twitched. "I'll be back in a half hour. Don't use the toilet. I'm going to have to snake it."

After the door closed, I lowered myself back down the brass ladder of the daybed until my head rested on the propped-up pillows. I thought about Ma kneeling on the floor, her pink cotton bathrobe knotted tight around her waist, her head bald, her face scared. I thought about the meaning of "proof." I had ninety percent proof that I was a total loser.

I'd hate to have me for a daughter. I didn't deserve Ma, didn't deserve Jesse. I knew I was going to lose everything. Still thinking that thought, I closed my eyes and slept.

Pa didn't wake me up for a few more hours, and when he did burst back through the door, he was in a better mood. He made me drink a full glass of water, then hoisted me out of bed. "Get dressed and come upstairs," he said. "We need to talk."

I searched around my room. My clothes from the night before were lying in a rank pile by the closet. Leaning over to pick them up was agony, but I gathered them and shuffled to the laundry room. The walk to the bathroom felt impossible, but I lowered myself onto my hands and knees and gathered up the bathmats and towels lying there abandoned. I put them in the washer too, then dumped soap on everything and started the cycle. With the sound of rushing water, I determined to make it up to them, especially to Ma.

I returned to my room, tripping twice on the carpet before finding a pair of jeans and a sweatshirt. Out of habit, I paused to look at my body in the mirror. I'd lost so much fluid my veins stood out like snakes on a board. I didn't like the way that looked.

I paused to look back at my comforter as I left the room and resolved to wash it next. Maybe if I just kept washing things, it would all go away.

I took the stairs on hands and knees, my abdominal muscles and head lurching painfully with each step. When I reached the top, I forced myself upright. I didn't want them to think I was being dramatic. I wanted them to see me differently than they ever had before. Like I could take whatever they had to give.

Ma and Pa sat on the couch facing me. The tree had been uprighted, but the ornaments lay in a haphazard pile in the corner. I tried not to look at them as I crossed the room and lowered myself onto the loveseat across from them. Late-afternoon sunshine streamed through the window with a cool, white light.

"I'm sorry," I said again.

Ma looked exhausted. Dark circles lined her eyes, which appeared watery and sick. Her face seemed bloodless, especially under the white handkerchief she'd wrapped around her head. Next to my father, she looked twenty years older. She held Pa's hand and avoided my gaze.

"Diana, what the hell did you drink last night?" Pa finally said, after a long silence.

"The bottle said 'Everclear.'"

Ma raised her fingers to her lips, then looked angrily at Pa. "I told you we should've taken her to the hospital. She probably had alcohol poisoning!" Tears were streaming down Ma's face as she talked, her eyes narrowed to puffy slits. "She's still a child."

I felt all the resolve to appear dignified drain from my body. I fought the urge to crawl onto Ma's lap and cry, *Yes, I'm still a child! Why is this happening? Why are you so sick?*

Pa sighed, aging before my eyes. His shoulders slumped. I could see the effects of the night before taking hold of him. He'd been checking on me for twelve hours.

"Who were you with?" Ma shouted, her voice breaking. Pa laid a hand on her knee.

"Amanda, Jennifer, and Karen," I whispered. My throat felt raw again, but I was thirsty. "Can I have a drink of water?"

Pa nodded, patting Ma's knee. I pushed myself up from the loveseat and shuffled around the corner to the kitchen. My feet seemed weighted with sandbags. The glass felt heavier than I remembered, but the water tasted better. I drained the glass in huge gulps, then refilled it and brought it back to the loveseat, sinking down and wondering if I'd be able to get back up again when the talk ended.

Ma leaned back on the couch now, her eyes closed. When I sat, she opened them and looked at me sternly. "You're grounded from cars for the next month. You'll not leave this house except for school."

Panic rose again in my throat. "But Ma, what about Jesse?"

Ma blew her nose into a crumpled lavender tissue. "How do we know Jesse wasn't part of this?"

I snorted. "Ma, he wasn't even there."

"How do we *know*? Diana, you always blame everything on Amanda, always have, and we always believed you because we trusted you. Now I don't know if you're telling the truth about anything, if you ever were. We can't trust you, can't trust your friends. You'll be here until we decide you'll be anywhere else. We are your parents, and we're still in charge."

This speech seemed to drain the last of Ma's energy. She stood shakily. "Now I'm going back to bed. I just got out of the hospital, and I don't need this."

Her words hung in the air as she gripped the stairwell for support on the way to her bedroom. The door closed with a solid click.

"But Pa, it's not fair to Jesse."

Pa rubbed his eyes with his hands. "Your actions weren't fair to anyone, Diana. Especially not yourself. Next time, think for a change. Now go get something to eat and go back to bed. Tomorrow's school, and you're going."

****

My stomach muscles still hurt the next morning, but I was able to sit up in bed without pulling myself up. The last of Jesse's flowers had dropped their blooms in the night, and I pulled them out, their stems rancid and rotting, and threw them into the trash can.

The shower felt good, despite my dark mood. As I bent to shave my legs, I noticed how few razor strokes it took to get all the way around my ropy calves. I had to keep my muscles slack or risk nicking myself in the sharp angles of muscle on bone. I circled my thumb and fingers around my thigh almost halfway up. Even then, I felt relieved to be able to trace them up, touch my ribcage and hip bones.

The drive to school was silent. Ma shifted quietly. She hadn't even dressed, wearing her pajama bottoms and a ratty green sweatshirt with my elementary school mascot airbrushed on the front. She said nothing when I climbed out of the car, driving away when I turned to look back at her.

All the doors felt heavy. I didn't make eye contact with anyone. Amanda wasn't at school, no doubt faking sickness again. I knew I had to find Jesse, had to tell him what had happened. I was going to have to make the first move. When he appeared in the door during biology on his way to take the attendance list to the office, I raised my hand to use the restroom.

"Jesse!" I whisper-yelled, scooting down the hall to catch him. He stood still as a deer, silhouetted by the light streaming through the atrium windows. My chest ached with longing for him, for the way things were with us before.

"Diana, God. What happened? Everyone has been talking about how drunk you were on Saturday." His voice sounded pissed. I wished it didn't. I wished it were friendly, loving, the way it always was before I ruined everything.

"I was. It was really dumb. I never really drank like that before. I didn't know it would hit me so hard. I'm sorry, Jesse. I wasn't thinking. I was just upset."

"After our fight."

I stared at my shoes. "Yeah. I don't want to fight."

"But you don't want to eat, either."

I stared at him, hard. He seemed to see in my face what he was looking for, but I wasn't sure what that was or if I wanted it to be there. I didn't know how to explain I wasn't trying *not* to choose him. I wasn't trying to make him mad. I wasn't trying to push him away. It was happening, and I was just watching it happen.

"Did your parents find out?"

"Um, yeah. I'm grounded for a month."

Jesse looked pained. "Seriously? From everything?"

"Yeah. I'm so sorry." I paused. "I'm sorry about this, I'm sorry about shutting you out, I'm sorry about how things have been. I miss you. I can't stop thinking about you." My words rushed out before my mind could stop them. "I don't know what is happening to me; it's like I can't even feel normal anymore. I'm just so mad all the time."

Jesse turned then and punched a locker. It dented and the sound ricocheted down the hallway. He stood facing it, rubbing his hand. "Can I call you?"

"I don't know. I doubt it."

He slammed the locker again. "Fuck!"

"I know, Jesse. I'm sorry. I've ruined everything." I still felt like I was just watching this

203

happen from somewhere else, like there was nothing I could do. I reached for his hand, but he pulled away.

A teacher's head appeared out of a doorway, questioning the sound. Jesse turned toward the office, not meeting my eyes. "Are you eating more now?"

"Jesse?" I started to cry. "Jesse?" I just wanted him to hold me without looking for anything, to understand, to accept me and my rules. I didn't want to have to choose. It was too hard; everything was too hard.

He turned again, hands in his jeans pockets, the muscles of his back showing through his t-shirt.

"Ma's home."

"I'm glad, Diana. Maybe that will help. I want it to help."

Then he turned and walked away.

Chapter Sixteen: Poison

Stuck in my room, I wrote six letters. I ripped up the first five and mailed the last.

Jesse,

You think I don't know you've been waiting. I do know. I've been waiting, too. I've been waiting for Ma to get better. I've been waiting to feel normal. I've been waiting for you to look at me the way you used to. I've been waiting for everyone to understand that it's just different for me—this is the way it has to be. I can't gain weight. I can't go back to being Amanda's fat friend. I know you didn't know me then, but I can't go back there. I don't even know who I am now, but I'm not that girl anymore.

You're the first new thing to happen to me that wasn't bad news. I miss you. Please talk to me. I love you.

D

I looked up his address in the phone book and walked down the driveway to mail the letter. The mailbox creaked as it opened, swaying in the wind on its wooden post. I stared at the letter lying there against the aluminum. It looked small inside the huge mailbox, so I tipped up the little red flag and shut the door.

There was no going back.

****

At school, I tried to catch Jesse's eye when he rushed past my biology class door, looking for some sign he'd gotten my letter, but he always seemed to be moving too fast. Amanda tugged my hair when Jesse flew past, clearly late. The note poked me between my shoulder blades, but before I lifted my hair to seize it, I already knew what it would say.

Lover's quarrel?

I didn't turn around, just nodded my head. The tears welled, and I rested my elbows on the desk, shading my eyes with one hand as I leaned over my algebra book.

I felt Amanda's palm in the middle of my back, making gentle circles. She smoothed my hair as I watched the tears drop onto the equations, smearing the logic.

****

Hiding my eating habits became impossible during my punishment. Ma had completed her last round of chemotherapy. As the pneumonia completely abated, her eyes grew clearer and brighter than they had since she'd been sick. Food tasted better to her, too, and she began cooking up a storm and insisting I eat dinner with them every night. Even Brussels sprouts, God help us all.

At first, I tried pushing the food around as I always had, but Ma eyed my plate, following my every bite until I put my fork down and glared at her. "What?" I asked.

Ma leaned forward. "Diana, you look really thin, and you're not eating much."

I glanced at Pa, who was looking at me as though seeing a long-lost relative. I pulled the sleeves of my sweatshirt down over my hands, which were now sitting in my lap under the table.

I set my jaw. "I'm not that hungry," I said, holding her gaze.

Ma placed another bite of pork chop delicately in her mouth, barely touching the fork with her lips. She seemed to come to a conclusion of sorts and picked up her fork and knife with confidence.

"Diana, I love you. I know I haven't been around properly the last few months, but I'm getting better all the time. And I am your mother. You need to eat. You're way too thin. You don't look healthy. Are you dieting?"

My fingers under the table circled my thigh. "No."

"Well," said Ma, passing me a basket of rolls. "Prove it. Eat. I don't care if you're not hungry. Just eat."

I reached for a roll, my fingers bouncing back off it as though it were a live wire instead of a soft, doughy ball that came in a gingham cardboard pack of twelve at the grocery store. I gripped it and shoved it in my mouth whole, then sat glaring at her, chewing. I knew it was a stupid move, but I didn't care. I was already grounded. What was she going to do?

207

Pa reached for my arm. "Diana, really, that's enough," he said.

I looked from one of them to the other, blinking like Mr. Hartman. Their voices sounded different since the night with the Everclear. They were in charge again.

I removed the outer part of the roll from my mouth and dropped it listlessly to the plate, turning to discern what Ma had seen outside.

Ma folded her hands in her lap and leaned forward again, her voice low and controlled. "Diana, if you don't want us to put you on the scale once a week, you'll eat like a normal person. This has really got to stop. You've been shrinking for months. I noticed a difference from when I went into the hospital to when I came home. We love you, but we're not going to sit by and let you hurt yourself."

My hands went cold and my head buzzed. I felt like I might barf around the roll still clamped in my jaws. I nodded, tears rolling down my cheeks. They couldn't take this away.

I didn't have anything anymore.

Ma reached across the table and patted my arm. "That's more like it, sweetheart," she said. "We've all been through a lot, but it's going to get better now. I promise."

I stared down at the picked-apart pork chop and finished chewing the roll. When I looked up, they were both staring at me again. "I understand what you're saying, but you just threatened to weigh me weekly like a sow. I think I'd like to be alone. May I be excused?"

Pa looked quizzically at Ma, who was clearly in charge of their intervention. I wondered for a minute if Mr. Mitchell had called them, before dismissing the thought. It didn't matter either way—when Ma got something in her head, she was going to do it. They were going to be on me from then on, nothing more to say. I needed a plan.

Ma nodded, picking up her fork again. "Please take your dish to the sink before you go downstairs," she said.

I carried the dish to the sink and scraped the rest of my food into the garbage. The buttered peas and pork chop fat looked like puke in the trash. I stared at them longer than I meant to, so that Ma called out to me. She was definitely paying attention again. I finished scraping the plate and stalked past them, not meeting their eyes as I disappeared into the stairwell.

****

The next day at school I could feel Mr. Mitchell's eyes on my back as I prepared my salad. Mark shoved his way past me on his way to the lunch line. He was shouting across the cafeteria to Jake, who'd just kidney-punched him. I looked over to see Mr. Mitchell heading toward Mark and Jake and sighed with relief.

Amanda sat down at our table. "Did you break up?" she asked immediately.

"I don't know," I said, afraid I might cry again. I focused out the window on a blue jay hopping across the stone bench of the atrium. "I hope not. I don't want to." I heard my voice creeping up an octave into a whine. "But I can't even talk on the phone."

"Well," she said, looping a spaghetti noodle around the tines of her fork with her fingers before popping it into her mouth to slurp off the sauce, "you've got to convince your parents to let you talk to him on the phone. It's been two weeks of the four. Even murderers get time off for good behavior."

I stabbed another forkful of lettuce and looked pointedly at Mr. Mitchell as I shoved it in my mouth. Amanda was totally right. I didn't know why I hadn't thought of it myself. I turned to her, both fascinated and disgusted by her bizarre spaghetti-eating practices. Anyone she caught staring at her earned a seductive, slow pull of her finger as she smacked her lips and sighed dramatically before haughtily looking away.

"Do you have a chance to talk to him in English?" I asked. Amanda shared only one class with Jesse, but it was one more class than I did. I suddenly felt panicked, as though too much time had already passed. I had to talk to him. Amanda nodded from behind her chocolate milk carton, not looking at me.

"Tell him to call me. Soon," I said.

Amanda nodded again, setting her milk carton down and wiping her mouth with a paper napkin before threading an individual spaghetti noodle between the tines of her fork, one in front, one behind, one in front, one behind. I was still watching her weird ritual when the lunch bell rang. I walked to the garbage and slid the contents of my tray into the gray plastic can, staring at Mr. Mitchell the entire time.

****

That afternoon when Ma pulled up the school's circle drive, I was waiting for her. I slid into the passenger seat and accepted the Twix bar she handed me, ripping off the wrapper and forcing myself to take a single bite. I assumed she wouldn't notice if I didn't take any more, and she said nothing after visibly relaxing at the sight of my chewing.

She carefully signaled to pull out of the drive. "How was your day?" she asked brightly. She'd wrapped a bandana around her wig. I wanted her hair to grow back faster, to prove the cancer was gone.

"It was good. I learned about filibusters. But Ma, I have to ask you something."

She smiled at me. "Sure, kiddo," she said. "What is it?"

"Can I please talk to Jesse on the phone?" I spoke quickly to get my argument out before she had a chance to shut me down. "I understand that I'm grounded, but I can't do anything wrong over the phone, and I'm supposed to be earning your trust back anyway, and Jesse and I had a fight, and I'm afraid he's broken up with me." At the end, my carefully planned argument dissolved into a shrill and desperate whine as I flung my face forward into my hands and cried.

Ma reached over and patted my back. Every day her movements lost more of their now-familiar weight as she returned to the Ma of before.

"Yes, Diana, you can talk to Jesse. I highly doubt he's broken up with you just because you got grounded, though. He seems nicer than that." She paused, remembering. "Although sometimes high school boys are idiots. Probably wouldn't hurt to call. But I'm sure it's not that."

I pressed my fingers into the spaces above my eye sockets. My head pounded. I felt sick almost all the time now: hungry, tired. Sometimes my heart would race when I tried to push open the steel front doors of the school.

"Okay," I said. "I'll call him tonight."

"After dinner," she added.

****

Jesse answered on the first ring.

"Hey."

"Hey, Diana," he said. I remembered those first few phone calls we'd shared, his voice so close in my ear. "I'm sorry about the way that night went," he said, his voice strange. "I didn't plan for it to go that way."

I paused, trying to decide whether to react or ask about the letter. I sat there with the phone pressed to my ear, thinking. The longer I waited, the harder the silence seemed to break. I felt panic run up my back. I was going to ruin this conversation, too.

He cleared his throat. "I qualified for state," he said.

And then I didn't have to think, and the awkwardness passed. "Shut up!" I screamed, jumping to my feet in my bedroom. "You did not!"

He laughed. "Yes, I did. I did it. I can hardly believe it. It's the only thing I've ever worked really hard at. I didn't even know how bad I wanted to go to state until I qualified." I could hear the smile in his voice, and

I wrapped my arms around my shoulders, tucking the phone under my chin.

"*I* did."

"Yeah…I know you did. Diana…" He paused. I could tell he wanted to talk more about that night, that conversation. I didn't. Thankfully, my two-minute time limit saved me.

"Diana, time's up," Ma called from the top of the stairs. She must've set one of her million egg timers. She even used them to time the commercials in "All My Children" so she could figure out when to pee without missing Kelly Ripa.

"Jesse…"

He laughed. "I heard her," he said. "I think I'm just now starting to really meet your mom."

"Obviously, my mom is a control freak. *"*

"*You* are a control freak."

"Touché. Call me later this week, okay? And congratulations. I think that's awesome."

"Thanks. I knew you'd be excited."

Ma's footsteps sounded on the stairs. "I love you. Bye," I whispered as I returned the phone to its cradle. Ma knocked on my door.

"Diana? Are you broken up?"

I opened the door a crack. Ma was standing outside my door, shifting from foot to foot. "No."

"Oh, good."

I looked at her, trying to figure out why she seemed so nervous.

"Let's go to the movies," she said. "All of us."

"But I'm grounded," I said.

213

"You're grounded from other people, not us," she said.

I looked down at my slouchy sweater and sweatpants. "I'm not exactly dressed to go out," I said, though the thought of a movie sounded good.

"So?" Ma said. "I'm bald." Then she threw her head back and laughed, gales of laughter rocking her body until she wiped her eyes. Seeing her laugh made me laugh, and then I ripped the wig off her head as though to check, and *Yes! She was bald!*

Ma reached over as we both forced our breathing to slow down. She grabbed my hand and squeezed. "I missed laughing with you. Hell, I missed laughing," she said.

"Me too. What should we see?"

Ma held up a folded newspaper. "Anything but 'Steel Magnolias,'" she said, which set us off in another fit of laughter. The sound of it drew Pa down the stairs, and when he arrived he found us rolling around on the floor holding our sides.

"You two," he said, "are very hard to understand sometimes."

Chapter Seventeen: Achtung Baby

It didn't happen overnight, but it sure felt like it did. One day I could still encircle the top of my thigh with thumbs and forefingers, and the next day, I was halfway to my knee.

Shortly before Jesse left for state wrestling, I stood in front of the mirror and realized my thighs were almost ready to touch. How much weight had I gained?

After Ma's threat to weigh me weekly, I'd hidden the scale. I ran into the back storage room and slid aside a stack of folded plastic-backed tablecloths and Grandma's crocheted afghans in myriad blues and greens until I found the scale. I was afraid to see the number. Too many people were watching to be sure that I ate.

I stripped off the jeans that weren't as baggy as they used to be, pulled off my sweater, my t-shirt, and then for good measure, my bra and underpants. I stepped onto the scale and took a deep breath, thought better of it, stepped off, exhaled long and low, then stepped back onto the scale, watching the metal circle of judgment swing wildly back and forth, first toward the numbers I wanted, then away, before finally settling underneath the orange needle.

I'd gained ten pounds.

I couldn't breathe. I stepped off the scale. Then I stepped back on. The needle floated over the numbers, swinging, swinging, then settling in the same place. I picked up the scale and carried it to the cement of the laundry room. I thought maybe the carpet was giving me a bad read, even though I'd weighed myself on the carpet of my bedroom so many times. The cement gave me a number one pound lower than the storage room.

I picked up the scale and threw it back into the storage room, grabbing my clothes and running naked through the basement back to my room. When I got there, I ripped clothes off hangers and threw them around my room, wanting to destroy something, tear something in two. I *knew* it would happen if I didn't follow the rules. And nobody believed me. I'd tried to explain it to Jesse, and he hadn't wanted to hear it, and now I was right.

I picked up a t-shirt and tore it from neck to hem, liking the whining sound it made as it ripped. I sank naked to the floor, staring down at my legs, which had filled out. How had I not noticed? How had I not known that, after months of subsisting on less than eight hundred calories a day, even adding the slightest mouthful would make me gain weight?

I'd let myself down. I knew it.

I hated myself.

I heard footsteps on the stairs and threw my robe on. Ma thumped down the hall and knocked on my door. "Diana? Are you okay?"

"What?"

I heard her pause, shift her weight. I imagined her tugging at her wig, which was starting to itch now that the baby hairs covered her head. I'd seen them, new and chestnut, curly. She'd never had curly hair before, but it was coming in curly. Proof that in an instant anything could change.

"Honey, we heard thumping. What are you doing down here?"

I threw open the door, my face burning. "I'm getting ready to take a bath. God, why are you always spying on me?" I spat the words out, furious at her. If she weren't back home, weren't better, nobody would be forcing me to shove the stupid food in my mouth and chew and actually swallow it. "Just leave me alone."

Ma looked shocked. Her face relayed a stream of emotions: confusion, concern, then hurt. She squirmed in the hall.

"Seriously, Ma? I just want to be alone."

Ma tucked a strand of wig behind her ear. "Are you okay?"

I just looked at her. Then I brushed past her down the hall to my bathroom, where I slammed the door and locked it.

I turned on the water in the bathtub and watched it pour out, a miniature waterfall tumbling to the tub basin. The tub had always been loud, and I didn't hear Ma turn and walk away.

When the tub was full, I sank down into it, keeping my eyes closed, keeping my hands from encircling my thighs, knowing it would just make me mad. I lay in the tub, forcing my breathing to slow, in and out, sinking lower and lower into the water. I stayed there until my toes pruned and began to ache from the water log, until the bath cooled to tepid, until I felt sleepy. Surely when I woke up the next morning, I'd be skinny again.

It didn't work. I woke up the next morning looking exactly the same, but I promised myself the restrictions were back on. I'd just have to find a way to hide things better.

At school, I felt like everyone was staring at me. Like everyone could see I'd gained ten pounds and was laughing at my lack of resolve, my lack of control. That I'd failed. I'd pulled it off for a while, but I'd failed in the end.

When Jesse passed by my classroom, I glared at him for not believing me. His face changed with a jolt from expectant to hurt, and then he hurried past. The instant he disappeared from the doorframe, I wanted to call out to him and pull him back, beg him to understand, just understand.

I spent trigonometry class doing calorie calculations in my notebook. It wasn't going to work. Ma and Pa were making me eat too much, and they paid too much attention to how much time I spent on the jogging trampoline. I leaned into my pencil so hard the lead broke. What was I going to do?

I waited in the front lobby for Ma to pick me up that day after school. The solution came to me while I watched the snow plows clear the newly fallen snow from the school parking lot. They backed up and then scraped the thin layers into thicker ones, shoving them into dirty piles at the edges of the concrete. What had looked like nothing on the cement grew to towering walls.

I had to just get rid of it—in whatever increments I could. They could make me eat it, but they couldn't make me keep it down.

As I set the table that night, I watched Ma cook. Soup, which was absolutely perfect. Soup took forever to eat, for one thing, and it wasn't that heavy in calories; at least the canned chicken noodle shit Ma was stirring over the stove wasn't. She'd made rolls and butter to go with it. I shredded mine and dropped it into the soup, watching it expand and soften as it soaked up the salty liquid.

Pa poured his soup into a mug and sipped it as he studied the evening paper. After wanting Ma to notice me for so many months, I hated her stare.

After dinner, I cleared the table quickly, then grabbed my school bag.

"Where are you going?" asked Ma, as she settled onto the couch with the TV remote.

"I'm going to take a bath and do my homework. I thought maybe I'd call Jesse. He's practicing late to get ready for state wrestling next week."

"Oh, that's nice," said Ma, flipping on the television. Pa looked up from his chair over the edge of the paper and smiled, nodding like a bobble head doll.

I waved and thumped down the stairs, wondering how to cover the noise I was about to make. I'd hoped the thundering bath water would be enough.

I ran to the bathroom and locked the door behind me, turning on the water as high as it would go. It roared out of the faucet. I positioned myself over the toilet, pulling up the seat and resting it against the lid as quietly as I could so it wouldn't clank.

I'd heard sticking a toothbrush down your throat worked, but I didn't like the idea of sticking sharp plastic into my soft throat. I thought about the last time I'd puked, and that was all it took—remembering the ethanol-like stench of the Everclear. I conjured up that smell, and my stomach immediately contracted, but nothing came. I reached a finger down a little into my throat, wondering if there was a magic spot I could touch that would project the contents of my stomach neatly into the toilet. As I fumbled around, a loud belch erupted from my mouth. I clapped my hand over my mouth and listened, but all I heard was the pounding of the bathtub water. The water level in the tub was getting higher. I was going to have to hurry.

I tried again, and this time the still-warm soup came pouring out of me, almost silently, the sound of it hitting the toilet water falling in with the pounding of the bath. I tried again, but nothing else came. I gauged the amount, trying to decide if I'd gotten it all. Sweat stood out on my brow, but I didn't want to cry like I usually did when I threw up. I felt triumphant. *High school girl pukes on command. Woo–hoo.*

Until I tried to flush the toilet.

After the Everclear incident, Pa said he'd snaked the toilet, but I wasn't so sure. The soup and noodles swirled sluggishly but refused to go down. There was no way anyone was going to believe it had come out the other end. I panicked. The scent of vomit hung in the air. I carefully set the lid down, thinking. I poured bath salts into the tub to take the smell out of the air in case Ma or Pa came downstairs, and lowered myself into the bathtub, letting the hot water rinse the sweat from where it stood out between my breasts and under my armpits. How was I going to get that soup down the toilet?

After a few minutes, I rose and tried flushing the toilet again. The concoction of soup and the toilet paper I'd dropped in to hide the mess made a drunken half-circle and paused, then the water started to rise. It was going to overflow.

I remembered the plunger in the mudroom bathroom all the way at the other end of the hall. I threw on my robe and ran down the hall as quickly as I could, not wanting to leave my toilet unguarded for a minute. I worried Ma would get suspicious up there, as she seemed now to be always listening, always watching. I figured I had about ten minutes before she would come investigate.

I found the plunger and raced back to my bathroom, locking the door behind me. I shoved the plunger in the midst of the muck, which was now threatening the levee at the top of the bowl. I shoved it in over and over, then held my breath and tried flushing again.

It worked.

Most of the mess went down, but a few stubborn noodles remained floating in the now-clear water. I was going to need another flush, but how many flushes could I make before they thought something was going on? I thought about it while I brushed my teeth twice, wanting to get all the traces of food out of my mouth. I realized I felt light, felt good, felt free again. I felt skinnier already.

Right before leaving the bathroom, I gave the toilet one more flush, and the evidence of my crime finally disappeared down the hole at the bottom of the bowl.

I opened the door to find Ma standing in the hall, holding a plunger. "I heard you flushing and flushing. That toilet is just not working properly. Did you need this?" she asked.

I wondered if she could tell what had happened. I kept my chin low, wondering if my eyes betrayed me. "Um, no. It was going to overflow, but I found the other plunger. Don't worry, the green carpet lives on to fight another day."

Ma sighed. "I told your father to snake that toilet. That's so gross. Just don't use that one for a while. Use ours or the mudroom."

I looked back into the bathroom. My new plan was down the drain as soon as I'd concocted it. "Okay."

Ma rested her hand on my shoulder. "I'm going back upstairs, Diana. Let me know if you need any help with your homework."

I shrugged her hand off. I was so mad at myself that I needed to be mean to her.

"Diana," Ma began, her voice hurt.

I thought of the last time I'd clogged the toilet puking—her tired face hovering over mine the night she came home from the hospital—and felt horrible. I turned back and patted her shoulder, not wanting to get too close lest she smell anything on me. "I'm sorry, Ma, I'm just busy," I said. "I have a test tomorrow."

"I love you," she said.

"I love you, too, Ma," I said, and as I closed my door I realized Jesse hadn't said it back to me on the phone.

Chapter Eighteen: Nevermind

Jesse was one of only five wrestlers making the trip to Des Moines. The wrestling team took one of the school vans up, and the cheerleading squad—Amanda among them, giggling with excitement and prancing like a pony in running tights and an oversized sweatshirt—took another. At least half the town, turned out in full Snowden regalia, gathered in the parking lot by the wrestling room to send them off. As I stepped into the boisterous crowd, I couldn't shake the feeling I was losing Jesse forever.

Pa waited in the car while I wandered over to stand by Lin, Hutch, and Seth near the bleachers. Everyone watched the wrestlers, their serious faces hidden by sweatshirt hoods, as they filed from the wrestling room and got into the van like soldiers going off to war. I tried to catch Jesse's eye, but I couldn't see his face past his hood.

"They look like they're going off to boot camp," said Lin. "It's like some historic photograph."

"Yeah, I guess," I said, staring at Jesse's back. "If boot camp were in Des Moines."

When Jesse climbed into the van, I hoped he would turn to wave, but he stayed facing forward, his Walkman wires just visible trailing out of the hood. When the van pulled away, I felt tears spring to my eyes. The wind picked up, and I felt Seth's long fingers interlace with mine. I didn't look at him but squeezed hard, then dropped his hand as the crowd dispersed.

"*The wrestling team is leaving*," I said pointedly to Seth, needing to play.

"*They are in a van.*"

"*I'm worried about Jesse.*"

"Why?"

But I couldn't think how to answer.

"What are you doing tonight?" asked Lin, leaning into Hutch against the building breeze.

"Nothing," I said. My punishment had been lifted just in time for everyone to leave.

"Do you want to hang out?" asked Lin.

I looked over at Seth, who smiled. "I have no life. I can take you home," he said.

"It's my birthday," said Lin. She looked at her Keds.

"Oh, my God, Lin. Happy birthday! I…" I put my hands over my face. I couldn't believe I'd forgotten her birthday. What kind of friend forgets a birthday?

"It's okay, Diana," she said. "You've had a rough year." She took my hand, squeezing it. "I know you didn't mean to forget." Her eyes were sad.

"Fortunately for you, kid, I already bought her a pony," said Hutch.

I looked over at Pa and gestured to my friends, pantomiming driving and pointing at Seth. Pa smiled and waved, then started the car and slowly pulled out the gate from which the wrestling van had left only moments before. I turned and followed Seth toward his car. "Where are we going?" I asked.

Seth nodded toward Hutch. "His parents are gone for the night. We were just going to hang out," he said. "Hop in, m'lady."

I hadn't been in Seth's car since our breakfast, and I now remembered what he'd told me, feeling guilty again that I hadn't called more. I was a shit friend to everyone.

"Seth, um…"

He shot me a sideways glance. "I know what you're going to ask. She was lying."

"What?"

"Yeah, she wasn't pregnant. I was going to give her money, you know. I even offered to go with her to have it done, but then she started crying and admitted she made it all up. What a crazy bitch."

I had no idea what Jesse and I were doing, what Seth was doing, but I kept hoping it would all be okay. *Hoped* instead of making sure, when it would be so easy to make sure. But that would be like admitting I wasn't a virgin.

"Are you sure she was really lying? What if something else happened?"

He dismissed me with a wave. "Of course she was. I never want to talk to her again. I can't believe I was so worried about it." But the muscle in his jaw flexed when he gritted his teeth. He turned onto Hutch's street.

"But Seth, what if she really had been pregnant?"

He stopped the car a block up from Hutch's house, dangling one hand over the wheel, and turned to face me. "Look, Diana, I told you about it, but now that it's done, I don't want to talk about it anymore. Hutch and Lin don't know. I don't even know why I told you. Don't make me regret telling you."

I pulled my head back as though I'd been slapped. "I'm sorry, Seth. I've been thinking about it a lot, that's all. I worry it'll happen to me."

Seth's face hardened, and he grabbed my shoulder. "Don't be an idiot, Diana. It *can* happen. I thought my life was over. It wasn't a good feeling." He turned the key in the ignition and muttered again, "Don't be an idiot, Diana."

My hand was on the door handle before Seth stopped the car, and I was up and out, running toward the house. Lin opened the door and I pushed through, blinking in the bright light of the kitchen. Lin and Hutch had rented movies, and Lin picked one up and pushed it into the player while Hutch pulled a bottle of Kahlua out of the liquor cabinet. He poured four full cups, then used a funnel to distribute milk back into the bottle.

"Don't they notice when you do that?" I asked, thinking any parent who had an unlocked liquor cabinet and a habit of leaving their high school kid home alone

228

was either very naïve or very careless. "I mean, it must totally taste different."

Hutch laughed, pulling out the funnel. "They hate Kahlua. Someone gave it to them as a gift, and they opened it that night to be nice. I don't know that they will ever even open this bottle again. Bully for us," he said, handing me the glass.

I carried it to the coffee table and set it down, knowing I wouldn't actually drink it. I looked at Seth apologetically, but he waved his hand at me again, still annoyed.

The movie seemed to drag on as I thought about Jesse in that van. I stared at the screen, but I was remembering lying on this couch with Jesse for the first time. How had we gone from understanding each other so well to not at all?

Seth had fallen asleep, mouth slightly open, head tipped back. His bangs fell over his eyes, like a sheepdog. He looked like he had when we were kids racing down the halls at church, pretending the green tiles were grass and the blue tiles were oceans where man-eating sharks dwelled, waiting to take us down to hell forever.

I curled up beside him and put my head on his shoulder. I still felt bad about pissing him off. In his sleep, he drew me in closer, wrapping his arm around me. I realized that for the first time in our lives I was smaller than he was. I put my hand on his chest, feeling it rise and fall. He smelled like cigarettes and pinecones.

The movie ended, and the screen went blue. I looked at the clock. It was almost my curfew. I needed to wake Seth up to take me home, but I hated to do it. His arm against me was warm, strong, wrong.

I raised my head, stroked his cheek. I heard a noise behind me and turned to see Lin standing in the darkness. I pulled my hand back quickly.

"What're you doing, Diana?" Lin whispered, her glasses flashing in the faint light of the television screen.

I sat up as carefully as I could. "I don't know."

She dropped down onto the armchair across from me. "I get it. Seth, I mean. He can look so sweet when he's not bouncing off the walls."

I stared at my hands. "How would you know? You don't see anyone but Hutch."

"What's that supposed to mean?" Her voice held hurt. I wanted to stop, but I couldn't seem to quit saying the wrong things.

"You don't even listen to me when I talk anymore. You're always mooning over Hutch."

"You think I should hang out with you and Amanda and her loser friends instead?" she hissed. "Has it ever occurred to you that you might've ditched me for them or for Jesse a time or two? At least Hutch doesn't go back and forth about who he's going to be loyal to. He never makes me feel like whether he's going to hang out with me that day depends on whether someone else won't."

"Lin…" I knew she was right. I wanted to take it all back.

Lin stood up and looked at the ceiling. I could tell she was trying not to cry.

"Wait. I'm sorry." I reached out for her hand, but she was already four steps away. She walked back down the hall to Hutch's room without a reply. I heard the click of the door as it closed.

Seth stirred on the couch. I shook his hand. "Seth," I whispered, then used my normal voice. "Seth. Wake up."

He squished his face up. "Oh, man. I am so tired," he groaned.

"I'm sorry you have to take me home. I can't call Pa, though—he'll wonder why we're here and Hutch's folks aren't."

Seth sat up, hair flopping back over his face. "I know. Ugh. I'll take you. Just give me a minute."

I turned off the television and flipped on the hall light. Seth squawked and hid his eyes.

"Sorry, but it's almost my curfew."

He stood and pulled on his hoodie, jingling the car keys. "I shouldn't have drunk that Kahlua. It's like sleeping pills, man."

I eyed my untouched glass. "It was wasted on me. I can't stand the stuff."

The drive home was mostly silent. "I'm sorry I asked so many questions about Vanessa," I said finally, as we pulled into my driveway two minutes before my curfew. I jiggled my keys, thinking about how much I'd screwed up that night between Seth and Lin. Right after screwing things up with Jesse. I hated myself. I needed someone to see that and cut me some slack, but every time I tried to show them, I pushed them farther away.

Seth patted my hand awkwardly. "It's okay. It's *okay*. I'm not mad at you. I'm mad at Vanessa. And her flute."

I smiled, hand on the door. Then I reached across the car and wrapped my arms around his neck, feeling his long bangs tickle my ear. "I love you, Seth," I whispered. I couldn't leave with them both pissed at me. I felt so awful.

Seth patted my back, then hugged me back, hard. "I'm easy to love."

Then I got out of the car and ran to the door to the sound of Seth reversing quickly and peeling out of our driveway, sending rocks hurtling out into the night as he went.

****

On Friday night, Ma and Pa took me to dinner to take my mind off state wrestling. "I wish you could've gone, Diana, but we just couldn't afford to stay in a hotel," Ma said, letting her voice trail off. She didn't need to say why—we all knew how high the hospital bills were.

I looked over at them, trying so hard to cheer me up with dinner at Perkins. "It's okay. It's on the radio. And if Jesse wins, we can watch his final match on TV."

Pa grinned as though Jesse were his own son. "Do you think he'll win?"

I realized my parents had no idea how far wrong things had gone with Jesse and me. To them, we were just kids cruising around in a LeSabre or going to the movies. To them, we were just sophomores in high school, worried about winning wrestling meets.

232

I shrugged, poking at my chicken pot pie. I hadn't thrown up since the plunger incident, afraid to try it again at home, but I hadn't needed to—I'd been able to eat like I wanted to all week with the hubbub of state coming up. There'd been a school event every night, and I just kept telling Ma and Pa I'd already eaten when I got home, subsisting instead on apples, string cheese, and rice cakes. It was easy to push the pot pie around without them seeing how much I'd eaten under the cave I'd constructed out of the crust.

I'd hoped Jesse would call from Des Moines, but I knew the wrestlers were under lock and key from Coach Davis. Amanda called Friday night when we got home. I could barely hear her.

"I'm on the pay phone," she screamed. "He made it to the qualifying round, Diana!"

My breath caught, and my fingers went tingly. I could hear Janine screaming something in the background, pictured Amanda standing in her cheerleading uniform, her long fingers wrapped around the aluminum casing of the cord, standing on her tiptoes, legs taut.

"Diana, I have to tell you something," she said, her voice funny.

"What is it?"

"I…" But then the phone cut off and went dead in my hands. My stomach lurched.

"What, Amanda?" I yelled into the phone, but she was gone. There was no way to call her back. I hit the button over and over, but there was just a beeping dial tone on the other end. I threw the phone down in frustration.

"What happened?" asked Ma, who was standing in the middle of the living room, ironing and watching the news. She looked over at me as I paced around the carpet.

"Jesse qualified for finals."

Ma stopped ironing and threw her arms in the air, whooping. She ran over and hugged me, then lifted my chin with one finger, as she'd done when I was a little girl. "Aren't you happy?"

I sank onto the couch, crazed with worry. "Amanda said she had to tell me something, but then the phone went dead."

Ma sat down beside me. "Honey, I'm sure she just wanted to tell you what's been going on there. You know how dramatic Amanda is."

I leaned over, grasping my roiling gut. "I don't know. She sounded funny."

Ma rolled her eyes and adjusted her turquoise turban. "She always sounds funny to me," she said. "That girl has been a drama queen since she was eight years old." Then she peered at me. "Are you worried something happened to Jesse?"

"No, I..." I looked up at Ma, embarrassed by the tears streaming down my face. "I just wish I was there. I hate not knowing what's going on."

Ma looked at her watch. Then she looked at the television and the iron. "Well," she said, "Des Moines is only three hours away. What time do the meets start?"

I blinked at her. "I thought you said we couldn't afford to go."

She shrugged. "We can't afford to stay in a hotel for two nights. But we could get up early tomorrow and drive there."

I leapt off the couch. "Are you serious?" I shouted. "That's amazing! You're the best mom ever!"

She smiled. "Well, I wouldn't have offered if I weren't serious," she said, laughing.

I hugged her, hard. "Oh my God, thank you! I have to go figure out what to wear."

She shook her head as though trying to discern what had come over her. "I'll tell your father when he gets home," she said. "We won't be able to stay the night. We'll have to just go and watch and then turn right around and come home. We'll get home late," she said.

I didn't care. I was going to see Jesse wrestle at state. That was all I cared about.

"That's fine. That's perfect." I ran toward the stairwell, then turned. "Thank you, Ma," I said.

She smiled at me from her perch on the couch. "I love you, honey," she said.

"I love you, too, Ma."

****

I was up before Ma and Pa. I put on my side-zip jeans, which I filled out more than I wanted to. My starvation mode had caused me to shed four pounds, and I felt better about the way I looked. I didn't have the nerve yet to circle my thighs with my fingers, but when I traced my ribs at night, I could feel them again, safely tucked under my skin.

235

I knocked on my parents' door at five-thirty a.m. with two steaming mugs of coffee. Ma and Pa were shuffling around the bathroom in their robes. Pa looked particularly rumpled, but he smiled when he saw me with the coffee. "Now this is service," he said. "Can I get a standing order?"

"That will be expensive," I said, "but, you know, anything's possible."

Ma smiled and touched the back of my head, careful not to muss my hair. "Scoot, kiddo, and let us get ready."

I ran back out to the living room and rifled through my purse, making sure I had powder and lip gloss. Then I paced up and down the kitchen floor, watching dawn break over the broken cornstalks in the field behind the house. As I watched, a deer crested the hill and stood silhouetted against the rising sun. It paused and looked straight through the glass door at me, maybe forty yards away. I froze in my pacing, and we stared at each other for a second before the deer flipped up its white tail and bounded away down the hill, toward the trees.

I kept my Walkman strapped to my ears for the drive, trying to drown out Pa's talk radio. Ma flipped through her cooking magazines as we sped down the highway. I listened to song after song and thought about Jesse. And Lin. I couldn't believe I forgot her birthday. I totally forgot her damn *birthday*.

When we arrived, we had to park in an overflow lot and trudge almost a mile to Veterans Auditorium. Banners covered the busses parked outside, and it seemed every car had windows soaped with schools' or wrestlers' names. As we entered, I saw roving bands of kids in school sweatshirts and parents wearing oversized plastic buttons showing their kids' pictures. Boys jogged around the perimeter of the halls, their Walkman headphones perched on their ears. Others sat quietly on folding chairs by the locker rooms, their hangdog expressions belying they'd lost—today, the day before, it didn't matter: they'd lost.

I grabbed a schedule from a girl wearing a bright orange t-shirt with "Event Staff" across the front in black block letters. I turned around to look for Ma and Pa, not wanting to lose them in the crowd, but Ma had already located one of the other Snowden wrestling moms and had her head down next to the short round woman's ear, listening and nodding.

"Diana," she called. "Jesse wrestles at three."

I looked at the large black-and-white clock hanging in the hall. It was eleven a.m. "Does she know where he is?"

Ma leaned down and whispered in the woman's ear, but the woman only shook her head.

Pa strode over, clearly annoyed with the crowd. "Three?" he said. "I'm going to go read. I can't stand to be around that much parental angst in one room." He pulled his computer magazine from under one arm and headed for a folding chair in the hall.

"Albert," Ma called. "Meet us here, by this clock, at two-thirty."

Ma and I entered the great hall and blinked in the bright gym lights. I'd never been at Vets Auditorium before, and I couldn't believe its size. Four full-size wrestling mats shouldered up against each other on the floor, each flanked with cheerleaders slamming their reddened palms against the mats and screaming for their wrestlers. Coaches stood on the edge of each mat, alternately holding their heads and bobbing from side to side, as though they themselves were sweating on that rubber mat.

I didn't see anyone I knew. Jake had already wrestled and lost, and Jesse was the only other Snowden wrestler who'd made the finals. I looked around, wishing for a friend. I wondered where Amanda was, but I assumed she was hiding out in some back hallway somewhere before she had to cheer again.

I read the program. "He's going to be on mat two, so I want to try to find a seat there," I said.

Ma looked around, bewildered. "Don't you want to find your friends?" she asked. I could tell she was wishing she'd brought something to do.

"Evelyn! Diana!" I heard a voice calling behind us. It was Jesse's mom. "I didn't think you were coming. Jesse will be thrilled."

I hugged her and reached down to squeeze his little sister Janey's hand.

Ma smiled. "When we heard Jesse made the finals, we decided to drive up for the day."

Jesse's mom looked us up and down. "Now that is dedication," she said. "Come and sit with us."

Ma looked at me. "I'd like to get something to eat. I'm already starving," she said. "I'll meet you over by mat two. Do you want anything, Diana?"

238

"Just something to drink. I'm too excited to eat," I said, hoping that lie would work, but Ma bought it easily. I followed Jesse's mom back toward mat two. "Where is Jesse?" I asked. "Can I see him?"

His mom shook her head, studying my face. "He says it messes up his mojo if he sees anyone before a meet. I think it would make him nervous to know you are here, sweetie. You can congratulate him after he wins," she said, winking.

We filed our way back up the bleachers and found a seat. Little kids hovered on the bleacher bases, coloring and racing Hot Wheels along the edges of the wooden slats. I caught Jake's mom staring at me and self-consciously encircled my lower thigh with my fingers as I sat.

I made Jesse's mom give me a play-by-play of his Friday meets. He'd almost lost the qualifying match, she said, nearly pinned before suddenly reversing and pinning his opponent before the kid even realized Jesse had slipped out of his grasp. "The boys have been pretty sequestered," she said. "I've hardly seen him the entire time I've been here."

Ma returned with a hot dog. I immediately began salivating at its smell and wished she'd hurry up and eat it to make the scent go away, but food odors hung over the crowd everywhere—funnel cakes and hamburgers and nacho cheese and cotton candy. I popped two pieces of gum in my mouth and chomped down hard, filled my mouth with Diet Coke, and leaned forward.

My stomach was tight the first hour, but by noon I was bored. I spotted one of the Snowden cheerleaders standing in the double-door leading out to the closest snack bar. "Ma, I see one of my friends," I said. "I'll be back in a little bit, okay?"

Ma looked over from the magazine Jesse's mom had lent her. "Okay, honey," she said. "Do you need any money?"

"No," I said. "Plus, I know where Pa is hiding."

Ma looked annoyed. "Tell him to come in, will you? We have seats."

I nodded, already halfway down the bleachers. "I'll send him in," I yelled.

On my way past the last row, I overheard a voice: "I know, it's sad, but it's kind of hard to feel sorry for her acting this way when her mother's been so sick."

I slowed involuntarily, careful not to turn my head, and waited behind a tall man in a fleece jacket who'd stopped directly in front of me.

"Apparently she doesn't eat at lunch, just stares at everyone else."

"Didn't the guidance counselor talk to her?"

"I thought so. It just seems awfully selfish to me, just saying."

The man in front of me scooted up the bleachers and I forced my feet to move again. The old Diana was fat. Apparently, the new one was selfish.

By the time I reached the door, the cheerleader had disappeared like a white rabbit down the hole. I circled back and found Pa exactly where we'd left him, his leg crossed right over left, in the way of farmers. I ran up to him and leaned down so he could hear me.

"Ma says to go in and sit with her," I said. "She's near mat two with Jesse's mom. Seriously, you should go in there before she loses her grip on reality. You know how she is in crowds." I grinned, trying to catch his eye.

Pa looked up, his eyes glazed as he broke his focus. "Oh, okay," he said. "Where are you going?"

"I saw the cheerleaders. I'm going to try to find Amanda."

"Well," he said, "good luck with that."

I swept the snack bar crowd for about fifteen minutes, but I couldn't find the cheerleader again. After walking the entire outer perimeter of the auditorium, I checked the clock and started opening stairwell doors and listening. I found a few other cheerleading squads hanging out on the stairwell steps and figured I was close. On my fourth try, I found the Snowden cheerleaders.

I stood in the doorway, excited to see them. "Hi, guys," I called up the stairwell.

They were sitting on the stairs, four in a row, skirts flared around them like tulip petals. They looked down, faces frozen in awkward smiles. I furrowed my brow. Something was wrong.

Amanda stood and smiled brightly. "Hi, Diana. I didn't think you were coming."

I climbed the stairs toward them, sweating suddenly in my thin t-shirt. The air in the stairwell seemed close and thick, stifling. "I wasn't, until you called. Ma said we could come watch Jesse in his final meet."

"Oh," said Amanda, looking at the other girls, who were suddenly tying their laces or straightening their vests.

Rosemary stood and said something about going to the bathroom, and the other two rose and followed her. I sat next to Amanda, not caring about the other girls, whom I'd never really liked anyway.

"He wrestles in a little bit," said Amanda, twisting her hair and staring at my t-shirt. "I like your t-shirt."

"I've had this shirt forever, Amanda. What's up with you? You're acting weird."

She looked through me, then at me. She leaned forward, then away. She sighed. "I didn't think you'd be here," she said again.

"Well, I'm here. What's going on?" The stairwell seemed to be getting hotter by the minute.

Amanda pulled at her skirt. "Diana, I kissed Jesse."

I felt like she'd punched me. My head swam, and I reached up for the banister, suddenly afraid I'd fall off the stairs even though I was sitting down. I sat listening to my breath and willing myself to stay calm. "I'm sorry. What did you say?" I asked, my voice low. I wanted her to say it again. I wanted him to say it. I couldn't believe what I was hearing.

"It's not his fault. He won his match, and I was so excited and proud and everything, and after he walked off the mat, I just ran up to him and kissed him."

I exhaled again. "Like on the cheek, you kissed him? That's no big deal."

She smoothed her ankle socks. "No, I mean I kissed him. For real."

I stared at her dumbly. "Did he kiss you back?"

She nodded.

"In front of everyone?"

She nodded again. "Diana, I'm so sorry. It was stupid. I don't know why I did it. I think I just got swept up in the moment, and we were all so excited and..." She trailed off. "And it wouldn't have been such a big deal," she continued after a moment, "because it will totally never happen again, but everyone saw it, so I knew I had to be the one to tell you. That's why I called you yesterday, but then I chickened out."

Fury mounted in my chest. I wanted to throw Amanda down the stairs. I pictured doing it, watching her long legs flail as she tumbled ass-over-elephant to the bottom and lay in a pool of her own cheating blood. I don't know how long I sat thinking about this before she took my hand.

"Please don't be mad at me, Diana," she said. "You know I love you and would never want to hurt you."

I threw off her hand and stood on shaking legs. I hadn't eaten anything since six a.m., and suddenly I felt weak and dizzy. I didn't look back at Amanda, just felt my way down the stairs and burst out of the stairwell door, headed for my parents.

The wrestling parents were beginning to rustle about for Jesse's meet. Ma looked at me quizzically, but I told her I was just nervous. Pa didn't look up from his magazine until the Snowden wrestlers appeared at the edge of the gym, milling about in their sweat suits, all except Jesse, who wore his singlet and headgear and paced without looking at the crowd. Now I knew why he hadn't called me.

I watched as the cheerleaders filed up the mat and took their seats. I didn't know if I could watch Amanda cheering for Jesse, but I took my head in my hands and stared forward, wishing we were home watching this on television so I could just enjoy it and find out the bad news later. I felt like such an idiot.

How could Jesse kiss her back? How could he touch her? I hated them both.

Jesse paced until the referee called both the wrestlers onto the mat. They shook hands and backed away, bouncing lightly on their thin-soled shoes. The other kid reached out, trying for a set-up, and Jesse batted him away. They circled again. I looked over at Amanda and felt my stomach roil with jealousy.

And so I missed it. The other kid's takedown. I knew something was wrong from the panic on Amanda's face, her color high in her cheeks, her chapped hands slamming down on the mat over and over.

Jesse lay on the mat, balanced on one shoulder blade, his weight braced against one big toe that was starting to slide. The other kid was on top of him, bearing down, trying to break Jesse's concentration. For a second, it looked like Jesse was in trouble. Then his foot got traction on the mat, and he reversed. In a flash, Jesse had both of the other kid's shoulders on the ground. The ref slapped the mat and the people around me rose to their feet as one, screaming and hugging each other.

Jesse hauled himself up and shook the other kid's hand. He turned to face the Snowden fans as the ref raised Jesse's hand high.

Jesse looked into the crowd and locked eyes with me. As he lowered his arm, I could tell what he saw on my face. And I was glad.

He would take third that day, but I didn't wait to see him stand on the platform. After Jesse saw me, I grabbed Ma's hand. "Can we go home now?"

"But Diana, don't you want to see if he places?" She looked confused.

I shook my head, my adrenaline gone. "I'll tell you in the car."

I didn't want to stay and talk to him, not here, not now. Not in front of Amanda. I never wanted to see Amanda again. Ma nodded and whispered in Pa's ear.

I motioned to my parents and ducked into the crowd before Amanda could extract herself from the other cheerleaders, and by four o'clock, we were on the highway, headed back home. I told them I'd had a fight with Amanda, a bad one, maybe the last one. Once I was safely in the backseat where no one could see me, I put on a pair of sunglasses and let the tears silently stream down my face.

We stopped at a diner at the halfway point. Ma was looking tired, but Pa looked as he always did, like he could drive forever. I looked down at the menu, still furious and sad and betrayed. I ordered an omelet and a milkshake.

Ma took forever to eat, but I ate like Pa, barely chewing huge bites of egg and cheese, warm and good. I hadn't eaten all day and was starving, and I didn't care about the calories. I wanted to hate myself later. I hated myself already, so why not pile it on?

I finished my meal in ten minutes, and looked over at Ma. She was barely a third of the way into her ham sandwich. My stomach felt full to bursting. I slid my hand over my distended belly. "I have to pee," I said. "I'll be back."

During the walk to the bathroom, I started to panic about all the food I'd just eaten. It wouldn't do to gain weight now, I decided, my mind turning over so many emotions I didn't even know which one to focus on.

The bathroom was a one-seater. I didn't even hesitate as I leaned over the toilet, heaving and retching until I felt empty and hollow again.

Chapter Nineteen: Listen Without Prejudice

On Sunday, I awoke alone in my room, the vinyl shades shut against sunlight, my pink vase empty and glowing softly against its white plastic backdrop. My head felt swollen. Then I remembered Jesse and Amanda. *The betrayal.*

Before Ma and Pa woke up, I ate chocolate pudding and puked twice into the plastic grocery bags I'd found in the kitchen the night before and carried like a zombie into my room. I was afraid to use my bathroom toilet, so I sealed and double-wrapped the bags, spraying the outsides with Lysol before hiding them in my backpack.

The smell reminded me of the scent of Everclear. Perhaps it would all come full-circle, I thought, remembering with a jolt the feeling of Seth's bony shoulder against my forehead. It was all so complicated.

Ma and Pa left me alone most of the day. Amanda tried to call once on Sunday morning, but I told Ma I wasn't talking to her. I sat in my room, listening to the radio and staring out at the woods beyond my room. The vase caught the light as it changed throughout the afternoon and I sat motionless at my desk.

Though I was glad I hadn't actually seen it, I pictured Amanda and Jesse's kiss. I went over and over in my head every time he'd blushed when he looked at her. Obviously he was attracted to her. Everyone was attracted to her. I still couldn't believe he did it. He must not love me anymore at all. Well, who could?

Everyone knew. Everyone who'd seen it was probably home by now. School was going to be horrible, worse even than Ma's first diagnosis. I couldn't hide behind her problems anymore. I had problems of my own.

I would've tried to fake being sick, but that would mean an entire day with Ma and a double-wrapped bag of vomit that was already starting to smell from the depths of my backpack. I picked it up and carried it to the garage, where I set it in the corner.

Jesse called at eight, but Ma told him I'd already gone to bed.

Pa drove me to school early the next morning. I told him I had study group at seven. The backpack sat in my lap, and I'd chosen Pa to drive me for his nose: he had no sense of smell.

When he dropped me off, I waved until I saw him pull out of the circle drive, then headed around back to the dumpsters. I hid behind the gutter when I saw a car turn around in the back parking lot, but it soon pulled out again. I fumbled with the backpack zipper and pulled out the bag. It was cold, but I felt the liquid swishing inside and saw the splatters through the thin white plastic. I pictured Amanda putting her hands on Jesse's shoulders, slick with sweat, and almost dropped the bag.

"Diana!" Lin swung her car door shut and started across the parking lot toward me. Panicked, I heaved the bag at the top of the dumpster. But I missed. The bag ricocheted off the green metal and burst open at my feet, covering me in day-old puke. My shoes immediately began to absorb the liquid, and tiny globs of rancid pudding mixed with stomach acid ran down my jeans. I tried to brush it away, but slime covered my shaking fingers.

"Diana, what the fuck?" shouted Lin as she ran toward me. I sank to the ground, sobbing and trying to brush it off. She reached me and immediately recoiled at the smell. "What the fuck?" she repeated, looking down at the bag.

I looked up at her, tears clouding my vision. "I don't know."

She squatted next to me. "I heard what happened. I called this morning, but your mom said you had early study group."

I put my head in my hands, getting it in my hair. I began to howl in fury, screaming over and over again, "No, no, no…"

"Come on," said Lin. "Get in my car before someone sees this."

I let Lin lead me to her car and stuff me inside as I began to thrash around like an animal, trying to get the vomit off me.

She just kept yelling, "What the fuck? What the fuck?" over and over as we drove to her empty house.

She led me to the bathroom and commanded me to undress. I was screaming still, writhing, over my limit and furious at everything: Ma's cancer, Ma's recovery, Mr. Mitchell, Amanda, Jesse, my body, the bag of puke, missing the dumpster, not being normal. I ripped at my hair and shrieked.

Lin waited.

After a few more minutes, my throat—already sore from the retching—started to burn. I stopped howling and fought to take deep breaths.

Lin just kept nodding her head up and down, like she was talking to herself, but her eyes were wide with shock. She went to her room and reappeared with sweatpants and a sweatshirt. "You're taller than I am, but these should fit," she said, pulling my soaked jeans off and holding her breath. As my jeans slid off, she looked at my hip bones in shock. "Diana, you're so skinny," she whispered. I nodded, hiccupping.

I pulled off my sweater and looked in the mirror, seeing my body the way she saw it, bony, weak-looking. My ribs protruded. Immediately, I began to shiver. "I'm sorry, Lin. I've been such a shit to you all year. I can't seem to stop ruining everything."

Lin shook her head, staring at my ribs. She ran the shower, and I stepped in, letting the water rush over my head until I was warm again. When I emerged in a cloud of steam, Lin wrapped me in a towel like a child and handed me a comb. When I'd dressed and put my wet hair in a ponytail, she got up from the toilet, where she'd been watching.

"This is bigger than just Jesse and Amanda, isn't it?" she asked. I nodded. "How long have you been like this?"

I looked over at her. "Months. I hid it. I didn't want anyone to know."

"I know things have been bad with your mom, but why would you starve yourself? Why would you do something to make your life *harder?*"

I stared up at the ceiling tiles, trying to answer that question myself as the tears coursed down my face and landed on the block letters of Lin's sweatshirt: COLORADO.

"Because I've always been fat."

"Diana, you know what fat is. You weren't fat."

"But I felt fat. And then everything else went wrong. And I couldn't do anything about any of that. Not eating makes me feel better. I can't explain why—it just does. You have to understand."

Lin held her forehead as though it hurt. I could see her struggling to understand, really trying. I could see it in the expression in her eyes as she stared at me, her mouth still wide open in shock. "Fat is not a feeling," she finally said.

I looked down at my leg, tried to encircle my thigh with my fingers. The feeling that rose up was not fat. It was pain. I was so tired of feeling miserable.

"I don't know how to feel better," I whispered. "I don't know how to make myself feel better except to starve."

Lin shook her head. "That makes you feel *better?* I don't understand. I would think that would make you feel cranky and hungry."

I looked down at my ankles protruding from the ends of Lin's too-short sweatpants. "Even that feels better than hating myself."

Lin squatted next to me. "Diana," she said. "You've had a really rough year, but your mom is on the mend. You know Jesse didn't mean to kiss Amanda. Nobody *means* to kiss Amanda."

Despite myself, I laughed wryly. I looked up at the ceiling tiles again, trying to make the tears stop. I knew it was nearly time for school. We'd be late. People would already be talking about me because of what had happened with Amanda and Jesse. But now that I was telling Lin, I couldn't stop until I'd said it all.

"Jesse knows how skinny I am. He had an older brother in Kansas City who died. Of cancer. And he just wants things to be normal here. He's so mad at me about this. I can't seem to explain it to him. I am just so tired of hating myself."

Lin sat with a thump. "Well, yeah," she said. "I can see how that would be exhausting."

And it was. It had been. The six months had been exhausting. Going to bed hungry had been exhausting. Running those bleachers had been exhausting. Hiding everything, puking, counting calories, pushing food around and hoping nobody would notice—all of it was exhausting.

Lin leaned over and wrapped her arms around me. I started sobbing again, pressing my face against her shoulder and shaking. Lin just rocked and patted my wet ponytail as I bawled into her shoulder and clung to her. "I'm so sorry," she whispered. She kept saying it, over and over, *so sorry, so sorry, so sorry.*

When I finally stopped, I pulled back and wiped my eyes. She smiled and pushed a bobby pin into my bangs, pulling them back from my face.

"I look horrible. I can't go to school," I moaned.

"You can," she said, reaching behind her and pulling out her make-up case. "Close your eyes." She pulled out a huge make-up brush and dusted powder over my hot, puffy cheeks. I kept my eyes closed as she followed with blush and touched my eyelids with cream eye shadow. "Open."

I looked in the mirror. My ponytail was half-dry. I could tell I'd been crying, but my color had returned to normal. I took a deep breath and looked into her almond-shaped eyes.

"You can go, and you will," she said. "Nobody else has to know about that bag of puke. It doesn't have to hurt all the time. Normal life doesn't hurt all the time."

I looked at my hands and nodded, considering. I was terrified of gaining weight. I was also pretty scared of what normal would be like after all this time. What would I focus on?

But I was also scared of spending the next twenty years or more hiding food and vomiting into restaurant bathrooms and constantly living in fear of the needle on the scales.

I was terrified of never feeling happy again.

I was scared of losing Jesse.

253

I was scared of killing myself.

I didn't know if I could stop.

I didn't know if I could *not* stop.

I didn't, actually, know anything about myself.

Lin picked up my rancid jeans and dropped them into the trash can. "Come on," she said. "We're going to be late."

Chapter Twenty: Out of Time

It got worse.

I fingered the edge of Lin's sweatpants all through the morning. When lunch came, I walked to the edge of the lunchroom and saw Amanda sitting at our table. Lin was there too, looking around. I couldn't face them.

I detoured past them and headed for the nurse's office. She took one look at my expression and motioned me to the cot. "Are you sick?" she asked.

"Yes."

"You look sick," she said. She held one cool hand to my forehead. "But you don't feel warm. What's the problem?"

"I have a blinding headache." It wasn't a lie.

"Okay," she said. "Is your mom home?"

"Yeah, she should be." I took a deep breath. I really didn't want to see Ma, but there was no other way to get home. And I had to get home, immediately.

"Go to the office and call her," said the nurse, reaching for her notepad. She scribbled something out and handed me a slip of yellow paper. "Give the office ladies this, and you can go home. I hope your head feels better."

"Thanks," I mumbled. Suddenly I felt so tired I wasn't sure I'd be able to function long enough to get home. I stood slowly and snuck down the hall, rushing past the lunchroom door as though on an errand.

When I opened my locker, an envelope slid out from where it had been jammed in the vents. The outside had "Diana" scrawled in Jesse's handwriting. I picked it up and shoved it in my backpack.

Ma showed up in the Honda ten minutes later. She pulled over expertly, flipped the automatic locks to let me in. My knees practically buckled as I heaved myself into the seat next to her.

"Diana, you look horrible. What's wrong?"

"I have a really bad headache."

"What are you wearing?"

I looked down and realized I was still wearing Lin's clothes. "Oh. I fell on the way into school and ripped my jeans. Lin loaned me her gym stuff." It had gotten so easy to lie to her that I didn't even have to think about it anymore.

Ma reached over to feel my forehead, and I pushed her hand away harder than I meant to.

"Ma, can you please just take me home?"

I tried not to see the hurt look on her face as she pulled out of the circle drive and took me away from school.

When we got home, Ma tried to get me to lie down on the sofa so she could make me some scrambled eggs, but I headed straight for my room and lay down on the bed. I was just drifting off when I remembered the envelope.

I ripped open the envelope and there was my letter. At the bottom he'd scribbled one sentence in black pen: *I can't do this right now.*

Though I didn't remember falling asleep, I was startled to feel Ma shaking my arm. "Diana? Can you wake up? I brought you something to eat," she said, concern in her eyes. A tray sat on the bed, with dry toast and water. I closed my eyes again and shook my head.

"Not now, Ma."

"Diana, please tell me what's wrong with you. This isn't like you."

"How would you know?" I heard the words coming out of my mouth, didn't mean them, but wanted to hurt her, hurt anyone. Hurting someone else might make me feel better, I thought. Or maybe I just didn't care.

"What do you mean?" Her confusion pissed me off even more.

"Nothing. I'm sorry. I feel horrible. I just want to be alone. Please."

She pulled her face back, swallowed. She seemed to be processing what I'd said, trying to decide if she accepted it or not. Then she stood up and walked out of the room. I locked the door behind her and pulled out the letter again. *Can't do what?*

257

But I knew. He meant he couldn't do *me* anymore, couldn't be with me, couldn't deal with me. He'd kissed Amanda and had plenty of time to think about all the happier, prettier, better girls than me he could be spending time with. And this was his answer. Happy, Better Girls: One. Diana: Big Fat Zero.

I didn't make any noise—I'd thought I'd scream if he ever broke up with me—but instead it was just this silent and constant outpouring, no matter how hard I stabbed at my eyes with tissues. Just an endless stream of what could have been.

Pa knocked on the door when he got home from work. He rattled the knob. "Diana? Can I come in?"

I unlocked the door and flopped back on the bed.

He stood in the middle of the room, rocking back on his cowboy boots, clearly unsure where to sit, so he stood. "What's wrong?"

"I have a really bad headache and my stomach hurts."

He looked at the toast untouched on the tray. "That might be because you're hungry. Even if you're sick, you should eat something. Toast sucks up the gunk."

I looked at the tray. "I know. But I'm just not hungry."

"Well, when you're sick, you don't get hungry. It doesn't mean it won't make you feel better to eat."

"Is that kind of like you telling me that just because I'm paranoid doesn't mean they're not out to get me?" It was one of my father's favorite expressions. I smiled with half my mouth, my best effort.

"Something like that."

"You're making me nervous. Sit or something." He walked over and sat heavily on my bed. I crawled over to him and put my head on his shoulder. "Daddy, Jesse broke up with me."

He nodded and started rubbing my back. "How do you know that?"

"He wrote me a letter. I went to the nurse's office even before I saw it, but it didn't help."

I started crying again, that same strange, silent stream. Pa pulled a handkerchief out of his pocket and handed it to me. It smelled like him, like the inside of a tractor—grease and cold and corn.

"I'll make a deal with you. If you eat a piece of toast, I'll leave you alone the rest of the night. I'll even divert your mother. I'm sure you'll feel better tomorrow."

That made the tears come faster. I could barely talk around the pain in my throat as it constricted. "Tomorrow's only Tuesday. Pa, Amanda kissed Jesse at the state wrestling meet. I found out when we went there. And now he's dumped me. How can I go back to school?"

He rubbed my back some more. "Well, Diana, you'll walk through the door, and there you'll be."

****

I asked Pa to drive me to school on his way to work again the next day. I wanted to be there ahead of everyone else so I could see them coming. I slunk into my first-period classroom and pretended to do homework until the kids started filing in. I could feel them looking but not looking. By now the whole school would know what had happened with Amanda and Jesse, what had happened to me. They probably thought I went home because of the note, which was just number one in the million things that were wrong.

Lin was waiting by my locker when I got there. My first reaction was to be nervous, even though I'd already told her. I was so used to hiding everything from everyone.

"Hey, I'm washing your clothes," I said, trying to avoid her eyes. "I promise I won't shrink them."

"Can you come over after school?" she asked, sticking her face in front of mine so I had to look at her. "I really want you to come over." She wasn't telling me what to do, just asking, sincerely asking.

I sighed. It felt good to have her be on my side again. "I think so. I'll have to see if Ma will let me, when she comes to pick me up. I was pretty mean to her yesterday, though, so I don't know. I told her I was sick."

"That's the world's biggest understatement, huh? I'll wait for you at the front door," she said, and then she squeezed my arm and disappeared into the rush of kids running for their next class.

I dreaded third period. Amanda sitting behind me meant it was impossible to take my seat without having to look at her. I didn't want to look at her. I wanted to kill her.

When I got there, I saw I needn't have worried. She was turned around chattering to Rosemary when I slumped into my seat, and when the bell rang at the end of the class, she lurched out of her seat and was out the door before I could see the expression on her face.

The other kids seemed to be giving me a wide berth, but I could've been imagining it. Not eating was easier than it had ever been: I had absolutely no appetite. When lunch came around, I skipped it and hid out in the balcony near the VCR, dreaming of "Buns of Steel" and Jesse loving me again. All I saw in my mind's eye were the wrestlers fighting against their plastic suits that didn't breathe, just like my rules.

When Ma pulled up, Lin was waiting next to me. Ma rolled down the window. "Hi, Mrs. Keller. Can Diana come over to my house? We're working on a science project and all the supplies are at my place. I was going to tell her yesterday, but she went home before I could catch her. It's due soon."

Ma looked at me, and I nodded, forcing a pathetic smile. "I forgot," I muttered. "I guess my mind isn't totally a steel trap."

"Okay. But I'll give you girls a ride there," she said. I could tell she still wasn't sure what to do with me. She knew about Jesse by then—I knew Pa wouldn't have kept that a secret—but she also seemed to suspect I was up to something. It would be a relief to let her see Lin and me walk into the house, as I had no intention of going anywhere else. For one thing, I felt too weak.

Lin's parents both worked and weren't home. We ran up the stairs to her room, and she turned up the radio. "Are you okay? Where did you go yesterday at lunch?"

"I had to go home. Jesse broke up with me." I pulled the letter out of my backpack and showed it to her.

She stared at it for a long time, then leaned over and hugged me. I felt the silent tears starting again as I gripped her narrow shoulders. Something about tiny little Lin just seemed so solid, like scaffolding alongside a tall building. I held on as tight as I could.

"I can't believe it. I just can't believe it," she said, handing me a tissue. "I really thought you two were going to get back together after what happened. So did everyone else."

"Why did he break up with me? Why? Why?" I could feel my throat burning again. "Lin, I was trying. I was trying so hard, but this is so hard, it's all so hard, and everything horrible just keeps happening over and over and over. I want it to end." I blew my nose and pulled my knees up to my chest. My throat hurt again and I wanted to throw up, to just spit all the bad feelings into the toilet and flush them away. I sobbed into my knees. "I want him back."

"I don't know why. I don't understand. Sometimes things happen that we don't understand," said Lin, scooting over to sit next to me. She pulled my hair out of its ponytail and picked up a brush. As she worked out the tangles and the bristles started pulling through my hair without resistance, I felt the sobs receding again, until all that was left was hiccups—and the aftermath of what had been.

Chapter Twenty-One: The Way It Is

Lin became pretty much the only person I talked to at school. I hated it when she would look casually at my plate at lunch, but I understood her message. As much as I appreciated having her there, having her care, I was scared of gaining weight, but also scared of driving her away by not eating. So—like I did with Ma and Pa—I ate enough around her to be "enough," though I knew more about how many calories were in whatever I was eating than they did. I went by calories, they went by volume, and I walked around with a stomach bloated from eating enormous plates of unbuttered vegetables. Sometimes I wished they weren't so easy to fool.

When Jesse walked past my classroom door now, he didn't look in.

After a few weeks of hiding from me, Amanda tapped me on the back in study hall one day and handed me a note. She didn't pull my hair like old times, she just handed it to me.

I'm sorry, okay? We've been friends forever. Let's just get over it. Can we? I miss you.

I stared at the note, wishing I could play the Obvious Game with her, just this once. I wanted her to see how it was. I felt deflated, wrung dry. I'd looked losing Amanda's friendship in the face so many times over the past month, and I'd realized I just didn't care anymore, not after already losing Jesse. At the crux of it, he'd meant more to me. He'd known me better. Jesse wasn't just another of Amanda's conquests. He was not only my first love, but the rock I was clinging to in the midst of everything going wrong in my life. I felt like she'd stolen it all, all the good that had come from the past year.

There was just nothing left for Amanda and me. Even after all that time as best friends, it could happen. I felt okay with it, surprisingly—surprising most of all to me. What would be the point of going on like nothing had happened? What would be the point of getting even?

I sighed and wrote back:

I just can't get over you kissing Jesse. You of all people knew how I felt about him. Please don't talk to me anymore.

****

"Hey, did you hear?"

I heard Jake in the hallway, talking to one of the other wrestlers. I ducked my head and leaned in closer. Nobody noticed me anymore. It was easy to eavesdrop.

"Hear what?" The other guy shoved past me as though I were a reed on the side of a stream, a slight obstacle in his path.

"Sticks got in-school suspension. I could hear the band director yelling at him during Spanish. And Sticks yelled back. It was epic."

I hurried to the detention room and stuck my head in. Seth was sitting at a desk staring at a piece of paper. I knocked quietly on the doorframe. He looked up, and I shrugged questioningly, one eyebrow raised.

He scribbled something on the piece of paper and folded it into an airplane. It sailed past me and out into the hall. I scooped it up and unfolded it. It was a copy of the school handbook. Sticks had corrected the spelling errors in red pen. I'd had no idea he was so good with grammar. I smiled for real. He'd written something in the margin:

I was trying to fix the fraying ends of some rope in band. I may have accidentally set the gong on fire.

I looked up at him and saw his head buried in his hands, his shoulders shaking. I smiled, because I knew, despite everything, Seth was still laughing.

****

The birds came back. The days got longer. And at Ma's follow-up appointment, the doctor said the cancer was back and growing fast. This time, they were going to cut out more, radiate more, poison her more.

Ma and Pa told me after school. We walked out to the porch swing in the front, and as our feet left and retouched earth, they told me that the cancer was aggressive, that the treatment would be worse, that they were sorry.

This time, I did howl when I cried.

We held each other as we swung back and forth. From minute to minute, I'd let myself feel the pain, like touching a hot burner, then put it in the box inside my mind, the same box where I kept the hunger. Feel/not feel. And like the hunger, over the next days I grew more callused to the fear and pain.

They let me stay home from school the morning Ma went in for her surgery, and I sat with Pa in the waiting room, staring at the ceiling and looking for spiders. We sat there so long I'd started to go all fuzzy and unfocused, sort of in and out of my own thoughts, when Dr. Chang, the surgeon, appeared. She was younger than I thought she would be, with little square glasses.

"Mr. Keller, Diana—we were able to get the tumor, but the cancer has spread farther than I thought, into her lymph nodes."

Pa reached over and took my hand. His face was taut, skin stretched tight to control his features.

"So what does that mean? Does she really, you know, need her lymph nodes?" I asked, not sure if I was supposed to be asking questions, but not really caring. I wished someone would smile.

Dr. Chang sighed. "It means we're in unknown territory. I wasn't able to cut it all out, so we're going to try to get the rest with radiation and chemotherapy. And yes, she really does need her lymph nodes. I'm sorry."

"But what if that doesn't work?" I demanded. Pa's grip tightened on my hand.

Dr. Chang sat down beside me. "Diana, I know this is hard to hear, and I truly hate being the one to say it, especially to someone so young."

I saw her eyes were moist and felt tears pricking at the edges of my own, though I'd thought there were no tears left in my body. Would I ever be out of water?

"You might want to say anything you need to say to her. Your mom is really, really sick." Dr. Chang stood and touched my shoulder. "If you'd like to see her, she's in recovery, but she's still unconscious."

I ran for the door. The closest exit emptied out into a courtyard in the center of the hospital between the surgery wing and the cafeteria. I stumbled over to a bench and sank onto it, staring at my hands, at the veins. For the first time in weeks, I felt violently hungry.

A few minutes later, I heard the glass door open, boots on pavement. I looked up and saw Pa, his face no longer a mask but a storybook of grief. I ran over to him and hugged him. He wrapped me in his farmer's grip and held me as my body convulsed.

"Come over here, Diana," he said gruffly. "I want to tell you something."

We sat on the bench, not looking at each other, his arm around my shoulders, my head on his shoulder, just like when I was little and he would read me picture books before bed.

"Have I ever told you my SEE theory?"

"No. What are you talking about?"

"Well, SEE stands for Significant Emotional Experience."

"Okay." I waited. As usual, Pa took his time making everything in life into an acronym.

"It's been my experience that SEEs are inherently necessary in order to grow up and become a functioning member of society. You really need two SEEs before you can properly empathize with other people's pain."

"I don't know what you're talking about, Pa."

"What I'm saying, Diana, is that you're fifteen years old, and you've had your two SEEs. You're ready to handle anything now. Some people go their whole lives without ever really knowing pain, and because of it, they never really grow up."

I stared at the planter in the middle of the atrium. It contained ice pansies and tulips, flowers that can grow in the cold. I nodded. "So what do we do now, Pa?"

He ran his fingers through his hair. "In general? I don't know. At this minute? We go sit with your mother until she wakes up. She's going to want us there."

He stood up, held out his hand to pull me up. He seemed more centered than he had been the first time around, more in charge. I wondered if this was Pa's second SEE, too.

****

Ma was hooked up to a bunch of machines when we got there. I looked at her short hair wistfully, wondering how long it would take to fall out again.

When she woke up, we told her what Dr. Chang said. She just lay there, her face blank. Finally, after Dr. Chang herself had come and gone, Ma asked Pa to give us a minute.

268

"Come here, Diana," she said, patting the bed beside her. I sat as delicately as if I were sitting on Ma herself. Everything seemed breakable, even me.

I wanted to tell her how scared I was, how unfair it was, but I couldn't say it to her, because she already knew it. I finally understood that her fear could be greater than mine.

"I understand that Dr. Chang is going to do her best to get this cancer out of my body. But I also understand that it might not work or the cure might actually kill me, too." She took a deep breath. "You're fifteen years old. You're always going to be my baby. I want this to not be happening to you. I want to protect you from everything, Diana. But right now I need to talk to you as a woman."

The silent tears streamed again. I nodded.

Ma grabbed my hand and pushed up my sleeve, exposing my fragile forearms. "I've been asking how to help you eat again. The hospital has a program. Regardless of what happens to me, I want you to recover."

I opened my mouth to protest that there was nothing wrong with me—even as my mind raced over the calorie lists covering the insides of every one of my school notebooks, the stacks of cookbooks by the bathtub, the old yellow scales I kept hidden now under my bed. I hadn't topped seven hundred calories in a day ever since Jesse had returned my letter.

Ma waved her hand dismissively. "Listen, Diana, there's no time for you to deny it. I have a problem, and you have a problem, and I'm going to work on mine, and I need you to work on yours."

She seized my face in both hands, pulling my face near hers. She smelled like a sick person. "Diana, don't leave your father. He needs you, and if I don't make this go away, he's going to need you even more. Please get help. *Please.*" Her eyes held a fierce intensity.

"Mommy, I'm scared." I fell apart, the pain bubbling up from my gut through my throat and out my eyes. *Ouchouchouchouchouch. Having a sick mother hurts.*

She let go of my face and held out her arms. "Oh, honey, I am too. I just never thought life would turn out like this. I want to protect you from everything, even yourself." She rubbed my back, and I knew she was feeling my vertebrae. "We've run out of time for dancing around anything, though. I have my demons, and you have yours. We're a family of strong women. We're going to do our best, do you promise? Do you promise to be a strong woman? Like me, like your grandma? I need you to promise." Her breath rattled in her chest as she waited for my answer.

I nodded. "I love you," I whispered. Maybe if I couldn't do it alone, I could focus on doing it for her.

"Oh, honey, I know you do. It's not your fault. *It's not your fault.*"

I didn't notice when Pa walked back into the room, because I was busy trying to memorize the feeling of my mother holding me.

****

The school year had a month left. Pa called the principal from the hospital and asked exactly what I'd have to do to finish tenth grade without actually showing up. He was on the phone for a long time, and as I paced up and down the hall outside the phone booth, I could see Pa dropping quarters in again and again as his voice rose and fell in incomprehensible murmurs. Finally, he hung up and opened the door.

"Do I have to go back?"

"No," he said. "I told them your grandmother would tutor you with the work they send home. You were doing well enough before, so they agreed."

"Grandma's coming?"

"I called your grandparents while you were talking to Ma. They're on their way."

For the first time since Dr. Chang walked into the waiting room, I felt hopeful.

"Diana?"

"Yeah?" My mind was racing, thinking about what Ma had said.

"We should know within a few weeks whether the treatment is going to get Ma's cancer."

"I know."

"Can you please eat?"

"I'll try, Pa. I promise." The voice in my head tried to remind me of the rules, but I smacked it away. I was a strong woman.

****

Grandma and Grandpa walked into Ma's room while we were all watching "Jeopardy." Ma had already gone in for her first round of radiation. She clung to Pa's hand, not wanting to let go for even a minute. She still looked scared.

"Eva, how are you?" Grandma asked, moving immediately to Ma's bedside.

"I'm not great."

Grandma nodded. Grandpa came over and took my hand. "Want to go home for a while, kid?" he asked. "Hospitals aren't great places for fifteen-year-olds to hang out."

I smiled at him. "Whatever makes you think that? This is so awesome." I poked Ma gently in the ribs, and she put her hand on my arm and squeezed. I didn't want to leave her, but I wasn't sure how much more hospital I could take. Darkness had fallen outside, and I desperately wanted to see a friend.

Seth. I wanted to see Seth.

"I'd like to see Seth," I said. "Can you drive me to his house?"

Pa nodded, waved his hand. "It would be good for her to have someone her own age to talk to," he said.

On the way to Seth's house, Grandpa didn't try to talk to me. He held me in the parking lot as I cried again—how could I cry *again?*—and then we drove, accompanied by the low strains from a classical music station.

We knocked on the door and Seth's mom answered, surprised to see us on her doorstep at nine p.m. Grandpa held out his hand, introduced himself, told Seth's mom what was going on. She invited us in, but Grandpa shook his head. "We hate to bother you, ma'am.

I would be obliged if Diana could have a little time with Seth."

"Of course," she said. "Seth can drive Diana home after they talk. You must need your rest after coming all this way."

Grandpa turned to me. "I'll be at your house, Diana. Your folks think you should sleep in your own bed. We can go back in the morning whenever you want."

"Thanks, Grandpa."

Seth's mother put her arm around me, making little noises in the back of her throat like you would for a baby. Oddly, I found them comforting. She yelled for Seth, and when he appeared at the top of the stairs, I tipped my head all the way back to suck the tears back into my eyes before he could see them.

****

We went for a drive. I didn't want to be in a house—I wanted to be outside.

"Start from the beginning," he said, lighting a cigarette and heading toward the power station.

I told him everything, everything, from Dr. Chang stepping out of surgery to what Ma said about my eating.

"Let's play," I said softly. "*I'm sick. I'm going to the hospital tomorrow to check myself in.*"

Seth held my hand. He squeezed it softly. "Okay. *You are too skinny. You're scaring me.*"

"*You have to stop running away from your problems.*"

"I know."

"I know."

****

The next morning, Grandpa knocked on my door at seven. When he came in, he was holding two cups of coffee. I sat up, and he handed one to me. I peered into it, worried there would be cream or milk, but I relaxed when I saw it was black. I took a tentative sip. No sugar.

"Do you want to go see your mom?" he asked.

"Yeah, I do. They start chemo today. She hates that."

"If it's too much, we don't have to run right back."

"No, I want to go." I choked a little on a sip of coffee. "If it doesn't work, I don't know how much time I'll have with her."

"I'm sorry, Diana."

"I know, Grandpa. It's just so weird—she was better, then she goes in and *bam!* It's worse, and all of a sudden she's back in the hospital and they're cutting into her and radiating her and poisoning her and she could *die?* How does that even happen so fast?"

Grandpa sighed. "Did you know I had a brother?"

I sat up straighter. I knew Grandpa had a sister, my great-aunt Emily, but she'd died when I was a baby. "What happened?"

"There was an accident on the farm. He died. I was around your age."

"Oh. I'm sorry, Grandpa."

"The thing is, Diana, when bad things happen, they usually *do* happen fast."

"What did you do?"

"I went on." He put his hand on my arm. "Do you need your mom to die to get help for your eating problem?" he asked quietly.

I paused. I'd never talked openly about my eating like this, and now everyone in my life seemed to know what was going on. I didn't like it. It was my business, my body. I looked at Grandpa, though, and I saw that Ma's cancer returning had changed all that.

"I don't know."

"You know you're the only person who can do anything about it. If you don't want to get better, the only thing we can do is force-feed you. But I have a feeling you'd just throw it up."

"I would. I...do."

"You're not as sneaky as you think, Diana. Your father told me he's snaked your toilet four times in the past month."

My skin prickled. I felt betrayed that they were all discussing me behind my back. But I couldn't get mad at Grandpa. I knew he was just the one who wasn't afraid of me.

"I think about what it would be like to be normal. But I don't think I *can* be normal. I think if I started eating, I'd just gain weight so fast I'd end up huge. I don't think I can deal with that. I can't be the fat kid again."

"You weren't a fat kid, Diana. You were a little overweight."

"Grandpa, there is no difference between a little overweight and a fat kid. You don't know how it is to have kids afraid to ride a seesaw with you for fear they'd never get down again."

Grandpa laughed, even though I really wasn't trying to be funny. Maybe it *was* funny, in a sick sort of way. "That may be true, but I'm not sure your perspective is reliable, kid."

I sat there.

"Your dad says there's a doctor at the hospital where your mom is who's willing to talk to you about their program, if you're willing."

"I can't go anywhere right now. Ma needs me."

"I think what your mom needs is a reason to get better. You starving yourself isn't very helpful to either of you. She's going to have to fight hard, and she's convinced herself that you're going to kill yourself if you don't get help."

My heart raced. It had been doing that lately. Heavy doors did sometimes feel impossible to move. I knew I was getting weaker. I was scared of getting help and of not getting help, but I'd promised Ma I would try—and I was going to have to start keeping promises to someone besides myself if I wanted anything to change.

"Okay. I'll talk to the doctor."

"Good. I'm glad. Let's go see your mom," he said.

****

When we walked into her room, Ma was sitting up, retching into a green plastic basin. The nurse was unhooking the chemo tubes and clucking softly to her. Grandma held a towel, and when Ma finally stopped, Grandma gently wiped her face as you would a baby

276

eating yogurt. Ma leaned back on the pillows, her face contorted in pain.

I rolled my shoulders back and cleared my throat. "I'd like to meet with the doctor Grandpa told me about." They looked at me, unsure. "The eating doctor."

Ma's face immediately brightened. "Oh, Diana," she said, her eyes filling with tears, "that makes me so happy. It's the best gift ever."

I lowered myself carefully onto her bed and hugged her as gently as I could, afraid too much movement might make her puke into my hair. We clung to each other, two skeletons.

Chapter Twenty-Two: Infected

Grandma went with me to the appointment with Dr. Ross, which was in the mental health wing of the hospital. This waiting room was eerily pleasant, with chairs upholstered in shades of green and lavender, and silk flowers everywhere. It felt a little too reassuring, like something out of a movie set.

"Am I crazy?" I whispered to her. "This room is for crazy people, isn't it?"

Grandma clucked her tongue. "Hush now. Of course you're not crazy." She patted my knee, her rings rattling. "You're from a big family of brave women."

Her words hung in the air like Christmas ornaments. "Why is all this happening?"

"Diana, I stopped asking that question when I turned sixty. I decided questioning things was for young people." She looked at me, narrowing her pretty green eyes. "Find the answers instead of asking the questions, child."

The door opened. "Diana Keller?" a nurse asked. She was wearing yellow scrubs. I played the Obvious Game with myself: *Your clothes clash with these chairs. I'm terrified.* In my mind, I gave her a flowing blonde wig. Then I followed her inside, Grandma behind me, her hand on the small of my back.

"I got your referral from your mother's doctor. I understand your mom is undergoing treatment in the oncology ward," said Dr. Ross.

I nodded.

"And did that help you decide to come in?"

I nodded.

"Do you think you're ready to get help?"

"I don't know." I gripped Grandma's hand. *A big family of strong women.*

"That's not unusual. We have several programs here. Normally we do a physical and mental assessment to determine the appropriate level of care. In your case, I'd like to admit you to in-patient care."

"Why?" My throat tightened. He wanted to lock me up.

"Because your mom is here, and she's fighting a pretty good battle herself. It might be good for you to be close to each other. I'd want you to be able to see her, to work with her as she gets stronger."

I looked at Grandma. "Do you think she'll get stronger?" I asked Dr. Ross.

He smiled kindly. "We always assume the best until given reason to think otherwise." He shuffled the papers on his desk. "We can start the physical assessment now, if you like."

It didn't take long. I found myself in a paper gown being weighed and measured. They took my heart rate, my blood pressure, drew some blood. In the past few days, I'd lost two more pounds. I could feel my heart beating through my chest all the time.

When I was dressed again, we sat back in Dr. Ross's office.

"I'd like to admit you tomorrow morning," he said. "We can do the mental assessment as part of your intake."

"What happens if I do that?" I asked. "Will I be able to leave?"

"Well, you can always check out," he said. "You're not in prison here. But I really think you need twenty-four-hour care if you're seriously going to get better. As I said, I want you to be able to see your mother, your family. This isn't the time to restrict visits. But I also want you to follow a structured program of mental and physical rehabilitation."

"How long will it take?" I asked.

Dr. Ross took his glasses off and began polishing them. "I hate to keep being so vague, but I don't know. Everyone is different. It all depends on how fast you progress, what recovery looks like for you." He put the glasses back on, pushing them up his nose with his pinky finger. "You're young, Diana, and your body has tolerated what you've put it through very well. I was surprised to see your labs weren't worse. I have very high hopes you can make a good recovery and this part of your childhood will be something you can put behind you. But it will take hard work on your part, and this is a hard time to do hard work. Do you think you can do it?"

Grandma put her arm around me. "Diana, we all want you to get better. Even if your mom hadn't gotten sick again, we've been worried about you for months. This is a real opportunity. Please do it. Please," she said quietly, stroking my hair. She looked older than she had before, and I could see that she was begging me.

"Okay," I said, my fingers tracing my ribs.

When we got to Ma's room, Grandpa and Pa were playing cards. Ma was sleeping. "I'm taking Diana home to pack," said Grandma simply. "We'll be back in a few hours."

Pa dropped his cards and crossed the room in two strides. He picked me up like a child and swung me around the room, holding me tight. Then he set me back down and strode out of the room, but not before I saw him crying.

****

The nurse in pink scrubs smiled at us as Pa and I filled out my paperwork. "You can come visit her tomorrow," she said to Pa. "Call us if there's any change with Mrs. Keller that Diana needs to know about, but we'd like the first day to do our mental assessment and get her settled in."

Pa nodded. It felt like the first time I went to sleep-away camp. I'd pretended I had something in my eye as the car pulled away and I saw Ma's waving arm grow smaller and smaller. But then the counselor had grabbed my hand and immediately started a game, and I forgot how sad I was. I hugged Pa quickly and turned

282

away. I didn't want to watch him walk out the door. I didn't forget how sad I was.

The nurse smiled at me. "We're going to see Dr. Mottenson," she said. "He's very good."

I followed her down a long hall filled with framed letters from former patients. I looked at them as I walked past, catching phrases here and there. "You saved my life," said one. "I'm free now," said another. I supposed they didn't frame the failures, or maybe they kept those in another hallway.

Dr. Mottenson sat behind a big mahogany desk. The walls were that same crazy-person green. He stood when I entered. He had flowing silver hair and a big beard. He looked sort of like a lion, or maybe Abraham with a trim.

"Hello, Diana," he said, holding out his hand to shake.

I shook it, hard, not wanting to seem weak. I felt weak.

And so it began.

****

Dr. Ross had told me the first thing they needed to do was stabilize my body. I understood that to mean they wanted me to eat. They did. I had three meals a day and one snack, and I had to eat it all. They wouldn't let me use the restroom for at least an hour after I ate, so I wouldn't throw it up. Someone followed me everywhere I went. I hated it, but it was also a relief to have no say in eating or not eating or puking or not puking. I didn't have the energy to fight with myself.

After breakfast, one of the nurses would walk me over to the oncology ward to visit Ma. They were all there, Ma, Pa, Grandma, and Grandpa. I could tell they were surprised to see me accompanied. "You don't have to stay here," Pa said, when he saw the nurse sit in the corner of the room.

She smiled. "Actually, I do," she said. "Diana needs a chaperone as part of her treatment."

Pa opened his mouth to say something—probably to say he could be the chaperone—but I could almost see him thinking, and he closed it again without comment.

Dr. Chang was in and out during our visits. The cancer did seem to be responding to treatment, she said. She didn't want to overpromise, but things were looking good.

In the meantime, Ma looked like hell. The chemo was strong, much stronger than before, and she was constantly sick and thinner every time I saw her. But she made a point of eating in front of me, even on the days when she was so ill Grandma had to spoon broth into her mouth and wipe her face with a napkin after.

I held Ma's hand every minute I was there, whispered to her that we were both going to get better, that we'd take vacations like we'd never taken. We watched "All My Children." Then the hour would be up, and I'd walk back to treatment with my nurse, wishing I could bolt out the nearest door and run away from everything, from my life.

Lin called, I know, and Seth. They left messages, but the nurses said right now I needed to focus on recovery. Seeing Ma was distraction enough.

284

After a week, I knew I'd gained weight, at least the ten pounds I'd lost since losing Jesse, though they didn't let me see the number on the scale. Frankly, I didn't want to know—the way I was getting through it was to float. Every time the thoughts crowded into my mind about Ma, about Jesse, about eating, about gaining weight, I imagined a huge eraser wiping them away. Every time I walked into Ma's room, her smile told me something was working, that I looked different to her already, and I wanted that to keep happening.

I wanted to protect my body from my mind.

****

In the afternoons, I had therapy with Dr. Mottenson.

"What do you feel like when you eat?" Dr. Mottenson asked, his pen poised.

"Fat."

"Fat isn't a feeling," he said.

"Yeah, that's what Lin said."

He pushed his glasses up and laughed. "Well, maybe she'll be a psychologist. So what's the real feeling?"

"Guilt. Anger."

"Why are you feeling those things?"

"Because I'm not supposed to eat."

"Why in the world not? Don't people need to eat to live?"

"Because if I eat, I'll get fat. I'm different."

"Why are you different?"

"Because all my friends can eat whatever they want and stay skinny. I eat what they eat and I gain weight."

"And you think you're the only person in the world with a different metabolism than two people?"

"No."

"So intellectually you understand that what you're saying doesn't make sense."

"Yes, but it doesn't matter."

"You're right."

I raised my eyebrows.

"I think it's not so much about stopping the feelings as recognizing the feelings for what they are. They're not right or wrong, they just are. Feelings are like dirt. They're just there. You have to decide what to do about them."

"So if the feeling is just there but the action is right or wrong, why do I have guilt about feelings?"

"Because you haven't realized they're just feelings."

"And I can't control my feelings?"

"In thirty years of practice, I've never met anyone who can control their feelings."

"I have rules," I told Dr. Mottenson.

"Why?"

"Because without the rules, I am Fat Diana. I didn't like being Fat Diana. I tried to do it the normal way, but it didn't work. My way was working."

"No, it wasn't working. You had extremely low blood pressure, and your heart was working way too hard. Now you're gaining weight through our structured program, and you haven't gotten fat."

"But I feel fat," I insisted, my fingers reaching for my ribs. "I can barely feel my ribs anymore."

"Why would you want to feel your ribs?"

"Because that means I'm following the rules. That means it's working."

"I still don't understand what that gets you."

"It means I get to be the skinniest person in the room. It means I'm in control."

He folded his hands in his lap as I shifted again on the couch. Even with a little more weight, sitting was still extremely uncomfortable.

"And if you're not the skinniest person in the room, if you're just of average weight, what does that mean?"

"That I'm not special."

"According to whom?"

****

I'd been in treatment for three weeks when I couldn't get my jeans on anymore. There weren't any mirrors in my room, and I hadn't made any friends. My roommate had checked out a few days after I checked in, and so far they hadn't replaced her. From her face when she left, I was sure she'd be back. When I left, I never wanted to come back. But it was so hard. When I couldn't get my pants zipped, I'd screamed and the nurse had come running.

"I can't zip them! I can't zip them! It's happening! I'm fat!" I howled, picking up my shoes and hurling them across the room. One bounced off the window with a sharp rap.

She grabbed my arm. "You've got to calm down, Diana. Take some deep breaths."

I looked at her, wanted so badly to calm down, but she couldn't know how it felt, couldn't know the fear, couldn't know this just proved I had been right the whole time. This was never going to work.

"Get your hands off me!" I screamed, throwing her off. The nurse sighed and pushed a button. I threw myself on my bed, sobbing, and a few minutes later an orderly brought a pill and I found myself on Dr. Mottenson's couch.

"What happened?" He knew, of course.

"My pants don't fit."

"That's good. Your pants were too small for a girl your height."

"I'm sorry, that's not true according to every ad in *Cosmo*. Have you ever been a girl?" I glared at him.

"No, I haven't. That's fair. Tell me why that's important."

"It's not good. It's happening. It'll just keep going up from here, and then I won't get what I want out of life. And that terrifies me."

"No, it won't. When your weight stabilizes, we'll teach you how to keep it there in a healthy way without starving yourself. With your progress, you'll be able to go home, help choose your meal plans, get less structured."

"So what does 'fixed' look like?" This was new news. I hadn't thought about what I would do differently

288

once I got home—I was just thinking about going home, more and more every day. I wanted to go home, and I wanted Ma to go home.

"Most people are able to go with the flow. Some days they eat more, some days they eat less. But nothing is the end of the world, and the rules are just not that severe. There is no punishment for failure. That's the ultimate goal."

"The ultimate goal is not skinny, then. Do you read?"

"Yes, I do. And it's really unfortunate we as a culture have grown so superficial. What would the ancient Greeks say?"

"Indeed."

"Indeed."

A thought nagged at the back of my mind. "Does everyone who leaves here get there?"

He took his glasses off and began polishing them with a handkerchief before he answered. Finally, he shook his head sadly. "No. Let me tell you a story, Diana. When I was a kid, we lived on the south side of Chicago. Our apartment got broken into all the time, which blew my mind, because the door was always locked. So one day I asked my dad why the locks never kept the robbers out. You know what he said?"

I didn't look up.

"He said, 'Jerry, locks are psychological. You might think that door is locked, but you've just deterred someone from getting in by slowing them down. If someone wants to come in, he will.'"

"Is that supposed to make me feel better?"

"I'm not done. Then he said, 'The fact is, though, that most people don't want to come in. Ninety-nine percent of people in this world mean you no harm. But don't put too much stock in locks.'"

I rubbed my eyes. Dr. Mottenson spoke in parables. "Can you please explain in plain English what you're trying to say?"

"What I'm trying to say, Diana, is that there is no 'can't'—only 'won't.'"

"So you're saying I can get rid of my rules, I just won't."

"That's what I'm saying."

I looked at the clock. "Time's up."

Chapter Twenty-Three: Strange Fire

The next day when I walked to the oncology ward to visit Ma, she had a surprise for me. "They're releasing me, Diana," she said.

I jumped back. I was glad she was better, but if she left, then I'd really be alone here.

"Um, that's great, Ma," I mumbled. "What did Dr. Chang say?"

"She said we're out of the woods. We're done with radiation but not chemo, but they're going to reduce the amount since I seem to have stabilized and the tumor isn't growing or spreading any more. It's out of my organs, Diana!"

Her eyes pleaded with me to please be happy. I forced a smile.

"Oh, and there's this," she said, pulling a Gap bag out from behind the bed. She held it out to me. "I heard you could use a wardrobe update."

I pulled three pairs of jeans out of the bag and immediately checked inside the waistband. The tags had been cut out.

"Grandma thought it might be better not to know for now," said Ma. "I think if I were you, I'd rather not know."

I reached over and took her hand. "Ma, I didn't think you understood," I said.

Ma sighed. "Let's just say my college roommates had their bouts with dieting, too. I didn't want to believe it was happening to you, not when I was so sick. I was selfish, Diana. I just wanted everything to go away. I'm sorry I let you down."

"I'm sorry you got sick, Ma."

"I kept thinking when we got to a safe place with my cancer, I'd swoop in and save you with the eating thing. We just never seemed to stay in a safe place."

I laughed. "Dr. Mottenson told me the other day that locks are psychological. He would say there are no safe places, only places."

"Do you want to try them on?"

"No."

"Okay," she said.

Pa walked in then. He looked better than he had in weeks. "Diana, I was afraid I was going to miss you. I had to fill out a bunch of paperwork. I suppose your mother told you she posted bond."

"Yeah."

He walked over and folded me in his arms. "Are you okay?"

"I don't want to stay here by myself," I said. "I want to come home."

He rocked back on his heels and pulled a toothpick out of his pocket. He put it in his mouth and rolled it back and forth a few times, waiting to speak.

"Ah," he said finally. "I suppose that's up to you then, kid."

****

Every meal dragged at first. With Ma gone, I doubled down on my efforts to walk around the wall of my eating disorder. My gut didn't stop clenching at the thought of food, and even if they would've let me see the numbers on the scale, I wouldn't have looked at them. I forced myself to stop circling my thumb and forefingers around my upper thigh—it was pointless; I knew they wouldn't touch anymore. I couldn't look at my body yet. I just let it grow.

The last night in my room at the hospital, I clung to my lavender and green bedspread in terror. I was as afraid to leave as I'd been to stay. How could I go back to the bathtub at home, to the toilet Pa kept snaking, to my life, to my friends? School was out, thank God. But still.

Grandma and Grandpa came to pick me up. They were going back to Nebraska after I got settled back in at home. I sat in the waiting room with my suitcase, waiting for them, when the door opened and in walked Seth.

"Hey," he said, running his hand through his hair. He looked older than the last time I saw him.

"How did you know I was coming home today?" I asked. We hadn't talked since that night.

"It's Snowden, Diana."

I gulped. "So everyone knows everything, huh?"

He laughed and slumped in the chair next to me. "Everyone knew everything before."

"Well, not everything. Not about Vanessa."

"Diana, I can't talk to you about that. It would upset my girlfriend."

"You have a girlfriend?"

"Don't act so surprised."

"There are a lot of crazies in the world."

He laughed easily. "Yes, and this one plays bass."

I leaned over and hugged him. "Thanks, Seth. Thanks for everything. Thanks for being there for me that night."

He hugged back, hard, then stood to go just as Grandma and Grandpa walked in.

"Hello, Seth," said Grandma. "My, you're looking tall and handsome these days."

"Thanks, Mrs. Keller," he said. "Same to you."

Grandma leaned back and laughed. Grandpa held out his hand to take my suitcase.

"Come on, Diana," he said. "Let's get you home."

Chapter Twenty-Four: Little Earthquakes

"You got everything?" said Lin, shielding her face from the sun with her left hand. A tiny diamond sparkled on her ring finger. I smiled.

"Yeah, I'm all good." I hoisted the last suitcase into the back of the Honda. Ma and Pa were inside, and Lin was my last goodbye before making the trip to the University of Iowa, to college. My ticket out of Snowden.

"Are you scared?" she asked, staring at the car. She made circles in the gravel of my driveway with her tiny toes. Lin was going to the community college and making plans for her December wedding to Hutch, who had enrolled in the police academy. Her life seemed to be all buckled up while mine could go anywhere. But I no longer wanted to know everything ahead of time, anyway. The road to hell is paved with good intentions.

"No. I mean, yes."

There were still days when I wanted to reach for the cookbooks and apples, the steam of a hot bath and the satisfaction of puking my guts out, but I knew that wouldn't fix anything, had never fixed anything. If I messed up, I'd have to start all over, and I didn't ever want to start all over again.

****

Currier Hall loomed large in the windshield. It was one of the oldest dorms at the University of Iowa. By lottery I'd gotten a single room, one that Ma worried about. She thought, I knew, that left to my own devices with no one to watch over me, I'd regress. I knew living with anyone else, having no escape from people, would be far worse.

Pa spent a few hours building a sleeping loft in the room that was so tiny if I sat down with my back against one wall, my feet would hit the dorm fridge on the other side.

"Well, that's the last of it," said Pa, hoisting his tools back into the bucket. Ma helped me make up the bed, fretting over me falling off. I pushed her hands away as she tried to tuck the sheets.

"Ma," I said finally, "you've got to let me try. I swear I mastered hospital corners years ago."

She smiled and tucked back a lock of my hair behind my ear. Pa carried the tools out to the car parked six blocks away, and I plopped on the floor, leaving her the desk chair, the only seat in the room. It was a room for one person, not two.

"Ma, I'm going to be okay. I have Dr. Mottenson's number. I have a local referral if I get scared. It's going to be amazing. I'm ready, Ma. I want this."

She reached for a tissue from the bright lavender box on the fridge and blew her nose. "I know. It's not that. I trust you to take care of yourself. You've done so well since then."

And I had. I'd gone to see Dr. Mottenson five days a week at first, then weekly, then—at the point at which I could hear his voice in my head as clearly as I'd previously heard the voices that told me I wasn't good enough, that I was still Fat Diana—once a month. Since summer began, I hadn't seen him at all, because I already knew what he would say. Dr. Mottenson called that pronounced me "recovered" and deemed me a graduate right after Snowden High did.

Ma reached for my hand and patted it. "I just feel like I missed part of it."

"Part of what?"

"You. I feel like I missed part of your life. I wasn't there."

I sniffed. My throat felt tight. "It's not like you could help it, Ma. Nobody asks to get sick. Especially in such a grand gesture of ultimate sickitude."

"I just thought it would last longer, Diana."

"What?"

"You being at home. You're going to have so many adventures, and I'm so excited for you, but I miss you already." She turned her head then, but I knew she was crying. I stood up and went to hug her. Her frame no longer felt skeletal, and neither did mine, but we both, I think, remembered that hug in the hospital when we were sisters of a sort.

Before we got better.

I told my parents they had to leave, immediately, because otherwise I'd be a snotfest, and that would not earn me any popularity points in my new home. Pa laughed and refrained from honking out "Taps" on the horn as they pulled away. I watched Ma's arm waving and waving until I couldn't see the Honda anymore.

Then I went up to my room and lay down on my new loft bed and cried until the huffing aftermath left me exhausted, and I fell asleep.

****

When I woke up, it was dark outside, and a party was heating up at the yellow house across the street. I peered at it through my window from the safety of my loft, where no one would see me watching. A tall blond boy with a scruffy ponytail and pathetic five o'clock shadow was hauling a keg of beer up to the porch, a stack of red plastic glasses in one hand. Suddenly, I felt panicked. Ma and Pa were gone, and I didn't know anyone. A new life, no direction. My first instinct was to hide, watch, and wait.

I crawled down the ladder and sidled over to my basket of snacks. I was hungry, which was a feeling I didn't like anymore, a feeling that now scared me. In this new place, with no friends and no Ma and Pa, I knew I was the only one responsible for feeding me, and I wasn't about to let anything happen to myself again. I had to stay ready for whatever was going to come next.

I ripped the wrapper off a cheese-and-cracker pack and wolfed it down, then drank a huge swig of water from my little sink. I grabbed my new keys and headed down to the bathroom with the lock on the door and took my first shower at college. Then I wandered back and opened the window—it was hot. As the party raged on in the yellow house, I drifted off into a fitful sleep.

Pink clouds ringed the sky when I woke up. The tiny room felt tight with the heat of the past night. I decided to walk down to the student union to buy a fan, but as I found my way down the trail, the Iowa River attracted me with its sluggish flow. I walked across the bridge, my sneakers slapping softly against the pavement. A mist hovered above the river, twisting into eddies in places where the wind blew it.

As I descended the bridge on the other side, I saw a figure by the river's edge near the boathouse. I veered off to the side, suddenly scared. I wondered if it was totally dumb to be wandering around at six in the morning in Iowa City by myself.

Then I recognized him.

Jesse looked up from where he sat, thick fingers folded in his lap. His eyebrows shot up.

"Diana?" he called hesitantly.

"Hey," I said, quickening my pace. I sank down beside him as he had beside me that first day at the pool, the day I'd told him my mom was sick.

"I knew you were coming here, but I guess I didn't expect to see you so soon," he said, smiling.

"Yeah, same here. Or maybe, you know, ever." My stomach knotted up, but it wasn't because I was hungry.

We sat in silence then, watching the geese picking their way across the opposite shore.

"When did you get here?" I finally asked.

"Last night. My roommate was going out, but I just wanted to ease into college. I guess I fell asleep pretty early."

"Me too."

"Who's your roommate? Mine just joined a fraternity. Ugh."

"I don't actually have a roommate. I got a single."

"How'd you manage that?"

"I have no idea. I don't think I want to know."

He laughed, pulling up a piece of grass and wrapping it around his index finger.

And so we continued to sit. I decided to just ask the question I'd pushed aside so much in the past two years, while I focused on treatment and Ma, and Jesse dated around and placed at state wrestling two more times. I'd avoided that question until it didn't hurt to look at him anymore, until I could pass him in the halls without feeling punched in the throat.

"So why did you write that note on my letter?" I asked.

He sighed and took off his ball cap. The sun hit his bare head—he was completely bald. It reminded me of Ma's head during chemo, and my breath caught.

"Why don't you have hair? Answer that first."

"It's nothing, Diana. I just shaved it. A change."

My breath shuddered out. "Okay. Then go back to my first question."

He pulled the grass tighter around his fingers. "I was weak."

"What?"

"I didn't mean to kiss Amanda, but she was suddenly there, and I was feeling good, and mad at you, and I just did it. Then after I got back from state, someone told me about what happened with you and Lin and the dumpster, and it felt like your problems would never end when all I wanted was to be normal."

I cringed.

His hand shot out and grasped my shoulder. "Don't. I'm not proud of how I acted. That was when you needed me most, and I hurt you and then I bailed. I've never forgiven myself."

I sucked in my breath. *Nobody is blameless.*

"I didn't…" I started, but he cut me off, staring at the river.

"I tried dialing the number of the hospital a couple of times while you were in there, but I never could let it ring more than once."

"Why not?" I asked, remembering the nights in that lavender-and-green room, wishing for nothing more than to talk to Jesse.

"What could I say? I was wrong. I hated myself. I couldn't see how you could possibly not hate me. I was afraid of what you would say."

I reached for my own piece of grass, pulling three and braiding them together. "Nobody has a corner on that market, Jesse."

He reached over and touched my arm. "I wanted to be with you, Diana. After school started again, I wanted to be with you so bad, but you were just in your own world. You never came to games, you never came to meets. You were just…gone."

"I had therapy appointments every day after school. I had to stay in out-patient or I would've been right back in that hospital. It was part of the deal."

"I know...or I thought I knew. That's what I told myself, anyway. But I've never stopped missing you."

"I thought about you, you know."

He turned to face me, pulled me toward him. His stubby hands on my knees set my stomach afire.

"You did? Because I thought about you every single day. I just thought it was too far gone. I never really expected to see you again after graduation, and then this morning you just walked out of the mist."

I smiled. "I couldn't sleep. The neighbors were partying, but I never felt so alone." I paused. "I know you tried. I see that now, but *then* all I could do was be mad at everyone, hurt everyone. You weren't trying to interfere, but I couldn't even see that because I was so sick. I can't even explain what it was like to think that way—it seems foreign to me, even now, and I try not to remember it, because I'm scared I'll fall back into it. It was horrible. And I was horrible to you. I'm sorry."

His gaze was so intense it almost hurt to look at him. "You don't know how bad I wanted to hear that. I've still never felt as close to someone as I felt to you that fall before everything went off the rails. As if you knew everything I was going to say before I said it. No other girl has been able to read me as you can. I keep looking, but I can't find anyone else like you."

He touched my cheek; I felt the old jolt. I leaned in and inhaled; he smelled the same. He wrapped his arms around me, and it felt like home.

Jesse pulled back and looked at me. Students were starting to pour out of the dorms. The mist had cleared from the river.

"Let's play," he said. "One more time, Diana."

"*I miss you*," I replied.

"*I still love you*," he said.

My breath caught, all the feelings of the past few years collecting in my throat at once. "Wow."

"*You're blushing.*"

"*I still love you, too.*" I was back at the homecoming dance, when Jesse held me and I was fifteen and the whole world was in front of me.

"Want to bridge jump?" he asked, smiling wider.

"What's that?"

"My roommate told me people do it all the time. The water's not too deep off this bridge, so you jump off and swim to the side."

I looked at the river, rolling lazily toward the dam. "What about the dam at the end?"

"You don't let yourself float that far."

"Okay," I said. "I won't." And I meant it.

Acknowledgements

This novel is a work of fiction, but I did myself suffer from eating disorders for a number of years. I'm happy to say I've made a complete recovery, not only in my eating patterns but in my thinking patterns. Since I started writing on my blog about my experiences, I've received emails from people all over the world searching for frank talk about living with and dealing with eating disorders. It's my hope this novel will give hope to those afflicted, and understanding and compassion to their friends and family members.

Thank you to my parents, Jim and Sarah Biermann; my sister, Renee; my best friend, Stephanie; my cousins and aunts and uncles and friends and teachers and everyone who stuck with me through that ten-year haze during which I thought the rules were different for me. Thank you to my husband, Greg, and my daughter, Lily, who cheered me on through the three-year period in which I wrote this book.

Thank you to my early readers: Stephanie O'Dea, Kelli Oliver George, Michael Pritchett, Karen Gerwin, and my agent, Eric Myers. This novel is almost unrecognizable from where it started, thanks to you. Thanks to my teen readers RJ and Alison for your honest critiques.

For moral support, thanks to Matt Boyd, Bill Rose, Jean Kwok, Ann Napolitano, Jenny Lawson, Lori Culwell, Alice Bradley, Stacy Morrison, Julie Ross Godar, Denise Tanton, Maria Niles, Diane Lang, Karen Ballum and all the readers of Surrender, Dorothy (www.surrenderdorothyblog.com), who have been my friends and readers since 2004.

For more information about eating disorders, me, my other books, or to get the playlist that goes with the chapter titles of late-eighties/early-nineties albums, go to www.ritaarens.com.

ABOUT THE AUTHOR

Rita Arens is the author of *The Obvious Game* and the editor of the award-winning parenting anthology *Sleep Is for the Weak*. She writes the popular blog Surrender, Dorothy (www.surrenderdorothyblog.com) and lives in Kansas City with her husband and daughter. *The Obvious Game* is her first young adult novel. She is at work on a second.

Rita has been a featured speaker at BlogHer 2008-2012, BlogHer Writers 2011, BEA Bloggers Conference 2012, Blissdom 2011, Alt Summit 2010, the 2008 Kansas City Literary Festival and 2009 Chicks Who Click and appeared on the Walt Bodine Show in 2008.

She's been quoted by Bloomberg Businessweek, The Associated Press, Forbes Woman, the *Wall Street Journal*, *BusinessWeek* and BusinessWeek Online and featured in *Breathe* magazine, Get Your Biz Savvy, *The Kansas City Star*, Today Moms (Today Show blog) and *Ink KC*.

Website: http://www.ritaarens.com

Enjoyed This Book?

Try Other

Young Adult

Romance

Novels

From Inkspell Publishing.

Buy Any Book Featured In The Following Pages at 15% Discount From Our Website.

http://www.inkspellpublishing.com

Use The Discount Code

GIFT15 At Checkout!

The world is about to be cloaked in darkness.
Only one can stop the night.

Finding a new home has never been so dangerous.

Forbidden fruit can be the sweetest—or the most dangerous.